To Michael, Jo, Phill, Phil, Rian and Kezia

Chapter 1

Clearing away the breakfast plates, I noticed my husband's mobile lying on the worktop. It wasn't like him to leave his phone at home but he had been in a rush that morning, dropping Dan at school on his way to the station. There was plenty of time to finish clearing up before I had to leave, but I hurried nevertheless. Having recently started work as a part-time receptionist at our local medical centre, I was keen to make a good initial impression. It had taken me a while to summon up the courage to apply for paid employment.

Seventeen years earlier our son had been born with cerebral palsy, and I hadn't returned to work when my maternity leave expired. Only a few weeks ago I had finally given in to my husband's insistence that Dan was perfectly capable of looking after himself, and I had found a part-time job, three mornings a week. We didn't need the money, but Paul said it would be good for me to get out. I knew he was right, but it was a challenge. I was out of the habit of going to work.

I was planning to leave a message at Paul's office to let him know his phone was safe, so he wouldn't worry about it, but before I had finished stacking the dishwasher, Paul's phone beeped, and the opening of a message flashed up on the screen. To say what I read there startled me would be an understatement. It was impossible to ignore the message, so I picked up the phone and keyed in what I thought was his passcode, but he must have changed it because my birthday didn't work, and nor did our son's. Down to my last chance to access the phone before it locked me out and determined to read the message in full if I could, I made one last attempt to open it. It was risky because, if I failed,

1

Paul would realise I had tried to unlock the phone. Crossing my fingers, I tried his birthday, and succeeded.

Even though there was no one at home to see what I was doing, I went into the bathroom and bolted the door before opening the message. Invading my husband's privacy might have been indefensible, but my frisson of guilt was quickly dispelled by disbelief. What I read made me reel. For a few seconds the bathroom seemed to spin out of control. Feeling dizzy and nauseous, I sat down on the toilet. Holding onto the edge of the sink, I closed my eyes and took a deep breath before opening the message again. I hadn't misread it.

'See you tonight, sexy?' the message began.

Paul had a regular arrangement to play squash with a colleague on Tuesday evenings, and he had taken his sports bag with him that morning. Pecking me on the cheek as he left the house, he had reminded me that he would be home late. It had all seemed so normal. I've never been a jealous wife who becomes suspicious when her husband makes his own independent arrangements with friends. On the contrary, I was pleased he had a regular weekly squash game. But what followed didn't give the impression that Paul was planning to play squash that evening.

'Can't wait,' the message continued, before saying the writer would be 'wearing lacy black undies.' It was signed 'Bella', followed by a row of kisses and a smiley face.

If this was a joke from my husband's squash partner, he had a very odd sense of humour. It was possible that this really was two men fooling around, but I had to be sure. Paul would never find out that I was reading private messages on his phone, but even so my hands shook scrolling through previous messages from that number, each one more disturbing than the one before.

'Can't stop thinking about you.'

'Can't wait for Tuesday.'

'I'm naked.'

'Have you got a hard on?'

And there was more along those lines. A lot more. Some of the messages were merely suggestive, others were explicit. The ones sent by my husband were the most graphic. His correspondent was called Bella, but he addressed her as 'Sex Bomb'. Even more upsetting than their reciprocal flattery was her complaint that he was 'stringing her along'. In response, he urged her to be patient. Patient? What the hell did that mean? Reading on, I realised there was a theme running through the messages. Paul had agreed to leave his family to go and live with this other woman.

Most of the messages were confirming arrangements to meet, invariably on Tuesday evenings when his 'Sex Bomb' enjoyed regular encounters with her 'Sexy Beast'. It was hard to square that with a husband who was usually snoring as soon as his head hit the pillow. Our lovemaking had all but fizzled out after Dan was born. It wasn't that I was no longer attracted to Paul, I was just too exhausted after taking Dan for his therapy, and coping with the stress of protecting him, and doing everything possible to ensure his development was normal. Our sex life had dwindled to one quick shag a week, on a Friday night, the midpoint between the times he was screwing his 'Sex Bomb', Bella. Wondering whether he had been thinking about her when making love to me, I felt like throwing up. Stunned, I read on.

In one of her messages, Bella mentioned that they had been together for two years. The implications of that made me howl with rage. I hurled his phone across the bathroom. Paul had been seeing another woman behind my back for two years, and in all that time I had never once suspected he was cheating on me. To learn the truth in such an underhand way was like a physical pain in my guts. Wracking my brains, I searched my memory for any hints that he was unfaithful but all I could recall was that he had been excited about his squash games. Looking back, perhaps I should have suspected something, but I had just thought he enjoyed playing squash. He must have been laughing at me behind my back.

What hurt even more than the fact that he was seeing another woman was discovering he had been lying to me for so long, about something so serious. Even if he stopped seeing her, I would never be able to trust him again. After nearly twenty years, he had wantonly destroyed the marriage we had built together throughout almost my entire adult life. Only a complete idiot could fail to see the truth that was staring me in the face. Resisting the urge to call Paul straight away to tell him exactly what I thought of him and his despicable secret, I picked up the phone and switched it off. Whatever I decided to do, our son was on the point of taking exams. Until he finished, his interests had to come first. My husband's adultery wasn't going to ruin Dan's life as well mine.

While I was deliberating, I heard the front door slam. It was too early for Dan to be home. Wiping my eyes, I patted my short blond hair and went downstairs to the hall where Paul was hanging up his jacket. Clearly flustered, he turned and stared at me with a slightly wild expression which only enhanced his classic good looks. Just one year older than me, he generally appeared younger than forty-three, but today his face was taut with anxiety. His normally tidy dark hair was unkempt, as though he had been running his hands through it as he did when he was stressed.

'You're home early. What's up? You look terrible.'

'I've lost my phone!' he cried out. 'Have you seen it?'

Slipping the phone into my pocket, I shook my head.

'Shall I call it?'

I pretended to hit the speed dial number several times while Paul walked through every room listening out for it, unaware that I was calling an unallocated number. After that we spent a fruitless hour searching the house, until finally Paul sat down in the kitchen and dropped his head in his hands.

'I'm sure it'll turn up,' I said. 'Where did you last have it?'

He shook his head.

'Don't look so worried,' I went on. 'It's only a phone. You can replace it.'

'That's not the point. There was an important number stored on it that I won't be able to access anywhere else.'

'Surely you can get hold of it again?'

'No, I can't. You don't understand.'

I understood only too well.

'There's no need to panic. It'll be stored on the cloud,' I said. 'You can retrieve all your numbers from there if you have to.'

Still frowning, he stood up abruptly. 'You're right. I need to get this sorted out. There's an important meeting later, and I'm expecting a call.'

I nodded but didn't say anything. I knew all about his 'important meeting'.

Without another word, he strode out of the room and a moment later I heard the front door slam again . Through the front window, I watched his car pull out of the drive. As soon as he had gone, I took his phone out of my pocket and looked up Bella's number. I couldn't send her a message and risk Paul seeing it when he had his phone restored, so instead I scrabbled around for a pen and copied the number down on a scrap of paper. Then I took the phone out to the garage where Paul kept his tools and found a hammer. Having removed the SIM card, I put the phone on the floor, crouched down and swung the hammer. It took me a couple of blows to smash the screen which shattered with a satisfying crack. After that I set to work on the back of the phone. That proved more difficult to damage, but I managed to dent it.

Having demolished the handset, I googled "How to destroy a SIM card" and discovered that, without access to a shredder, the best way of destroying it was to use some sort of acid, or else risk damaging the microwave, neither of which suggestion was very helpful. Finally, I came across a practicable solution which was to cut the card along the centre line to disable the silicon chip, and then soak it in salt water to corrode the metal contacts. After doing that, the advice was to cut it into small pieces and dispose of them in various locations. It all seemed a bit excessive, but I decided to follow the recommendations.

Using my large kitchen scissors, I chopped the SIM card into four tiny pieces which I boiled in salty water. Satisfied that the metal contracts were ruined, I poured the hot water through a tea strainer, wrapped the fragments of card in kitchen roll, and stored them in my purse. Having dealt with the SIM card, I turned my attention to the handset. After wrapping that in kitchen roll as well, I stuffed it into an empty tissue box which I sealed in a plastic bag. With the packaged phone further concealed in an otherwise empty cereal box, I took it out to the bins which were due for collection early the next morning.

As soon as I went back in the house, I panicked that Paul might come home and check through the bins in case his phone had accidentally been thrown away. If he found the phone with a cracked screen and missing its SIM card, he would realise it had been thrown away deliberately. Grabbing the rubbish bag, I carted it back inside and rummaged through it, frantically hunting for the cereal box. Paul might return and find me searching in the rubbish. While I could safely explain that I was hunting for his missing phone, it was possible he might spot me finding my mysterious-looking packet.

Even though the cereal box was hardly difficult to find, it felt as though my heart skipped a beat when my fingers closed on it. Grabbing the box, I retrieved the plastic bag containing the phone, and threw the rest of the rubbish out once more. I would have to dispose of the phone away from the house, but that could wait. Paul might be back at any moment. Meanwhile, I needed to hide his phone temporarily, somewhere he couldn't possibly come across it by chance. This was turning out to be far more complicated than I had anticipated. It would have been so much simpler to tell Paul I had found the phone and hope he wouldn't notice the most recent message had been opened.

If disposing of the phone was proving unexpectedly difficult, it was going to be straightforward throwing Paul out of the house. In fact, I was growing impatient having to wait to toss all his clothes out of an upstairs window, preferably when it was raining. But first, Dan had to finish his exams. In the meantime, I needed to carry on as though everything was normal. That was going to be the most difficult challenge of all.

Chapter 2

Paul didn't like to eat in front of the television claiming that, on some days, supper was the only quality time he spent with Dan. We kept our dining room neat and formal rather than homely, because our kitchen was just about large enough to accommodate a small table pushed up against the wall, and three chairs, and we all preferred to eat there, only using the dining room on special occasions, or for guests.

'How did it go?' I enquired, as brightly as I could, when we were all seated with our food in front of us.

'The new phone's still downloading. It's taking hours-' Paul began.

He broke off, realising that Dan was speaking at the same time, also in response to my question.

'Useless,' Dan said and paused, glaring at Paul in sullen silence.

'Until it's working, I won't know what's there.'

'Dad lost his phone and had to get a new one,' I explained.

'Of course, that's much more important than my exams,' Dan snapped. 'Only the rest of my life depends on how I do.'

'You know you've done fine,' Paul assured him.

'Same old, same old,' Dan muttered, staring at his plate.

Paul and I had done our best to reassure Dan. I reiterated yet again how impressed we were with how well he was doing at school. His teachers had predicted he would easily pass all his GCSE exams with grades good enough to secure him a place at sixth form college.

'Predictions,' he hissed. 'That's not the same as results. You think it's so easy.'

'Nothing in life is easy,' I said quietly, avoiding Paul's eye. 'We understand you're under pressure. It would be strange if you didn't feel anxious. It's only natural. But you can only do your best, and if you mess up on the day, you can always retake.'

'So, you think I'm going to mess up and I'll have to retake them all?'

'No, of course not. You know perfectly well that's not what I meant.'

We got through dinner, but it was heavy going.

Paul wasn't the only one who had friendships outside the family, although mine were no secret. I had arranged to meet a couple of girlfriends that evening and set off as though nothing was wrong, despite my inner turmoil. Paul wasn't going to take my social life away from me as well as my marriage. There was no need for me to mention my painful discovery to my friends. My husband's affair was no one else's business. The situation was not of my making, so I had nothing to be ashamed of, yet somehow it felt like a guilty secret. Walking towards the station, I wondered whether it was wise to hide my problems from my friends. Admittedly I shouldn't have read Paul's private messages, but the first one of those had been displayed on the screen. The messages I had deliberately opened were merely an extension of what had already been revealed without any prompting from me. But gossip spread quickly, and I didn't want Dan to hear a whisper of what was happening. He had enough to worry about right then. Once Dan's exams were over, I wouldn't hesitate to throw his father out. My friends could hear all about it then.

The weather was mild, but it was drizzling as I scurried along the street. As I walked, I glanced around, pulling the collar of my raincoat up around my neck. Although the street was empty, I hesitated to drop Paul's phone in someone else's bin in case I was spotted. I wasn't sure whether information and contacts could be stored on the handset, so even though I had trashed the SIM card, I had to be careful about where to dump the phone itself.

Leaving it hidden inside my bag, I kept walking. If I dropped it down a drain, it might block a pipe and be recovered. Similarly, if it were left in a bin, someone could come across it. If there was any way its owner could be traced, Paul might be alerted. There was no reason why he might suspect I was in any way implicated in the disposal of the phone, but if it were discovered with the SIM card removed, it might arouse suspicion.

Arriving at the restaurant I saw one of my friends straight away. Her curly ginger hair was easy to pick out, even though she was sitting with her back to the door.

'Isn't Nina coming tonight?' I asked as I sat down.

'No, she's away.'

'Of course, I'd forgotten.' I forced a smile, trying to act normally. 'Have you lost weight?'

Katie's plump cheeks reddened slightly. 'I've been trying. I really need to get back to Weight Watchers, but it's hard to find the time. There always seems to be so much going on.'

I wasn't sure whether she noticed my conversation was stilted, but I was finding it hard not to mention what was on my mind. Finally, after a couple of glasses of wine, my resolution collapsed, and I heard myself telling her about Paul's phone messages. At once I regretted having blabbed, but my friends would find out about it once Paul left home, so my telling the truth straight away didn't really matter.

'But you must promise to keep this to yourself,' I stressed. 'Paul doesn't know that I know, and I really don't want Dan upset while he's doing his exams. Promise me, Katie.'

To my surprise, it wasn't difficult to admit what had happened. Katie's eyebrows shot up but, apart from her initial surprise, she didn't seem particularly shocked.

'Is there any chance you could be mistaken?' she asked. 'I mean, you were reading his private messages.'

When I told her Bella had called Paul a sexy beast, she giggled.

'It's not funny!' I protested. 'This is my husband we're talking about. How would you feel-'

'Okay, sorry,' she interrupted me. 'Come on, don't get upset with me. I'm your friend, Julie. I'm here for you. But are you sure you didn't misunderstand? I mean, could it have been someone messing about?'

Glancing around, I lowered my voice. 'I'm not making a mistake. It was perfectly clear. He's seeing someone else.'

'Do you think it's serious?'

I shrugged. 'How should I know? I'm not the one having an affair.'

'Could you be overreacting? I mean, perhaps it's just a drunken one-night stand? Maybe if you talk to him, he might come clean and be terribly contrite, and...'

'No, it wasn't a one-night stand. He's been seeing her for about two years.'

Katie gaped. 'Two years?'

'According to *her* messages, he's promised to leave me, and he's been begging her to be patient.'

'That sounds pretty serious. Is he really talking about leaving you? Shit, Julie, are you, all right?'

'I think so. To be honest I'm confused rather than upset. Is that awful of me?'

'You really had no inkling he was having an affair?'

I shook my head. 'Honestly, not a clue. I mean, you never really know what someone else is thinking, I suppose, but I didn't have a clue he was seeing someone else. Not a clue. He goes out every Tuesday to play squash with another man, well, that's what he told me. But all the time he was seeing this other woman. I feel such a fool. How could I not at least have suspected something was going on?'

She gazed at me. 'So now you've found out, what are you going to do?'

'I don't know. I don't know. It's all such a mess. He has no idea I read his messages. What would you do if you were me?'

'I'd chuck him out and change the locks,' she replied promptly. 'So, what happens now?'

I crumbled a piece of bread between my fingers. 'The trouble is, this isn't a good time.'

'Is it ever a good time to discover your husband's cheating on you?'

'No, of course not, that's not what I mean. The point is, Dan's right in the middle of his GCSE's, and you know how important they are. He's desperate to get into college to study for A Levels. He's been working so hard for so long, I can't let anything upset him now, not if I can help it. He's stressed enough as it is. It hasn't been easy for him.'

'Oh yes, how's he getting on?'

'Okay, I think.'

It felt surreal to be sitting there chatting about everyday things, almost as though I hadn't just told her that my husband was having an affair with a woman who called him her Sexy Beast.

'So, what do you think I should do, really? I mean, what would you do?'

'Listen,' she replied, 'it happens a lot. How many people do you know whose marriages have lasted after one of them cheats?' People split up all the time. It's sad, of course it is, and I'm sorry about you and Paul, but you shouldn't beat yourself up about it. This wasn't your fault. If that's how he's prepared to behave, then he's a shit, and you're better off without him. If I were you I'd get rid of him as soon as you can. Just throw him out. You know what they say, once a cheater, always a cheater.'

I wondered if she'd made up that saying, because I couldn't remember having heard it before.

She leaned forward, scowling. 'I've never told you this, but I never liked Paul. I know I've only met him a few times, but I remember thinking you could do so much better for yourself.'

I was genuinely surprised. 'What's wrong with him?'

'Apart from the fact that he's cheating on you? Oh, I don't know, he just struck me as a smooth talker, you know. The kind of man I'd never trust. A real bullshitter. All talk and no decency. I mean he's smart and attractive enough, but you've got to admit he's full of himself. The first time I met him I remember wondering how you put up with such a bighead.'

We both knew Katie was just saying that to make me feel better about what had happened. I appreciated her loyalty, but it didn't help.

'Remember what happened to Nina,' she added darkly.

'Don't worry,' I reassured her. 'I'm not going to fall apart. I can handle this. Like you said, he's a shit and I'm better off without him.'

We were silent for a moment, remembering how Nina had gone to pieces when her husband had left her a few years earlier.

'Yes,' I repeated firmly, 'I'm better off without him.'

The broken pieces of SIM card were still in my purse. Instead of walking straight home after we left the restaurant, I took a detour and stopped beside a bin at the top of a drive. Looking around furtively for fear of being seen, I put the smashed phone in the bin, pushing it down until it was out of sight. I dropped a piece of the SIM card down a drain as I walked away. Before I reached home I stopped again. Having made sure no one was watching, I dropped the other pieces of card down another drain. Then I hurried home, feeling like a criminal, even though I hadn't broken any laws.

That night I slept badly. In the morning, I remembered fragments of a nightmare where the police arrested me for illegally disposing of a phone. They produced the missing handset which rang, and my husband's voice ordered me to confess that I was guilty of war crimes.

Chapter 3

The following Tuesday, Katie and I met up again, and this time Nina joined us. Before I had even taken my coat off, Katie asked me whether I had thrown Paul out yet.

'Have you even tackled him about it?' she pressed me, a frown in place of her usual smile.

'Hang on,' Nina interrupted us, her face alert with curiosity, 'what's going on? What's happened? Have Julie and Paul split up?'

Unlike Katie, Nina seemed distressed to hear about the affair. She gave me a sympathetic grimace across the table and said how sorry she was. Her face always appeared anaemic in its frame of dark hair, but she looked even paler than usual. She seemed so disconcerted, I was afraid she might burst out crying.

'Are you sure you're okay?' she asked me, although she was the one who seemed agitated. Always jittery, she was more fidgety than ever. 'You can come and sleep at mine if you need somewhere to stay, you and Dan, until you sort yourselves out. I've got a spare room, and we can easily-'

'Paul's the one who should be moving out, not Julie and Dan,' Katie interrupted her. 'He's the one who's been playing away from home. If he were my husband, I wouldn't mess around. I'd get rid of him straight away.'

Meanwhile, having had a week to get used to the situation, my own stunned disbelief had turned to dull anger at Paul's betrayal.

'But who *is* this other woman?' Katie demanded. 'What do you know about her?'

'All I know is what I told you. He's been seeing her every Tuesday for about two years, at least that's what the phone messages said.'

'They've been seeing each other long enough for them to have discussed his leaving Julie,' Katie told Nina.

'Bloody hell. He's talking about leaving you? You're joking. That's awful. Throw him out, Julie,' Nina said.

'Where's his phone now?' Katie asked. 'Can we see the messages?'

I described how I had destroyed the handset and the SIM card.

'But that means you can't contact the other woman,' Katie pointed out.

I thought she sounded disappointed.

'Why would she want to speak to the woman Paul's been having an affair with?' Nina asked.

'She needs to call her and tell her to stay away from him,' Katie replied.

'I wrote her number down but then I was afraid Paul might see it, so I ripped up the piece of paper.' I hesitated to add that I had memorised Bella's mobile number before tearing it up.

'Didn't you learn the number off by heart first?' Katie asked. 'I know I would have done.'

'Yes, I did actually.'

'So? Have you called her? What did she say?' Katie pressed me.

'No, I haven't called her, and I don't intend to either. She doesn't know me. Why would I want to speak to her, and if I did, how could I explain who I am and how I even had her number?'

'You don't have to tell her who you are,' Katie pointed out. 'But don't you want to find out who she is and what she's like?'

'Why?' I asked again, although my interest was piqued, as well as my resentment.

'Yes, why would Julie want to see her? She's a marriage breaker,' Nina said. 'She knows he's married but she still kept on seeing him. This other woman was trying to get him to leave you. I wouldn't want to have anything to do with her if I were you.'

'Well if it were me, I'd call her and tell her exactly what I think of her. Or I'd phone her and tell her he's never going to leave me, and he doesn't want to see her again,' Katie said. 'Why should she get off so lightly?'

'But Paul's bound to talk to her and then she'll tell him what I said, and he'll deny it.'

'So? What if he does? Who cares?' Nina said, seeming to change her mind and agree with Katie. 'You can't just take this lying down, Julie.'

We ordered another bottle of wine. When I admitted I was curious to learn more about my husband's mistress and find out how long they had really been seeing one another, Katie suggested I call her anonymously.

'Here, you can use my phone,' she added, fishing it out of her bag as she was speaking.

'But what am I going to say?'

I wanted to know what kind of woman could have attracted my husband away from me, but despite my curiosity I don't think I would have made the call if I hadn't drunk so much, and my friends hadn't been there, egging me on. We were all quite sloshed, with Katie urging me to tackle the marriage-breaking bitch and thrusting her phone into my hand. Taking a deep breath, I recited the number. Katie dialled it and handed the phone to me.

'It's ringing!' she hissed.

A woman's voice answered, husky and a little breathless, as though she'd been running. 'Who's this?'

In a panic, I muttered an apology about a wrong number, and ended the call. Somehow until that moment I hadn't really believed Paul's other woman existed. A mistress was a character in fiction, not an actual person. Seeing my expression, Nina poured me another glass of wine.

'I wonder what she's like,' I muttered. 'He must be with her now.' I didn't want to think about why she had sounded out of breath.

'You could arrange to meet her and go along and just see what she looks like without speaking to her,' Katie suggested.

'I can't see the point in torturing yourself like that,' Nina said. 'Paul's the one who should be suffering, not you. Get rid of him as soon as possible. Cut him right out of your life. You can find someone better than him. He doesn't deserve you.'

I explained that nothing was going to happen before Dan finished his exams.

'One more day,' I said, 'and he's gone. Dan's got his last exam tomorrow and then I'll pack up Paul's things and chuck the case out on the street.'

'Why waste a suitcase?' Katie asked. 'Just throw all his things out of the window. When it's raining.'

I smiled at Katie for saying what I was thinking.

We ordered another bottle of wine and all drank far more than we should have done. Sharing a taxi home, we squashed together on the back seat and Katie pulled a bottle out of her bag and passed it round.

'Here,' she whispered, holding it down so the driver wouldn't spot it in his rear-view mirror. When I asked what it was, she giggled.

'A night cap.'

'I've already had too much.'

'So, a little more won't hurt, will it? Go on, it'll help you sleep.'

My husband had let me down, but at least my friends were there for me. I hoped that Bella would abandon Paul, and everyone else would shun him for ruining our marriage and destroying our family. Our home that had once seemed tolerably happy had been wrecked by his deceit. I felt strangely numb when I reflected on the end of my marriage. But when I thought about Dan, and how our break up would impact on him, I struggled to contain my fury. I wondered whether I ought to wait until he went away to college before confronting Paul.

Old enough to know better, the next morning I woke up feeling as though a heavy weight was pressing down on my face. It must have been getting on for twenty years since I had last been this hungover. All I wanted to do was go back to sleep, but my head was pounding and besides, I had promised to drive Dan to school that day for his last exam.

It was a physical effort to open my eyes. Afraid of throwing up in bed, I struggled to the bathroom where a quick glance in the mirror showed me that I looked almost as terrible as I felt. Splashing cold water on my face, I had to force my eyes to open properly. Feeling ill, I went back to the bedroom where Paul was lying on his side, facing away from me, sleeping peacefully.

'It's all right for you,' I groaned. 'I've got to take Dan to school today. He's got a nine o'clock exam.'

I was half hoping Paul would wake up, leap out of bed, and tell me he would drop Dan at school, so I could have a lie in. But he didn't answer.

I pulled on my clothes and tapped on Dan's door.

'Are you awake?'

'Yes. Leave me alone, will you? I'm getting ready.'

I smiled, remembering how he had struggled to learn to dress himself.

'Don't be too long. I'll go and get breakfast ready.'

'I don't want anything.'

Ignoring his reply, I left him to get washed and dressed. In the hall downstairs, I spotted an unfamiliar coat on the coat rack. Lifting it off the hook, I checked the pockets and found Katie's purse. I called her straight away. She was almost in tears as she thanked me.

'I was sure I was carrying it over my arm when we left the restaurant, so I thought I must have left it in the taxi, along with my purse! Thank you for taking it home and looking after it. I was going to call you and Nina later to see if either of you had picked it up for me.'

When I replied that I had no recollection of taking her coat from the taxi, she laughed.

'It'd be a miracle if you could remember anything about last night. You were out of it. I must say I feel rough today. Are you at home now? I can pop over right away and get my things on my way to work, if that's okay.'

'Sure,' I said. 'I'm dropping Dan at school for an exam, but we won't be leaving for about half an hour, or you can come over later after work.'

Katie said she would come over straight away as she would need her purse at lunch time, and we hung up.

'Come on, you can't go into an exam on an empty stomach,' I told Dan as he toyed with a slice of toast I had given him. 'Dad said to wish you good luck,' I added untruthfully.

'Where is he?'

'Still in bed.'

'Typical,' he muttered. 'He couldn't have got up a few minutes early to say it himself.'

'I think he was tired.'

'I'm tired. I'm the one who's working all the time.'

Katie arrived to collect her coat and we stood in the hall for a moment talking.

'Have you decided what to do about you know what yet?' she whispered.

I shook my head. 'I'll talk to you later.'

: She nodded her understanding. Calling out to wish Dan good luck in his exam that morning, she left. I shouted up to Paul that we were leaving, but he didn't answer. I knew he would be late for work if he didn't set off soon, but I didn't care. It would serve him right if he got in trouble.

Each preoccupied with our own thoughts, Dan and I didn't speak on the short journey to school. I glanced sideways at him a couple of times, but he was staring straight ahead, and appeared to be concentrating. Guessing that he was repeating formulae in his head, I didn't disturb him. Not until he was gathering his bags and preparing to clamber out of the car, did I wish him good luck. He looked back at me with his father's dark eyes, his limbs lank and gangly as Paul's used to be when we first met. Dan looked so young and thin, I felt a lump in my throat and had to turn away, blinking.

'Thanks, Mum. Sorry I've been a bit cross with you lately.'

'Don't worry about it, this is a stressful time, but as long as you've done enough work you'll be fine. Remember, it's the preparation that counts. And you've certainly...'

'Yes, yes, I know,' he interrupted me with a smile that was almost a grimace. 'I wasn't asking for a pep talk. I know you mean well but sometimes your fussing just isn't helpful, it's irritating. And I've got enough on my plate as it is.'

'Good luck anyway.'

'Thanks. And you too, have a good day.'

I returned his smile more brightly than my prospects for that day warranted, but the last thing I wanted to do was upset him just before an exam. As he turned and walked away, a group of other pupils walked past him.

'Oh well, at least they'll be finished soon,' another mother remarked.

Watching Dan lag behind the other kids, I nodded. 'I'll be glad when this is all over.' I wasn't thinking about the exams.

'I know, I can't wait for them to finish. It's insane, the number of tests they have to do,' she replied.

'I'm sure they'll be fine.'

It was bizarre, chattering about mundane issues as though nothing out of the ordinary had happened, when I knew my husband had been conducting an affair behind my back.

The other mother shrugged. 'You know what they're like at that age. He thinks the world owes him a living. But life is never that easy.'

'No, it certainly isn't,' I agreed.

With the image of Dan's worried face in my mind, I drove home. He had looked so vulnerable, walking in to school alone. What was about to happen was going to shatter his world. But the situation was not of my making. I was only reacting to Paul's betrayal. I hoped Dan would understand that.

Chapter 4

Reaching home, I was surprised to see Paul's car in the drive. Going inside, I called out to him, but there was no answer. He wasn't in the kitchen or the living room, so I went upstairs and was startled to see the mound of his body still lying in bed. I called his name, then reached out and shook him by the shoulder. He didn't respond, so I shoved him more strongly, shouting at him to wake up. His arm felt oddly stiff. Grabbing hold of it to heave him over onto his back, I barely registered that his eyes were open. Meanwhile he continued stubbornly unresponsive. In a panic, I slapped his face. He didn't flinch. Everything about him felt rigid. He just lay there, glaring up at the ceiling.

'Paul! Paul! Answer me! For Christ's sake stop it. Look at me!'

Kneeling up on the bed beside him, I studied his face. He didn't even blink. Leaning forward, I listened. He made no sound. I checked for a pulse, a heartbeat, a breath, any sign of life in his motionless body, but there was nothing. Sitting back on my heels, I gazed at him in horror, for the first time taking in his unhealthy pallor and fixed stare. It didn't take medical training to work out that he had passed away in the night.

It's difficult to describe how I felt right then. Numb is the best word I can come up with. I knew I ought to do something, but what? Should the doctor be called? Or 999? I stared at Paul. He would have known what to do, but he was dead. Nothing I did or failed to do could make any difference to him now. In a daze, I pulled the duvet over his face, so I couldn't see his eyes, staring in silent accusation. Then I clambered off the bed and went into the bathroom, as though he wasn't there. And it was true. He wasn't.

My mind seemed to have switched off, but I was aware that my body was physically shaking. All at once, I felt the bitter taste of vomit in my throat and ran to the toilet to be sick. Vomit splashed the sides of the bowl and flecked my jumper. Still shaking, I washed my face. I looked terrible.

'Come on,' I muttered. 'Pull yourself together. Do something.'

Before making any calls, I showered and changed my clothes, carefully avoiding looking at the bed. A hump in the duvet showed where Paul was lying, covered up. I felt as though I was in a nightmare, so that I half expected to wake up and find him snoring at my side. But this wasn't a terrible dream, and he really was dead. I had heard his mistress's breathy voice asking me who I was. Her words kept repeating inside my head, 'Who's this? Who's this? Who's this?' as clearly as if she were in the room with me, yet I could no longer recall the sound of Paul's voice. It was as if he had been deleted from my bank of memories.

I went downstairs to make myself a strong cup of tea and work out what to do next. I had never felt so alone, and there was no one I could approach for advice. Aware that I was procrastinating, I continued to put off making the call for as long as possible. While no one else knew what had happened, I could somehow carry on pretending to myself that Paul wasn't dead. So, I sat in the living room shutting everything else out of my mind and telling myself that a good cup of tea deserved my undivided attention. The whole situation was surreal. All the time I had been downstairs chatting inconsequentially with Katie, and then dropping Dan at school, Paul had been lying in our bed at home, dying or already dead.

After a while I stopped shaking and my mind cleared. Perhaps it was fortunate that, for the moment at least, my anger with Paul was so raw. My fury at his betrayal held back grief that might otherwise have overwhelmed me. But more than anything, I was afraid people would wonder why I hadn't reported my husband's condition as soon as I woke up. Should the police somehow become involved, would they believe that I had left the house thinking my husband was peacefully sleeping? If there had been any way

I could have simply got rid of his body without repercussions, I would have done it. He deserved to be disposed of in a rubbish bin, along with his phone. But that wasn't practicable.

I didn't know who to contact but had a vague idea that a doctor would need to sign a death certificate. And a doctor would be familiar with the correct procedure. Once I decided how to tackle the situation, it took a while to speak to someone at the medical centre. Several of the other receptionists worked part time, like me, and I didn't know the woman who took my call.

'I need a doctor,' I told her. 'No, I don't want an appointment and I can't come to the surgery. The doctor must come here. I think my husband's dead. That is, I know he is. He's not breathing, and I can't find a pulse. Yes, it's my husband. No, I haven't called the emergency services because there's no point. I told you, he's dead.'

Finally, after confirming Paul's full name and date of birth, and my full name and relationship to him, I was told a doctor would be with me soon.

'Wait there,' the voice on the line advised me, as though I might be contemplating going shopping instead of staying at home to open the door. 'The doctor will notify the coroner's office when he gets there, so you don't need to do anything else for now. Just sit tight and someone will be with shortly.'

Soon after my call, one of the practice doctors arrived. Tall and grey haired, he nodded solemnly at me. We had been introduced when I started working at the medical centre, but he had never spoken to me before.

'Where is he?'

Without a word, I turned and led him upstairs to the bedroom where I pulled back the duvet to reveal my husband staring up at the ceiling. The doctor frowned and glanced at his watch. It felt as though time stopped as I waited to hear what he had to say. I tried not to look at Paul's face, but my eyes seemed to have developed a will of their own. Paul lay, motionless, and his face appeared to have taken on a greyish hue so that he looked more like a statue than a man.

'Well,' the doctor said, turning to face me after he had examined the body. 'I'm sorry to confirm that your husband is dead.'

'What happens now?'

He gazed solemnly down at Paul. 'I'm afraid I can't issue a death certificate without knowing the cause of death. The coroner's office will need to know exactly what happened here.' He looked at me with a slightly quizzical expression. 'Your husband's been dead for around ten hours.'

I wasn't sure what the doctor meant but couldn't see why the specific cause of Paul's death mattered. It wasn't unheard of for an apparently healthy man in his early forties to drop dead. If he had suffered a heart attack because of stress from worrying about keeping his affair secret, it served him right. But I kept such thoughts to myself. All I wanted to do was get the body removed from the house as soon as possible. Uppermost in my mind was the thought that I was going to have to sleep in that bed, and I would have to throw out the mattress and sheets that were soiled and beginning to stink. Apart from the horror of death, the smell was making me feel nauseous again.

'Should I contact the undertaker's? I've never had to deal with a situation like this before and I'm not sure what to do,' I gabbled.

All I could think was that the body couldn't stay where it was.

'He can't be moved just yet.'

'What? Why not? He can't stay here.'

'Before any arrangements are made, you need to wait until the police have taken a look.'

'The police?' I felt my skin prickle. 'Why? What have they got to do with it?'

The doctor spoke gently. 'It's likely the police will want to investigate your husband's death.'

'Investigate? What do you mean?'

The doctor looked at me. 'There may be good reason to question whether your husband died from natural causes.'

For the second time that week, I felt the world spinning out of control.

Chapter 5

No time at all seemed to elapse before the police arrived to question me and search the house. They refused to tell me what they were looking for. Fortunately, Paul had replaced his missing phone straight away, because they might have thought it was odd if they hadn't found one. Even though I'd had no inkling of what was going to ensue, I was very glad I'd had the foresight to destroy his old phone.

'I'll tell you exactly what happened,' I told a police woman who was questioning me in the living room.

At that point I hesitated, aware that someone might say they had seen me dropping Dan at school. When you lie, it's best to stay as close to the truth as possible. That way it's easier to avoid being caught out. It also makes it easier to remember your story. All the same, I was careful to say nothing about Paul's infidelity.

'As soon as I got up, I went downstairs to make my son some breakfast. We'd arranged for me to drop him at school this morning, because he had an exam. My son has cerebral palsy and school has been a real struggle for him. He's worked hard to get where he is. It's important he has a proper breakfast.'

I stopped abruptly. Preoccupied with what to say to Dan when he came home, I was rambling inconsequentially. The police where there to investigate the cause of Paul's death. They wouldn't expect me to be more concerned with whether my son had eaten breakfast that morning than with the loss of my husband.

'So, you were busy attending to your son after you got up,' the police woman prompted me.

I nodded. 'I realise now, from what the doctor said, that Paul must already have been dead by then, but he was lying under the duvet and I thought he was asleep. I mean, I just assumed he was still asleep because he didn't move when I got up. I was trying not to disturb him because I thought he must be tired if he was still asleep at that time. He's usually awake before me. So, I got dressed as quietly as I could and went straight downstairs to make some breakfast. My son's not been diagnosed with an eating disorder, it's nothing like that, but I must keep an eye on him to make sure he eats properly, especially when he's feeling stressed. The thing is, I was focused on getting my son to school for his exam. Honestly, I didn't pay any attention to my husband. I just thought he was asleep.'

She frowned. 'So, your son had a school exam?'

'Yes. He's doing his GCSEs, and he's very conscious of the fact that he's doing them a year late. They're important exams because his sixth form studies depend on how he does, and he's been working so hard. I didn't want to upset him.'

Hearing myself babbling about Dan again, I had to force myself to stop talking.

'And your husband?' she prompted me. 'You didn't notice he was dead?'

She didn't hint by a single twitch of a muscle that she found my account hard to believe, but her question was unsettling.

'Yes, well, if I hadn't set my alarm early so that I could give our son a lift to school, I might not have woken up and discovered my husband was dead for another couple of hours anyway, so it didn't actually make any difference that I dropped Dan at school before I called the doctor. I mean, it could have been even later if I'd gone shopping and not come home when I did.'

She frowned and I wondered whether I had made a mistake in sounding so dismissive about Paul's death.

'So, you dropped your son at school. That would have been at what time?'

'At about half past eight. A friend came over first to pick up a coat she'd left in our taxi last night.'

'Your taxi?'

'Yes, I went out with a couple girlfriends last night.'

'The night your husband died?'

'Yes.'

'But he didn't go out with you?'

'No.'

She made a note of Katie's and Nina's contact details, and then there was an awkward pause. I wasn't sure what she was waiting for, so I didn't say anything.

At last she spoke again, and her voice was very quiet, inviting confidence. 'Were you and your husband on good terms?'

'Yes.'

'But when you woke up you didn't notice he was dead?'

'It's like I just told you, I was thinking about my- our son. It's what Paul would have wanted as well. Our son had an important exam, so I took him to school and left my husband sleeping. That's what I thought he was doing, anyway. I thought I'd let him have a lie in.'

I began to cry. If the police woman interpreted my tears as grief, so much the better. To tell the truth, I was crying from fear, because the police were bound to realise none of this was making sense. I had been alone in bed with Paul all night, and no one else had been in the room, at least not while I was awake. Admittedly, I had probably been semi-unconscious rather than simply asleep, after the amount I'd drunk, but the police had found no evidence of a break in. If I wasn't careful, they might suspect I was in some way responsible for Paul's death.

'I loved... my husband...' I stammered through my sobs, afraid my words were too late to save me from suspicion.

'We'd like to check all the electronic devices in the house,' she replied.

'All of them?'

Although horrified, I agreed, afraid they might suspect me of wanting to hide something if I refused.

'You can't take my son's laptop,' I protested. 'What happened with Paul has nothing to do with him. You can't punish a teenage boy who's just lost his father. '

'No one is punishing him,' she told me. 'But we have to go through routine procedures. You do want us to complete our investigation and establish the cause of your husband's death, don't you?'

My relief when the mortuary van arrived was almost overwhelming. I had only to hold my nerve and my horrible ordeal would be over. It seemed to take a long time, but at last the body was removed. Before she left the police, woman questioning me asked me to hand over my phone.

'What if my son calls me?'

'You have a landline here, don't you?'

I nodded dumbly.

Finally, the police left, apparently convinced by my account. I went up to my bedroom and was surprised to find the bed had been stripped. My only response was relief. I had already decided to make up the bed in the spare room and sleep there, so it didn't affect my arrangements

Dan was less easily satisfied. Stuttering and trembling, he was direct in his accusations when I tried to explain what had happened that morning.

'How could you not have noticed he was dead? It's unbelievable.'

'I was focusing on you, Dan. You had an exam-'

'Stuff my exam. We're talking about my father's life. You can't shift the blame onto me and my exam. I could have missed one. It wouldn't have mattered. I'm probably going to fail them all anyway. Neither of us should have gone out this morning. We should have been here, with Dad.'

'It wouldn't have made any difference. Your father died hours before we woke up.'

'How do you know? You're not a doctor. Maybe they could have saved him.' He began to cry.

'He was dead, Dan. The doctor said he died at about midnight. So, it wouldn't have made any difference if I'd discovered him at seven instead of at nine. And he wouldn't have wanted me to let you miss your exam for nothing.'

'How is it for nothing? And who cares about exams? I could have retaken it. I messed up anyway. But you could have saved him, and you didn't. I'll never forgive you.'

'Let's just calm down and-'

'Don't tell me to calm down. My father's dead!'

His discovery that his laptop had been confiscated prompted another outburst. He was only pacified when his grandfather offered to loan him an iPad. Dan's eyes were bloodshot and puffy. By contrast I was dry eyed. I told him I couldn't believe his father was dead and the reality hadn't sunk in yet, but it was hard to conceal my true reaction. The truth was, I was glad Paul was dead. It served him right, and it saved me a lot of trouble negotiating my way through a divorce. Plus, with his death, our mortgage would be paid off. If, after all his cheating and lying, his own heart had let him down, there was a kind of justice in what had happened. Of course, I would have summoned help immediately had be still been alive when I had found him, but he was already dead and there was nothing I could have done to save him. My conscience was clear.

But as the reality of the situation hit me, I struggled to come to terms with the shock of losing Paul. Apart from seeing my son in tears and refusing to eat, one of the most difficult tasks was calling Paul's parents to tell them the news. In their sadness at losing their only child, their sympathy for me was hard to deal with. Naturally they both wanted to know what had happened, but all I could tell them was that his death was being investigated.

'What do you mean, it's being investigated?' my mother-in-law, Stella, asked.

I had to spell out for her that the doctor had been unable to identify the cause of death. 'So, they have to carry out an autopsy.'

'An autopsy? Why?'

'It's what they have to do when there's a sudden death for reasons that aren't immediately apparent. It doesn't mean they suspect anything untoward,' I added quickly. 'They just don't know whether he had a heart attack, or a stroke, or what it was.'

'How's Dan?'

'We're coping.'

'Is there anything I can do?'

It was kind of her to ask, and she agreed at once when I suggested that we bring forward Dan's planned visit to see them. All I wanted right then was to be left alone. Coming to terms with Paul's death was difficult enough. His infidelity was a whole other matter. Adultery was the worst kind of deceit, and I would never have an opportunity to challenge him about it. For the rest of my life, I would have no idea how or why he had stopped caring about me. If he loved me, he wouldn't have promised Bella that he would leave me. He wouldn't even have had an affair with her. Perhaps he too had been waiting for Dan's exams to finish before confronting me with his plans for a new life with another woman. Or he might have just been enjoying a meaningless dalliance with her. I would never know.

Meanwhile, I had Dan's anguish and anger to deal with. Somehow, I had to convince him that I was as distressed about Paul's death as he was, while remaining strong and supportive, as his only living parent. I thought back to the early years of my relationship with Paul, before work and bills and Dan had distracted us from each other. When we had first met, I had thought only of pleasing him, but gradually we had drifted further and further apart. Nevertheless, I had never considered being unfaithful and it hadn't occurred to me that Paul might be having an affair. I had honestly thought we were happy enough, and that muddling along amicably was what most people did, once the first flush of romance faded. We were in our forties, hardly living love's young dream.

'So, you let me sit through my exams as though nothing had happened, and all the time he was dead, and you knew it? I can't believe you did that. Why didn't you call the school and let me know straight away?'

'He was dead, Dan. There was nothing you could have done.'

'Don't you care about my feelings?'

Keen to avoid a confrontation, I held back from accusing him of unfairly directing his anger against me.

'It hadn't sunk in,' I replied, desperate to restore his trust in me. 'I still can't believe it. I think I'm in shock. It just doesn't seem real. I found him like that, in bed, when I got home from dropping you at school, and- it was horrible...'

I broke off, briefly moved to tears. I wasn't crying for Paul, but for myself. Before he died he had destroyed my love for him, so I couldn't mourn his death. But my tears helped because, sobbing, Dan came over to me and put his arms around me.

'It's okay, Mum,' he said. 'It's okay. Don't cry.'

'We'll get through this,' I assured him.

I hoped I was right.

Chapter 6

A few months had passed since we had made plans for Dan to visit his grandparents in Scotland once his exams were over. He had been due to go there in a few days' time, but I wanted him to leave the following morning. Apart from the fact that it would be good for him to stay away from home for a couple of weeks, I needed him out of the way so that I could pursue my own plans.

The lure of an iPad waiting for him in Edinburgh helped persuade him to go.

He assured me he was happy to travel there by himself. 'But are you sure *you'll* be okay?' he asked. 'I'll be with Nan and Granddad, but I feel bad about leaving you on your own for so long. I don't have to go. Or you come with me.'

'I'll be fine. You don't need to worry about me. Dad would have wanted you to go, and he'd be right. We shouldn't let his parents down, especially now, after what's happened. And there's a lot for me to do here. It'll give me a couple of weeks to myself to start sorting out some of the paperwork.'

'What paperwork?'

'You don't need to worry about it, Dan. This is what happens when someone dies. There are a lot of documents to deal with. It takes a long time. It's a big hassle, but Miles is going to help me through it, and I can always call you if I need you.'

He nodded uncertainly. Miles was a friend of Paul's and a lawyer who dealt with wills and probate.

'I could stay and help you?'

'That's very kind, but I think Nan and Grandad might appreciate seeing you right now.'

'If you're sure you'll be okay?'

'Yes. I'll be fine. And I think it would be very kind of you to spend some time with Stella and Mark. They must be worried about you.'

Living in Scotland, Paul's parents hadn't seen us since Christmas, and Dan agreed it would be a comfort for them to see him. Privately I hoped that supporting them in their grief might help him to deal with his own feelings. And although I would never have admitted as much to anyone, it was going to help me to have him out of the way for a while.

Having seen him off at the mainline station, I turned my attention elsewhere. If I had any sense, I would never have risked delving into Paul's secret life. It was all over. He was dead. The other woman in his life was history. As far as I knew, apart from my two friends, the only other person who had known about her was dead. If it hadn't been for my chance discovery, Paul's secret might have died with him.

Rather than poking about in Paul's clandestine affairs, what I needed to do now was focus on rebuilding my life. In some ways that wasn't going to be too difficult because Paul's death had left me in a reasonably secure financial position. Once the police were satisfied, the mortgage would be paid off. Together with my modest earnings as a part-time doctor's receptionist, Dan and I would be able to afford to stay in the house for the time being. When he left to go to university, I might think about working full-time, or moving. I wouldn't need a four-bedroomed house once I was living on my own, and downsizing would release funds for Dan's studies.

Nothing but curiosity drove me to call the number I had found on Paul's phone.

It was answered by the same woman's voice as before. 'Hello?'

'Is that Bella?'

'Yes. Who's this?'

I hesitated before answering. 'We need to talk about Paul Barrett.'

'Paul? Is he all right?'

'He's...' I paused.

'What's happened? Why hasn't he rung me? I keep calling him but-'

'We can't talk about it over the phone. It's not that easy- '

I had so many questions. I wanted her to confirm she had been seeing Paul for two years, and to tell me where they had met, and whether she had been in love with him. More than anything else, I was curious to know what she looked like. I had nothing to gain, but it was like wanting to scratch an itch, or pick a scab. I had to know all about her. I had to see her.

'Who are you? How did you get my number?' she asked.

She sounded so hostile I nearly hung up, but I couldn't stop.

'Paul gave it to me, and he gave me a message for you. But I can't tell you over the phone.'

'Why not? I don't understand. Tell me who you are.'

With the conversation threatening to become tetchy, I suggested we meet at the top of the stairs by the Parcel Yard pub at King's Cross station. I would be able to sit on the terrace outside and watch her coming up the stairs. If I decided not to speak to her, I could slip into the lift and make my way out of the station without her seeing me. We agreed to meet at six o'clock that evening.

'How will I recognise you?' she asked.

'I'll wear a green jacket,' I lied. I had never owned a green jacket. 'What about you?'

She paused. 'A white shirt, and I'll carry a white bag. I've got fair hair. And I'll wear a red scarf.'

I nodded. That figured. Paul had always said my blonde hair was one of the reasons he had been attracted to me. But that was a long time ago.

I arrived at King's Cross station early to take up my position. I wanted to sit near the lift so I had the option of slipping away unseen. Although this was the woman who had destroyed my faith in my marriage, I felt vaguely excited about our assignation, as though I was some kind of spy. We weren't due to meet for nearly an hour but I climbed the stairs glancing around furtively in case she had also arrived early. A few of the tables at the top of the stairs were occupied. I went inside the bar so as not to attract attention. This was a pub, after all. Returning outside, drink in hand, I saw that a table close to the lift had become vacant. Taking a seat, I settled down there to wait.

I recognised her straight away, looking around anxiously, her long hair swinging around her head, just like mine used to do when I had been her age. She couldn't have been more than thirty and was possibly still in her early twenties. Undeniably pretty, she moved with a kind of natural grace. I was unexpectedly overcome by pity for this young woman who had been strung along by my feckless husband. It was hard to believe he could have been planning to leave me and Dan for a girl almost young enough to be his daughter. I wondered if she knew about Dan. Either way Paul had behaved despicably, planning to betray us or her. I would never know who he had chosen.

As if in a dream, I watched a stout woman in a green jacket toil up the stairs a few moments after Bella. They were too far away for me to catch what they said to each other, but there appeared to be altercation. The woman in the green jacket drew back, waving her arms as if to fend off the white-shirted girl who followed her inside.

'You're crazy! Crazy cow!' I heard the woman in the green jacket shouting as she disappeared into the pub with Bella at her heels.

I had watched Paul's mistress for long enough. There was no point in following her into the pub.

With a sense of closure, I stood up and left. My rival was like a younger version of me. I supposed Paul had been going through what was generally referred to as a mid-life crisis. Only in his case the crisis had come at the end of his life.

Chapter 7

When I arrived home that evening, there was a message on the landline from Nina who had phoned to say she wanted to speak to me urgently. It was only eight o'clock, so I called her back at once. She told me she had tried my mobile but that must have been while I was on the underground. Assuming she was concerned about my state of mind, I assured her I was all right, but without explaining what was on her mind, she insisted that we needed to talk.

'What about?'

'It's complicated.'

I was already late calling Dan. Sensing that Nina was going to take a while to get to the point, I said I would call her back once I had spoken to my in-laws, and she had to be satisfied with that.

'Don't forget to call me,' she insisted. 'It doesn't matter how late it is.'

Having satisfied myself that Dan, his grandparents, Stella and Mark, were coping as well as they could in the tragic circumstances, I rang off, after promising to call them again the next evening. By that time, I hoped to be able to give them more details about how Paul had died, and when we could start planning the funeral.

'It's all up in the air now,' I told Stella. 'As soon as they release the body we'll start discussing the arrangements. I won't do anything without speaking to you first.'

Almost as soon as I hung up, my phone rang. It was Nina.

'I was just about to call you back,' I told her.

'I really have to speak to you.'

'What is it?'

After all her insistence on speaking to me, she grew hesitant.

'What is it? What's up?'

'I don't quite know how to tell you-'

'What?'

'The police have been here asking questions.'

'What do you mean?' I felt a frisson of unease. 'What questions? What about?'

'They were asking about you.'

'About me? What about me?'

'I may have got this all wrong, but I think they suspect Paul was murdered.'

'What?'

Once again, the room began to reel. First, I had learned Paul had a mistress, then he went and died on me, and now this.

Remembering the police officers who had taken all our electronic devices away with them the previous day, I wondered what else they had found.

'That's ridiculous!' I protested. 'He was at home in bed when he died.'

'I know. Listen, Julie. You don't think they'll suspect *you*, do you?'

'No, of course not. Why should they?'

'Only that you were there with him.'

'But why would they think I killed him?'

'You had just found out he was seeing another woman,' Nina pointed out.

'So?'

'So, you had a motive.'

'But they don't know about that. Nina, you mustn't tell them,' I burst out, realising the danger that threatened me. 'Promise me you won't say anything. Promise me!' I repeated, my voice rising in alarm.

Assuring me she knew I would never have done anything to hurt Paul, Nina told me not to worry. But as we hung up, I remembered that Katie also knew about Paul's infidelity. I had to speak to her before the police did.

Her husband, Tony, answered the phone.

'Julie? Do you know what time it is?' he said when he heard who was calling.

'I know it's late, but I need to speak to Katie urgently.'

There was a pause during which I thought I heard muffled voices.

'I'm sorry,' he said, sounding faintly hostile, 'she can't talk to you right now.'

'Please, this is important. I have to speak to her.'

There was another pause. This time the phone went silent, as though he had put his hand over the receiver.

After what felt like ages, he came back on the line. 'I'm sorry, she's gone to bed.'

Before I could reply, Katie's voice broke in. She sounded upset, and almost shouted at me, 'Why did you do it?'

'What?'

'The police were here this evening asking questions about you and Paul and your relationship. Why would they do that? You know what they were after. I'm not an idiot, Julie. I can work out what happened-'

'Katie, I haven't done anything wrong. You must believe me. I'm the injured party in all this. But listen, don't tell them I knew about Paul's mistress, or they're bound to jump to the wrong conclusion.'

'How could you do it?'

'You're not listening to me, Katie. I haven't done anything. I wouldn't. I couldn't. I... I loved Paul.'

'How could you? However, much he hurt you, however badly betrayed you felt, nothing could excuse what you did. You could have left him, thrown him out, divorced him, but this-'

'Please, calm down and think about what you're saying. If I was seriously going to kill him, would I have told you about Bella?'

'All that proves is that it might not have been premeditated.'

'Katie, I didn't do anything. You must believe me. When I got home, I was so sloshed I could hardly stand upright, let alone overpower a grown man. I just crashed out straight away, and he was dead when I woke up in the morning. He might already have been dead when I got home, only I was too far gone to notice.'

She put the phone down. Panicking, I called her back, but Tony told me she didn't want to speak to me, and I wasn't to phone her again. If the police hadn't put such a terrible suspicion into her head, it would never have occurred to her to accuse me of murdering Paul. I found it hard to believe she would think that of me. But whatever happened, I had to protect Dan from suspecting his mother had killed his father. Whether or not it was true, he would never recover from hearing the suggestion. It was nearly midnight, but this couldn't wait. I had to persuade Katie that she was mistaken in suspecting I had killed Paul, and she had to be convinced of my innocence before Dan returned. I still had two weeks to change her mind, but I didn't know what she had already told the police.

By midnight I was knocking on Katie's front door. After a few minutes, an upstairs window opened, and Tony peered out.

'Who the hell is that?'

'I need to speak to Katie.'

He disappeared. I waited. When nothing else happened, I knocked again.

'Go away before you wake the neighbours,' he hissed at me from the same window.

'I'm not leaving until I've spoken to Katie.'

'If you don't go right now, I'll call the police. And we'll tell them how you've been harassing her and warning her not to talk to them.'

'I never said anything of the kind!' I replied, aghast at the turn things were taking. 'Please, I just want to talk to her.'

'Go away, before I call the police. She's already upset enough about all this.'

'*She's* upset?'

'She thought you were her friend.'

'We still are friends, as far as I'm concerned. Please, just let me talk to her.'

The window slammed shut.

'Some friend you turned out to be!' I called out.

I hesitated, but I couldn't risk Tony calling the police. It would hardly help my case, if I were found pestering a potential witness at midnight. Such desperation was bound to suggest that I was afraid because I had something to hide. Muttering a curse, I turned away, bitterly disappointed in Katie. As I drove home, I realised that it couldn't be left like that. I had to confront her and clear up any misunderstanding. She worked in a school only a few miles from my house, so I resolved to go there first thing in morning and speak to her.

The next day I left home early to speak to Katie. I waited for her, fretting at the reception desk after she was summoned, but she didn't appear.

'I'm sorry, Mrs. Barrett,' the school secretary said at last. 'I'm afraid Katie's tied up. Our teachers are generally very busy during the school day. Can anyone else help you?'

Peering up at me through the thick lenses of her glasses, she raised her eyebrows slightly when I shook my head.

'Would you like to make an appointment. What did you say your child's full name is?'

'Oh no, I'm not a parent. That is, I am, but I don't have a child at the school. My son's seventeen. Katie's a friend of mine and I need to speak to her urgently.'

'I'm sorry,' she repeated, more coldly this time, 'but she's not able to speak to you right now. If she's a friend of yours, perhaps you could call her this evening?'

'Can I at least leave a message for her? Please ask her to call me. And tell her it's urgent.'

'I told her that you're here, and you're very anxious to see her, but she said she knows what this is about, and she can't spare you any time today. I really don't know what else you want me to say.'

With a shrug, the secretary turned away. Short of running around scouring the premises for Katie, and probably being thrown out by security, or the police, there was nothing more to be done, so I left.

As I walked back to my car, I reminded myself that whatever happened, I had to behave normally. But that was becoming increasingly difficult. I no longer knew what it felt like to be normal.

Chapter 8

The police were waiting for me when I arrived home, their car parked outside my house. After watching me go through my gate, a man and a woman followed me. Tall and lithe, the man moved quickly to reach my side before I had crossed the threshold, while a dark-haired woman strode at his heels.

'Julie Barrett?' He held up his identity card and introduced himself as Detective Inspector James Morgan. 'This is my colleague, Detective Sergeant Mary Cooper.'

The woman nodded, poker-faced.

'Is this about my husband?'

'Yes,' the Detective Inspector replied. 'We're very sorry about your loss, Mrs Barrett, but if you'd like to accompany us to the police station, we can arrange alternative accommodation for you and your son if necessary, or perhaps there's a relative or a friend you can stay with?'

'Alternative accommodation?' I repeated stupidly.

'Just while we take a look inside your house.'

'Where is your son now?' the sergeant asked.

I wasn't sure whether they were entitled to refuse me permission to enter my own house, but there was nothing to gain from being obstructive, and it was important to act as though I had done nothing wrong.

'My son's visiting his grandparents in Scotland. We arranged it months ago,' I added, feeling I needed to explain why he had gone away at such a time. 'We thought it would help them, and I thought it would be good for him to get away for a while, have a change of scene.' It sounded lame, but it was the truth.

'Please, come with us.'

'What's this about?'

'You know why we're here. Now, please, we'd like you to accompany us to the police station.'

'Do I have a choice?' I muttered.

'We would like to ask you a few questions about your husband's death.'

'I've told you everything I know, I don't understand,' I spluttered, doing my best to look surprised.

Katie was right. The police suspected I had killed my husband.

The Detective Inspector gazed steadily at me, his grey eyes unblinking. He was around my age, with hair beginning to turn white on his temples, and a face creased with laughter lines. Under other circumstances I would have found him attractive, but the situation was terrifying. I had to think quickly. Assuming my husband really had been murdered, if the police discovered I had known about Paul's affair, they might suspect I had killed him in a fit of jealous rage.

'What do you mean, you think he was murdered?' I asked, trying to stall them while I considered what to do. 'I need to speak to a lawyer...'

But the time for discussion had run out. A whole team of officers clad head to foot in white suits joined us by the door, looking as though they had just stepped out of a science fiction film. I trembled at the harsh reality of what was happening.

The Detective Inspector held out his hand. 'May I have the key, Mrs. Barrett?' It wasn't a question.

The Detective Sergeant spoke, and it took me a moment to process what she was saying.

'A search warrant?' I repeated. 'What for?'

'We need to look around your house,' she replied patiently.

'I don't understand. Paul's gone. They took him away. They took the bedding. They emptied his drawers. There's nothing left-'

'We'll be the judge of that,' the inspector said quietly.

'No, no, go away, all of you,' I burst out, shocked that these strangers intended to poke about inside my house. 'I just lost my husband. Please, leave me alone.'

Trembling with fear at what they might find, I was powerless to prevent them from conducting their search. The two detectives were very kind about it. The sergeant drove me to the police station where she sat me down and made me a mug of tea while out of sight a team of white-suited officers were busy rummaging through my belongings. At least Dan wasn't there to witness this intrusion into our privacy. That would have just about finished him off.

'They won't move anything in my son's room, will they?' I asked with a sudden tremor of anxiety. 'He's very particular about his things. He suffers from OCD and when he feels stressed he refuses to eat. We manage his condition, but it can be quite serious, and he's already out of his routine. He had to be hospitalised a couple of years ago when he refused to eat, and something like this could set him off again.'

'When is he due home from his grandparents in Scotland?'

'A couple of weeks.'

The Detective Sergeant nodded. 'That's just as well then. I'll make sure nothing in his room is disturbed. Don't worry.'

I didn't respond to her facile comment. She might as well have told me not to breathe. We sat waiting for what felt like a very long time until at last the inspector appeared.

'Just a few questions, Mrs. Barrett,' he said, sitting down, 'and then you can go. Is there somewhere you can stay?'

'How long is this going to take?' I asked. 'And when can I go home and collect my things?'

'I'm afraid that won't be possible today.'

'What do you mean? Why not? It's my house.'

It was ironic that now the house belonged to me alone, I was locked out of it.

'It is currently being treated as a crime scene.'

'A crime scene?'

'Yes. Is there anywhere you can stay for tonight? I assure you that you'll be allowed back home as soon as possible, but these forensic investigations can take a few days.'

'If it's just for a night or two, I've got a friend who'll put me up.'

Once I had assured them I needed no help from them to arrange my accommodation for that night at least, the detectives said they would like to ask me a few questions. I sat in a small room at the police station, sipping lukewarm tea, and they sat watching me drink, until I felt as though I had been drinking tea in front of my silent watchers for hours.

'There is just one small point we'd like to clear up with you, Mrs. Barrett,' the Detective Inspector said at last.

He spoke casually, but I was instantly on my guard, aware that Paul's death had placed me in a precarious position. I tried to sound confident in my answer, but I could hear my voice shaking. The detectives must have noticed it too.

'I did call the doctor as soon as I knew Paul was dead. Of course, I did.'

It was imperative I behaved as though I had never stumbled on Paul's adultery, but it was hard to pretend I was still in love with him when I hated him more than anyone else I had ever known. People say love and hate are closely related. That's a lie. Love is an overriding generosity that makes you smile on strangers as friends. My hatred for Paul was a barren passion. I was a robot programmed only to protect myself and my son, a machine for survival. Other people had been reduced to mere obstacles in my path. I had never felt so desperate before, or so strong.

'Your husband had been dead for nearly eleven hours by the time you called the doctor,' the Detective Inspector said quietly.

'I phoned them as soon as I found him. That is, it might have been a few minutes before I phoned, but I was too shocked to do anything at first.'

He looked thoughtful, no doubt analysing everything I said.

'What did you do for those few minutes between discovering the body and calling the doctor?'

'I can't remember. I don't think I did anything. I think I just cried. And I remember shaking his shoulder and shouting at him to wake up.'

'You didn't try to resuscitate him?'

'He was dead. I could tell there was no point, even if I'd known what to do, which I didn't. All I knew was that he was dead. What difference would it have made to him if I didn't get to phone straight away?' I added, trying to sound him out in case he discovered the delay had been considerably longer than a few minutes.

'My problem is the time of death was around midnight, yet you didn't call the doctor until ten to eleven the following morning.'

'I had to give my son a lift to school,' I explained. 'I was focused on that. He had to have some breakfast before he went to school. He struggles to eat when he's stressed. And my friend came over to collect her coat. She'd left it in the taxi the previous evening.'

When I had given my initial statement to a constable, she hadn't reacted to my account. Now, the inspector's expression gave nothing away. It was unnerving. I would almost have preferred it if he had looked sceptical. When people lie they talk too much, so I dropped my gaze and waited, while the two detectives stared at me in silence.

'Is there anything more you'd like to tell us?' the Detective Inspector asked after a few minutes.

I shook my head. 'What do you want to know?'

The Detective Inspector was abruptly called away, leaving me with the Detective Sergeant and a constable standing by the door.

'How would you describe your relations with your husband?' the Detective Sergeant asked in a low soft voice that seemed to promise discretion.

I wondered if the Detective Inspector's summons had been genuine. Probably they thought I would be more likely to confide in another woman.

'He was my husband. We were married for nineteen years. It would have been twenty this year. You don't stay together for that long if you don't want to be with each other.'

Realising I was sounding defensive, I shut my mouth. I had to be careful not to show my true feelings about Paul. Words spoken cannot be unsaid, and these detectives noticed everything.

'I hate to have to press you at a time like this, but we do need to ask these questions.' She gave me an encouraging smile. 'Were you happily married?'

'Yes. We were happy together.'

I hoped my answer didn't sound wooden. It was true that we had been happy together once. It wasn't my fault if that had changed.

When the Detective Inspector returned and told me I was free to leave, I struggled to maintain my calm expression. The questioning had been gentle, but it had still felt to me like an interrogation. And all the time a desperate part of me wanted to shout out the truth, that I had hated my husband and was glad he was dead. It was no more than he deserved.

'We'd like you to let us know where you're staying,' the Detective Inspector added as I stood up. 'Just in case we need to get hold of you.'

I walked out of there as quickly as I could.

Chapter 9

Although I hadn't seen the inside of a cell, I felt as though I had been locked up for hours. Leaving the claustrophobic atmosphere of the police station, I breathed in deeply, the cool evening air welcome after my hot tiring day. Calling a cab, instead of giving the driver Nina's address, I directed him to the nearest Travelodge which was a couple of miles away, near Northolt station. Without spare clothes or toiletries, I wanted to stay somewhere I could be on my own and not have to field any more questions. Nina would lend me whatever I needed, but I had talked enough for one day. I could hardly accept her hospitality and then insist on being left alone.

The young man at reception handed over a key with an impersonal smile. That suited me. I wanted to be anonymous, left alone to work out what to do. After pretending to listen to his patter about checking out, I made my way along the corridor. The hotel room was clean, with a firm comfortable bed, and the only noise was the gentle hum of passing traffic. I was so exhausted, I thought I would be able to sleep anywhere but, as soon as I lay down, my mind raced. It might have been the stress of everything that had happened, or just the result of drinking too much tea, but I couldn't settle.

Abandoning my attempt to sleep, I called Stella to ask about Dan. I didn't tell her the police were investigating the possibility that Paul had been murdered. As quickly as I could, I shifted the focus of our conversation away from me. When I asked her how she and my father-in-law were doing, she broke down, admitting tearfully that they were finding it hard to believe that Paul was dead. I said I knew exactly how she felt, although that wasn't true. I hadn't struggled to accept that Paul was dead even for a moment, perhaps because I had seen his cold corpse. Dan seemed to be coping, she told me, but he couldn't talk to me just then as he and his grandfather were out getting fish and chips.

After ringing off I lay back on the bed and tried to rest. The mention of fish and chips had made me realise how hungry I was. All I had eaten since the morning was a biscuit at the police station, but I was too tired to go out and look for something.

When the phone rang again, I answered at once expecting to hear Dan's voice, but it was Nina calling to ask how I was. I didn't tell her that I had been turfed out of my house. Somehow since Paul's death I seemed to be lying to everyone.

'Are you sure you're okay?' she asked me.

I assured her that I was fine. Another lie.

'The police came here to see me,' she said, and paused. 'They seem to think someone killed him.' She paused again. 'They'll understand, you know, after what he did to you. If you tell them.'

'What do you mean? Who's going to understand what?'

'Anyone would understand if you lost it in a fit of jealous rage. No one would blame you. I'm here, whatever happens.'

The realisation that Nina thought I had killed my husband shocked me so much I was speechless for a moment. What possible hope was there that the police would believe my protestations of innocence, if my two best friends thought I was guilty?

'I didn't do it, Nina. You have to believe me.'

When she assured me that she did, I wasn't sure if *I* believed *her*.

'You've got to be practical,' she went on. 'Most important, you need to find yourself a good lawyer, in case the police arrest you. It's a possibility, so you really need to think about getting your defence together. And don't worry about Dan. He can come and stay with me if you need someone to look after him.'

'What are you talking about? Paul's death makes no difference to Dan and me.'

'I'm talking about if...' She hesitated. 'If you have to go away for a while. I'm only saying in case. I'm not suggesting you're going to need it, but you ought to be prepared.'

'You really think they're going to arrest me for murder? Is that what you're saying?'

I could feel waves of hysteria rising in my chest, making it hard for me to breathe, but I managed to keep my voice steady.

'No one is taking Dan away from me,' I said.

'No, no, of course not. That's not what I meant at all. I don't want to take Dan away from you. No one wants that. And we won't let the police come between you either. I only meant I'll look after him while you're, you know, being investigated, if that's necessary.'

Her insistence that I shouldn't worry did nothing to calm me. On the contrary, I felt as though the nightmare was closing in around me. In all my confusion, only one thing remained clear in my mind: none of this was going to have any impact on Dan and me. He had already lost his father. He would never survive the shock of losing me as well. So, I thanked Nina for her support, and hung up. I was more determined than ever to extricate myself from my plight before Dan came home. I had two weeks.

To my surprise I slept well after that and woke up in the morning ravenous and thinking clearly. Paul had inexplicably dropped dead. I had to get past my emotional shock and work out what to do. As far as I knew, there was no obvious reason for his death, so the police suspected he might have been the victim of foul play. It was their job to think the worst of everyone, just in case some ostensibly innocent person turned out to be a murderer. It wasn't as if murderers flagged up their guilt. But at the same time, it was a lazy solution to the problem of why Paul had died. What they should have been doing was discovering what had really happened to him. So far, events had unfolded around me with a sickening inevitability. It was time for me to take control of my own fate, which meant it might be down to me to discover the true cause of Paul's death to prove my innocence.

Over breakfast at the Travelodge, I ran through the events of Tuesday evening, as far as I could remember them. My last memory was of sitting in the back of a car with my two friends, surreptitiously drinking from Katie's bottle and giggling uncontrollably. After that I could remember nothing until I woke up the next morning to find my husband's dead body in bed beside me. There was no way I could have killed him. Apart from the fact that I had been in no state to do anything, it just wasn't something I would do. And it was hardly something I would forget. But even I could see that temporary loss of memory due to drinking wasn't the most robust of defences. I had to come up with something better. And I didn't have much time.

The police forensic team were busy searching my house for clues to what had happened. God only knew what they were going to find. In the meantime, it would be best for me to stay out of sight. I had paid for my night's accommodation with my credit card which meant the police would easily be able to discover my whereabouts, should they decide to haul me in for further questioning. But I wasn't ready to be taken out of circulation just yet. First, I was going to do my own investigation. Realising that Bella had probably been the last person to see Paul alive, my next step was to arrange to meet her, face to face. But this time I wouldn't bottle it. There was more than mere curiosity driving my interest now.

To carry out my plan unimpeded, I would have to disappear. With Paul's death I was going to a wealthy woman, certainly wealthy enough to spend a few hundred pounds keeping myself out of sight. I would have to get hold of a new phone, and find somewhere to spend the night, and everything would have to be paid for in cash. Plus, once I had withdrawn enough money, I would need to travel around without leaving any trail, which ruled out using my car or public transport. There was no point in trying to cover my tracks before getting hold of the cash, so I caught a bus back to Harrow and went to an ATM. When I keyed in my PIN number, an error message appeared on the screen: Access Denied. I ran along the street to another bank, but the same thing happened.

I had just over eighty pounds in my purse, barely enough to live on even for a day, and somehow, I was going to have to disappear. And before that, I had to speak to Dan.

To my relief, he picked up straight away. If he had been out and not answering his phone, my plans would have been delayed, and with every passing moment I risked being tracked down if the police were looking for me. I chatted to him for as long as I could, and he sounded as though he was doing all right. When I spoke to Mark, he confirmed that Dan seemed to be coping. They were talking about Paul a lot, he said, but Dan was eating and sleeping, and although he was clearly upset and grieving, he wasn't making himself ill. Thanking Mark, I told him that I might not be able to call them for a day or two. When he expressed surprise, I struggled to explain that I was swamped with paperwork to do with the funeral arrangements and the probate. That wasn't true, but I couldn't think what else to tell him as I might not have access to my landline for a while.

'Does that mean you have a date for the funeral?' he asked.

'No, not yet. It's all taking forever. But I'll keep you posted. Don't worry, everything's getting sorted out.'

Suppressing a flicker of guilt at having lied, and a pang of jealousy that I wasn't the one comforting my son, I rang off before Mark could quiz me any further. It must have sounded odd that I wanted to cut myself off from them for a few days, but I hoped he would assume I needed space to come to terms with my loss. People grieved in different ways. Telling myself Dan was in good hands, I turned my attention to my immediate problems.

My priority now was to purchase a phone for cash, so I could contact Bella without the call being traceable. That proved trickier than I had anticipated. None of the first few phone shops I tried were able to sell what I wanted. Finally, I found a young man working in another shop who was prepared to swap my phone for a second hand pay as you go. Although the new phone had cost me more than it was worth, I was happy because part of the deal was that he wiped all my details off my phone. With fifty pounds in my purse, and a new phone that couldn't be traced, I was satisfied that I was off the radar, at least for the time being.

Seated at a corner table in Starbucks, with a coffee and a pastry in front of me, I called the woman who should have been my worst enemy. She was the only person who might be able to help me.

Chapter 10

As a rule, I ignore calls from unknown numbers, and I was afraid Bella might feel the same way. But on my third attempt, she answered. My persistence must have persuaded her that someone wanted to speak to her very badly.

'Bella?'

'Who is it?'

'You don't know me, but I need to meet you.'

'Have you called before? Is this about Paul? Was it you who was supposed to see me on Thursday?'

Admitting that was me, I apologised for failing to turn up at King' s Cross. 'Something came up that prevented me from making it,' I said.

That was true, in a way, but I didn't explain that it was my own cowardice that had stopped me from meeting her.

'Why should I trust you to turn up this time?'

'Because you want to know what's happened to Paul.'

She didn't argue with that, and we arranged agreed to meet as before.

Leaving the coffee shop, I went into a stationer's and bought a notebook which I threw away as soon as I left. I kept the carrier bag. The next few shops I visited were well staffed, but it wasn't difficult to find one where the changing rooms were poorly supervised. Taking a few T-shirts, a jacket and a handful of scarves, I slipped through into a cubicle. With the door bolted, I checked my haul for security tags. It was a cheap shop and as far as I could see, none of the garments were tagged. So far so good. Quickly I bundled my own jacket and shirt into the carrier bag I had brought from the stationery shop. Then I pulled on an innocuous grey T-shirt and denim jacket. The jacket was slightly too big, and the sleeves were too long, but that didn't matter. It looked fine with the cuffs turned up. In fact, it made the jacket less obviously stolen, because it didn't look new. Nothing about my outfit was likely to attract attention. Finally, I chose a turquoise scarf which I stuffed into my handbag. My heart was pounding as I hurried out of the shop, terrified of feeling a hand tap me on the shoulder, but no one challenged me.

Winding my new scarf round my neck, I sauntered into a charity shop and left my own shirt and jacket on hangers, ensuring they were as inconspicuous as possible by leaving them on rails of similar items. If the police *were* looking for me, I didn't intend to make it easy for them to find me. In a party shop I paid a few pounds for a pair of costume spectacles with plain glass lenses and black frames. As it happened they quite suited me, but the important thing was they didn't look fake. They put the finishing touch to my disguise.

So now I was a shoplifter. My new status as a murder suspect, and a fugitive from the law, was proving strangely liberating, since compared to that anything else seemed petty. I knew that I wasn't helping my situation, and I should give myself up to the police before I landed in any more trouble. But I was too angry to surrender my freedom willingly, because none of this was my fault. Paul was to blame for everything and he was the one who had escaped retribution. It wasn't fair. There was no way I was going down without first fighting to clear my name. I owed that much to Dan.

There were CCTV cameras all around the shopping centre, but I wasn't sure where else to go, so I spent the next few hours sitting in a coffee shop pretending to read a cheap book I had picked up in a bargain store. As a crime thriller it was fast paced and quite exciting, but it barely held my attention. All the time I was aware that I might be a wanted person, and I kept glancing up to make sure no one was watching me.

After about an hour, a couple of uniformed police officers entered and stood in the doorway, looking around. Feeling my heart hammering, I kept my head down pretending to be engrossed in my book. I didn't dare look up for a long time and had to remind myself to turn over the pages as though I was really reading. When I finally risked looking up, they had gone, leaving me to wonder whether they had been searching for me or were just passing through on a routine patrol.

I arrived at King's Cross early and sat down at an empty table to wait for Bella. This time I waved as soon as I saw her red scarf, and she came straight over to my table and sat down.

'Can I get you a drink?' I asked, reckless of the fact that I was virtually broke.

Her eyes narrowed. 'You're his wife, aren't you?'

'How did you know?'

'I recognise you from the photo on Paul's desk at work. That's where we met.' She sighed. 'You know, I'm sorry it had to be this way. I hate the fact that I'm sleeping with a man who's still married to someone else.'

'You didn't let that stop you.'

'Yes, but I didn't know about you when it all started.'

'How can you say you didn't know? You just told me you saw my photo, so you must have known he was married.'

'He told me you were estranged.'

'Why would he have my photo on his desk then?'

She shrugged. 'If I'd known you still cared about him I would never have let it go this far.'

'I don't care about him. He's nothing to me.'

'If you don't still have feelings for him, why would you bother to see me? And I know why you're here.' She paused. 'He told me you didn't love each other anymore. He said the only person you care about is your son and if it wasn't for him your marriage would have been over a long time ago. But I don't believe that's the case for you, is it? I think you do still love him. That's why you're here. You should tell him how you feel and let him make up his own mind what he wants to do. I'll understand if he chooses to stay with you. But I don't think that's even a remote possibility.' A faint smile flickered on her lips. Her smugness made me want to slap her. 'I know he loves me. He wants to leave you, so he can be with me. It's all for the best, our meeting like this, so now we can get him to sort this out.'

She seemed confident he would never give her up, as though my nineteen years of marriage to him counted for nothing.

'That's not why I'm here,' I said.

'He's going to leave you. He's told me he's going to divorce you as soon as he can get you to agree. He might not have persuaded you yet, but that's what's going to happen. You can't force him to stay with you forever.'

I shook my head. It would be needlessly cruel to tell her that Paul had lied to her about having asked me for a divorce.

'It's not going to happen now,' I said quietly.

'I don't think that's for you to decide. Let's go and ask him right now and end this once and for all.'

She pushed her chair back and began to stand up, but I reached out and put my hand on her arm.

'Wait, Bella. Please. You don't understand. It's already ended.'

Something in my tone must have startled her because she sat down abruptly.

'I came here to ask you a few questions,' I said. 'And to tell you that... There's no easy way to say this. I'm sorry to tell you Paul's dead.'

She put her hand over her mouth and her eyes grew wide. 'No!' she burst out. 'You're just saying that to stop me seeing him. That's a terrible thing to say. He might be dead to you, but–'

'Why else do you think he suddenly went silent? You haven't heard from him since Tuesday night, have you?'

'He told me he was leaving you. We were going to get married. We were going to start a life together.' Hiding her face in her hands, she broke down.

With a sigh, I explained that Paul hadn't knowingly deserted her. He couldn't help being unable to contact her. It was strange, feeling sympathy for this woman who had stolen my husband's affections away from me, but the reality was that the romance had fizzled out between us a long time ago. I felt an unexpected impulse to comfort Bella. She seemed like a nice girl. If I had come across her in any other situation, I think I would have liked her. I could even understand how Paul might have fallen in love with her.

'Did he love you?' I asked.

She shrugged. 'He said he did.' She raised her tear stained eyes and looked at me. 'Why would he say it if it wasn't true?'

Even she knew that was a stupid question.

'I suppose we'll never know, will we?' I answered my own question.

The difference between us was that I was no longer in love with my husband. I felt sorry for Bella. This wasn't how I had expected our meeting to go, but I needed to be strong and broach the subject I had come to address. It was awkward. If she didn't believe me, my situation would be hopeless.

'The reason I wanted to see you,' I said and paused. 'Paul died on Tuesday night.' Her eyes widened in horror. 'Did you see him on Tuesday evening?'

'Yes. But... What happened? How did he die?'

'I don't know. The police are looking into it.'

'The police?'

'Yes. They're not sure about the cause of his death. Did there seem to be anything wrong with him on Tuesday evening?'

She shook her head.

'Only I think you were probably the last person to see him alive and I wondered if you might be able to shed any light on his physical or mental state that evening? Did he complain of feeling ill? Or did he look as though anything was bothering him? Was there anything that struck you as out of the ordinary about him?'

Again, she shook her head. 'Nothing.' She frowned. 'Do the police know about me?'

'No. They would have been to see you by now if they did.' I hesitated. 'It's probably best if they don't find out about your affair. They'll only start pestering you.'

She nodded, and I breathed a silent sigh of relief.

'You will let me know how it happened, won't you? I mean, it doesn't change anything, but I'd like to know.'

'Of course.'

We both knew I was unlikely to contact her again, but we parted with a hug. It just felt right. Although we would probably never meet again, in losing the man we had both loved, we shared a bond of sorts.

Chapter 11

I found a Travelodge along Grays Inn Road, half a mile from King's Cross station. It was a case of hiding in plain sight. Although the central London streets were peppered with security cameras, I was confident my new appearance would go unnoticed. And the busy area gave me a greater anonymity than I might have found in a less densely populated area.

I had been wearing the same clothes all day and would have to wear them again the next day, but I didn't want to waste money buying more, or risk being stopped for shoplifting. Instead I bought a deodorant and doused myself in it after taking a shower. Rinsing certain parts of my clothes, I dried them with the hair dryer. It took a long time, but it was a kind of respite to be occupied with so mundane a chore.

The traffic outside was clearly audible even with my window closed, but I slept well. In fact, since Paul's death, my nights had been less disturbed than when he had slept at my side. Even the hum of the traffic was a constant drone while his snoring had been intermittent silences disturbed by sudden loud snorts right by my ear. In some ways, the silences had been worse to bear than the noise of his snoring because, ironically, I had often lain awake listening, afraid that he had stopped breathing. At least I no longer needed to worry about that.

All that concerned me now was avoiding arrest while I investigated Paul's death for myself. And meanwhile the clock was ticking. If necessary, I was prepared to try and arrange for Dan to remain in Scotland with his grandparents for another week, but I was wary of calling them on my new phone in case the police were monitoring *their* calls. But one way or another I was going to have to call them the following evening, and I would have to do so without leaving any trace of my location. I had a lot to think about, but I was too tired to make any more decisions that night.

The next morning, I tried to make plans over breakfast. I didn't have enough cash to spend another night in the Travelodge. The more I thought about my position, the more hopeless it seemed. In my desperation I had allowed myself to believe that Bella would help me. If Paul had been feeling unwell on his last evening with her, I could have persuaded her to go to the police with me, to put the case that he had been ill before he died. But her assertion that he had been fine led me nowhere.

Glancing up, I caught sight of a television screen in the corner of the breakfast area. Fortunately, my coffee mug was almost empty, or it would have spilt all over the table, and the last thing I wanted to do was draw attention to myself while my face was displayed on the London news with a subtitle: "Police would like to speak to this woman."

There was no longer any question that they were looking for me. Until then, I had always turned to Paul whenever I had a problem. For the first time in my life I really needed help and he had disappeared and was never coming back. Even knowing he had abandoned me for another woman would have been preferable to this. I could still have talked to him and asked his advice. Our relationship had been deeper than romance. He had been my rock for as long as I could remember. Overcome with emotion, I fled from the restaurant of suited business-men with their briefcases, and anoraked tourists with back packs.

Locked in a toilet cubicle, for the first time since my husband's death, I gave way to despair.

Only the thought of Dan kept me from losing the will to carry on battling to prove my innocence. Somehow, I had to speak to my son and reassure him that everything was all right at home, without revealing where I was or what was going on. I was reasonably confident that the item of London news I had seen wouldn't be broadcast in Scotland. If Dan saw it, any hope of protecting him from further distress would be wrecked. In the meantime, I had to proceed on the assumption that he knew nothing about my immediate difficulties. The death of his father was more than enough emotional trauma for him to have to deal with. It was fortunate he had such a close relationship with his grandparents, or I don't know what would have happened to him.

What was just as pressing as contacting my son, was the need to prove my innocence. Unless I withdrew more cash from an ATM, I had under twenty pounds left. There was no way I could continue to survive on my own. I wracked my brains to think where I could turn for help. By now the police would probably have spoken to everyone on my contact list, so it wasn't safe for me to approach anyone I knew. Nina might be prepared to help me, but even if I managed to get in touch with her in secret, the police knew she was my friend. There was no guarantee she wasn't being watched.

In the meantime, I was at risk of being recognised at the Travelodge now that my face had appeared on the news. I had to move on.

After checking out, I bought myself the cheapest pair of sunglasses I could find. They weren't too dark to see through, and they masked my appearance better than plain glasses. Next, I needed to find a bed in a hostel while I figured out what to do. Passing a church, I wondered vaguely about seeking sanctuary, but that wasn't a proposition nowadays. In any case, I couldn't hide out indefinitely. Somehow, I had to get help.

On my way back to King's Cross station, I passed a large phone store. I wanted to buy another mobile, so I could call Dan and while I was making the purchase, I had an idea. Researching in an Internet café, I made a note of a few likely numbers and called them.

'Do you have an office in London?'

'No, but I work all across the city and can arrange to meet you at a convenient location.'

'So, you could meet me in London?'

'Yes. I suggest we have a conversation on the phone for ten to fifteen minutes and you give me any information you feel comfortable telling me, and after that I'll be able to tell you whether this is something I can help you with.'

I took a deep breath. This wasn't going to be easy. Any hint of the trouble I was in was bound to scare him off, and quite possibly prompt him to contact the police.

'I want to investigate my husband,' I began.

'Go on.' When I hesitated, he asked, 'Do you suspect him of cheating on you? This kind of situation can be very upsetting but we're here to help you get to the truth if that's what you want.'

'No, it's not that, not exactly. I mean, he was having an affair. I know that.'

'But you're after proof?'

'No, no. I don't need proof. I know all about it. I've already met the other woman and she hasn't denied it.'

There was a short pause. 'What is it you need help with?'

'My husband's dead-'

'I'm sorry.'

'And I need to know what happened to him.'

'You want to know where he's been buried?'

'No, he's not been buried yet. He only died on Tuesday. But I need to find out how he died. The cause of death.'

'I see.' He paused. 'I take it there's no question of a police investigation into the circumstances of his death?'

'It's not quite that straightforward.'

'Perhaps it's best to leave it to the police?'

'I'm prepared to pay, whatever it takes, to get to the truth. You can name your price.'

My words sounded ludicrous. This wasn't a film, and he wasn't going to risk any trouble with the police.

'If you can't help me, maybe you can recommend someone who can?' I said. 'I'm desperate. Please, I really need help.'

'I'm sorry, lady. This isn't something we can deal with.'

After a few more calls, I began to lose hope. As soon as I mentioned that I wanted to investigate a death, and acknowledged that the police were involved, the private investigators I contacted were unable to help me. But I persevered, mainly because I could think of nothing else to do and, finally, someone said he was prepared to help me.

'I'll tell you what I can do for you,' he said. 'But this never comes back to me. It's more than my reputation's worth to be associated with anything irregular. Have you got a pen? Remember, you didn't get this number from me.'

I jotted down the number and he rang off before I could thank him. I gazed at the scrap of paper in my hand, presumably the number for a dodgy private investigator. But in my present circumstances, on the run from the police, that was the best I could hope for.

Before calling the number, I phoned Dan, aware that this was possibly the last time we would speak for a while. Stella answered the phone. When she prevaricated over passing the phone to Dan, I knew I was already too late to keep my status hidden. She asked me where I was and knew I couldn't afford to stay on the line begging to speak to my son. The police had all kinds of equipment that could trace calls. I just had to hope that he would be all right at his grandparents' house. For the time being, that was the only home he had.

Chapter 12

Clearly used to such assignations, the private investigator didn't hesitate to set up a meeting in a dingy café near Ladbroke Grove station. The windows were grimy and the table felt sticky, but the place was empty apart from a dowdy old man in a raincoat and a slovenly girl behind the counter. It was a depressing setting, and appropriate for what I had to do. Taking a seat at a corner table, as instructed, I waited.

It was only a couple of minutes before a man with a craggy face and mud-brown eyes sat down opposite me and leaned over the table. I stared at his crooked nose and unshaven chin, avoiding looking into his eyes, and wondered how I had come to this. In less than a week I had become a suspected murderer, and a fugitive from the law, as well as a thief.

'You're Julie.' Although we had never met, it didn't sound like a question.

'What's *your* name?'

'You can call me Ackerman.'

It was obviously a false name, but I didn't care. It was probably best not to know too much about him.

'Shall we get a coffee?' he suggested.

'Okay.'

He didn't move and I realised he was waiting for me to go up to the counter. As I pushed back my chair, he told me he drank his coffee strong and black with two sugars. I went over to the counter and ordered his black coffee, and a skinny latte for myself.

'No skinny,' the girl said.

Back at the table, I set two mugs down and Ackerman nodded at me. I took a sip of coffee and burned my tongue.

'Now,' my companion said, cupping his mug in one large hand. 'Tell me what I can do for you.' He smiled, showing a chipped front tooth.

Leaving out any mention of my current difficulties, I explained that my husband had died a few days earlier. The police, I said, were unwilling to investigate, but I was convinced my husband had been murdered.

'You're saying you woke up in the morning and found him dead in bed beside you?'

'Yes.'

'And you think he was murdered in his sleep?'

'Yes.'

'And the killer didn't disturb you?'

'That's correct. I was asleep. To be honest-'

'Please.'

'I'd had way too, much to drink and I was out cold.'

'I see.'

'So? Will you help me?'

'Help you?'

'Yes, to find out who was responsible for my husband's death. You see, the police don't believe he was murdered and- well, I need to know the truth.'

Ackerman stared at me for a moment, then his eyes narrowed as though he was calculating something.

'You think he was murdered, but the police don't?' he asked, speaking very slowly. He leaned forward suddenly. 'You're certain about that?'

I nodded.

'Very well,' he said. 'I'll help you. But it'll cost you.'

'Of course. Name your price.'

I wasn't sure if I was being reckless or wise, but I couldn't manage the situation alone, and so far, Ackerman was the only person prepared to even consider helping me.

'I don't care what it costs,' I insisted. 'I really need your help.' I stopped, afraid of sounding too desperate. 'Of course, if this isn't your line of work I can take it elsewhere. With the funds I have at my disposal, I'll easily find someone to investigate my husband's death. But I don't want the police to know I've asked you. This has to be kept just between us or the deal's off.'

He leaned forward. 'Five thousand pounds.'

He spoke so quietly, I wasn't sure I heard him correctly.

'What?'

'Five thousand.'

'Yes. All right.'

'As a deposit.'

'So how much will it be altogether?'

He shrugged. 'That rather depends on how much work I'm going to have to do. Let's start with the deposit, shall we?'

I agreed to his terms, five thousand pounds up front, the balance yet unspecified.

'Should we agree a maximum fee?' I asked, suddenly getting cold feet.

He frowned. 'It's tricky to put a figure on it, given we neither of us have any idea how much of my time this is going to take. I know what my time is worth. I won't rook you, but it's up to you to decide whether you want to trust me or not. It works both ways. How do I know you're good for the money? Anyway, it's your call.'

He downed his coffee in a few swift gulps.

'Yes,' I said, knowing only that if Ackerman walked away, I was on my own. 'Let's do this.'

He nodded. 'Now, about that deposit.'

I had agreed to pay him five thousand pounds, but all I had on me was a handful of change. When I told him I might have a cash flow problem, he frowned.

'I mean, I have the money. A lot of money. My mortgage is paid off and I have twenty thousand pounds savings in my own name, plus my husband's work pension and his savings. And I can sell his car. He has a new Mercedes. That must be worth something. It's just that I might not be able to get hold of any of it right now.'

'What about your own savings?'

I shook my head. 'There might be a problem. It's not something I can explain. It's to do with my husband's family.'

It was a stupid lie, but it was all I could think of on the spur of the moment.

'You're not being honest with me,' he said, getting to his feet.

'Where are you going?'

'Out of here, unless you level with me. And before you tell me exactly what you're involved in, you can pay me the deposit we just agreed. I have a contact who knows how to move money around without leaving any traces. Come on.'

Feeling increasingly like a criminal, I followed my new acquaintance out of the café. Ackerman had a rundown car parked nearby, an old kind of Ford.

'Hop in.'

It wasn't as though I had anywhere else to go, but as we drove off I had a feeling I might have landed myself in worse trouble than before, if not in actual danger. At least the police would have to charge me and subject me to a trial. I didn't know anything about this man Ackerman, yet I had willingly jumped in his car, allowing him to drive me to an unknown destination. And he had questioned whether *he* could trust *me*. Not for the first time, I wished Paul was there to help me. All I could do was keep my wits about me and hope for the best.

We drew up in a rundown industrial estate. Ackerman led me through a warehouse of electrical equipment to a small office where a sharp-featured man was seated behind a very large desk. He looked up and nodded.

'It's... err...?'

'My name's Ackerman,' my companion said promptly, holding out his hand.

They shook hands, and Ackerman introduced the man behind the desk as Martin. We sat down.

'This lady needs to pay me five thousand pounds,' Ackerman said.

Martin nodded. 'But you don't want anyone to trace the transfer of funds? I can't see any problem with that. So, let's make it seven thousand, shall we? How about an expensive non-refundable holiday? Or a new carpet? What works for you?' Seeing my expression, he paused. 'You do have the funds available?'

'Oh yes. I've got the money.'

Martin picked up a pen. 'Let me have your bank details then, and we'll sort this out before anyone even knows it's happening.'

'The thing is, there may be a problem.' I hesitated. 'You see, if I take any money out, my husband's family are going to know.'

'Your husband's family? But there's an account in your name?'

'They could stop me getting at it,' I said miserably, aware that my excuse didn't really stack up, seeing as it was my bank account. 'I tried to take out five hundred on Saturday from a hole in the wall, and it wouldn't let me.'

'She has funds but they're currently unavailable,' Ackerman said.

'Liquid assets frozen?' the other man replied, putting down his pen.

'Looks that way,' Ackerman said. 'As good as.'

'So, someone's placed a restraint on your account,' Martin said, giving me a shrewd look. 'Let's think about this. Who else might have access to your account? Your husband's dead. His family wouldn't be able to see your transactions. So, who could it be?' He stared at me with a slightly quizzical smile. 'Who could possibly have access to that sort of private information?'

I caved in. 'I think the police are looking for me,' I muttered. 'So, I might not be able to get hold of the money, because yes, they've probably frozen my account. They want to find me. I can't say why.'

Martin didn't even blink. 'I'm not interested in why the police might want to question you. That's why Ackerman brought you here to me. Have you got any other liquid assets?'

'I've got fifteen thousand pounds in an ISA.'

Martin shook his head. 'That would take too long, and they might put a stop to it before we get it out.' He looked thoughtful. 'What about that ring you're wearing?'

I clasped my hands. 'It was my mother's engagement ring.'

He grunted. 'Is it insured?'

'Yes, but-'

'How much for?'

'Five thousand pounds, I think. But I can't let you have it. It was my mother's.'

He shrugged. We both knew I had run out of options. With my own engagement and wedding rings, together with a diamond pendant Paul had bought me for our anniversary, and my diamond stud earrings, the jewellery I was wearing should fetch several thousand pounds.

'That'll do for now,' Martin said briskly as I placed my jewellery on the desk. 'I'll get those gems valued and sold. That'll give us your first instalment, Ackerman, and the rest will be yours, lady, after I've taken my cut, of course.' He smiled. 'Good to do business with you. I'll be in touch.'

'Do I get a receipt?' I asked.

Martin and Ackerman laughed as though I had cracked a joke. 'I'll have that money for you by tomorrow evening,' Martin said.

Afraid that I had just been shafted by a pair of crooks, I followed Ackerman out of the room.

'You mentioned a son?' Ackerman said to me as we walked back across the warehouse.

'Yes. He's staying with his grandparents in Scotland for the time being.'

'While you're here avoiding doing anything that might let slip where you are.'

I was suddenly too choked to speak.

'If you write to him I can post your letter with a postmark somewhere out of London. How about Tunbridge Wells? Don't worry. I'll make sure it gets to your boy.'

I could have flung my arms around his neck and hugged him.

'Thank you,' I said. 'I'd really appreciate it.'

'Had a son myself once. Do me a favour, lady,' he went on quickly, before I could say anything. 'Don't start asking me questions. This is just a job. Let's keep it that way.'

Chapter 13

After Ackerman dropped me back in central London, I had to find somewhere to stay for the night. On the assumption that Martin came through with the money, I could afford a hotel room. But I had another idea. Katie and even Nina might have told the police Paul was having an affair, but I was sure I hadn't mentioned Bella's name to either of them. Since I had destroyed Paul's phone, the police had no way of discovering her identity. So, I called her.

'Bella, it's me, Paul's wife.'

'Paul's wife?'

'Yes.'

'Have you found out what happened to him?'

'No, it's not that. I need your help.'

'You want *my* help?'

Listening to her, I realised that this was a mistake. She would never let me stay at her house. It was insane of me to have imagined she would.

'It's all right, forget I called.' I hung up.

I was on my own again. Too tired to find anywhere else, I returned to the Travelodge in Grays Inn Road, but without money there was no point in going in. As I was prevaricating, my phone rang. It was Bella.

'You called me. What do you want?'

'I was just wondering if you were at home this evening.'

'Yes. What do you want?'

I wondered if I had misjudged her when we had met. She had seemed sympathetic, but I could hardly blame her for sounding wary. In her position, I would have been extremely dubious about speaking to my dead lover's wife. She might even be wondering if I had been telling her the truth. For all she knew, Paul might still be alive. I certainly had a motive for persuading her he was dead, just to get her out of his life. But once again I was desperate. It was getting late and if I didn't find somewhere to stay soon, I might end up sleeping on the street.

Although the weather was warm, even for June, once the sun went down it grew cold. Worse than that, I was concerned about my safety alone on the streets at night in central London. Many homeless people kept dogs for protection, but I was alone. At least I was no longer wearing jewellery that could be stolen, but I was really scared. All my life I had been cared for, first by my parents, then by my husband. I wasn't used to coping with dangerous situations by myself.

'I have a problem,' I said cautiously.

'Really?'

There was no harm in asking her for help, if I felt my way carefully in case the police had been able to trace her. I reasoned that if they had warned her they suspected I was capable of murder, telling me where she lived was the last thing she would do.

'I just wondered if it's possible for you to put me up for tonight? If you feel you can?'

Her silence was almost audible.

'I know it's a bit late, but I've been let down...'

'Are you serious? You want to come and stay at my house?'

Her surprise was predictable. She was the last person on earth I ought to be asking for help. But that meant her home was the last place the police would expect to find me.

'There's no one else I can turn to right now. I'll explain when I see you. It's complicated.' She didn't answer. 'Please. I wouldn't ask you if I had anywhere else to go.'

'Don't you have friends who can help you?'

'No. That is, yes, I do have friends who'd be happy to help, but I can't go to anyone I have a known connection with.'

It seemed I had exhausted her patience because she snapped at me. 'I don't know what you're talking about. If you phone again, unless it's to tell me about Paul, I'll report you to the police.'

'Please, don't hang up. Wait, I'll explain.'

It wasn't easy describing my situation to her over the phone. When I finally admitted the police were looking for me, she interrupted.

'Has this got anything to do with Paul's death?'

'Yes. The thing is, they seem to think I was in some way responsible for what happened-'

'They think you killed him?'

'Yes, and-'

'Did you?'

'No!'

'Then why don't you tell *them* that. Why tell me? There's nothing *I* can do about it. They're not going to accuse you of something like that without good reason, and if you didn't do anything you haven't got anything to worry about.'

It was my turn to butt in. 'I know. You're right. The trouble is, I'm not sure I can trust the police. You see,' I paused, wondering how to word what I had to say. 'There's circumstantial evidence that points to my having killed Paul. I didn't,' I added quickly, 'only it might look as though I did. And of course, as his wife I inherit everything he owned, so the police are saying I had a motive, and that's why they think I did it.'

'So, did you?'

'No, I just told you, I didn't,' I insisted. 'You must know our marriage wasn't exactly happy. It was over in all but name a long time ago. So, once I found out about your affair, I decided to leave him, and yes, I was going to take him for every penny I could. But I never wanted to kill him. Do you really think I would want my son to lose his father, and risk him seeing his mother go to prison for it?'

I was close to tears, aware that my protestations sounded lame, so I was surprised when she told me I could stay with her. 'But just for tonight.'

I could have cried with relief. Quickly I made a note of her address and she told me her nearest station. I didn't let on that it would be too risky for me to use public transport.

'I'll be there in about half an hour,' I told her.

Bella lived on the third floor of a converted Victorian property in Hampstead, about three miles away. It was easy to pick up a taxi at King's Cross, and within twenty minutes I was ringing the bell for her to buzz me in.

She sounded surprised to hear my voice. 'I didn't think you'd be here so soon.'

That was fair enough, as it would have taken longer by train.

'Well, I'm here now. Can I come in?'

'Yes, yes, of course. Just a minute and I'll get the door.'

I waited and at last the buzzer sounded to let me in. There was no lift. I climbed the stairs and rapped at the door to her flat. She took so long to open it that I was already wondering if I would have to go down and sleep in her hall until the morning. At least I would be safe there. The problem with that was that I urgently needed the loo. I knocked again, more loudly this time, and finally the door opened. Bella looked paler than I remembered her, possibly because she was wearing a dark pink sweatshirt over black jeans and no make up, which made her look very young. Perhaps she was.

'I'm sorry,' I said, 'It's late. I probably shouldn't have come here at all.'

She appeared to be shaking as she led me inside but it was difficult to be sure because her hall was poorly lit.

After I used her bathroom, she showed me into her living room which was brighter, with white walls and beige furniture, and a few watercolour prints on the walls. Although the room was stylishly furnished, the atmosphere felt bland and impersonal, like a reception room in a hotel. There were no photographs on the shelves, just a few books and ornaments tastefully arranged. A large rug on the floor was no substitute for a functional coffee table, and the whole room seemed designed for effect rather than for convenience or comfort.

Perched on a chair, I wondered how often Paul had lounged beside Bella on the sofa. The thought of seeing the bed he must have shared with her was disturbing yet compelling, and I struggled to resist asking to be shown around the flat.

'This is very nice,' I said.

Bella's eyes flicked to the door, as though she was unconsciously willing me to leave.

'Would you like some tea?' she asked, glancing at the door again.

'Thank you.'

She scurried out to her kitchen, leaving me alone in the living room. I heard her clattering around with the kettle and cups, and then she was quiet. I felt trapped, up on the third floor. It had been a mistake to suppose I might feel at ease there.

Bella seemed to be gone for hours, although it could only have been a few minutes. All at once, I felt a pressing need to leave but it seemed churlish to follow my instincts which were screaming at me to walk out of there. A wave of tiredness washed over me. Lying back on the comfortable chair I closed my eyes, allowing myself to relax for the first time in days. Uppermost in my mind was the need to see my son, but I would leave off worrying about that until the morning. After all my rushing around I was safe, at least for one night.

The silence was disturbed by voices that reached me from the hall before the door to the living room was flung open and I heard a familiar voice.

'We've been looking everywhere for you, Julie. It seems you forgot to tell us where you were going.'

With a sigh, I opened my eyes and looked up at Detective Inspector James Morgan. I had been a fool to trust my husband's mistress.

Chapter 14

The inspector didn't waste any time in arresting me on suspicion of murdering my husband. His expression was cold, but I thought I saw a glint of satisfaction in his eyes. After the shock and humiliation of my arrest, the next few days passed in a blur. I did my best to block what was happening from my thoughts. Lying on a hard bunk in a police cell, staring up at the whitewashed ceiling with its painted compass, I pretended the last few weeks were just a bad dream, and I would wake up in the morning with Paul in bed beside me and Dan nearly late for school, as had happened so many times in the past.

The following morning, I was introduced to a lawyer, Andrew Parkinson, who had the job of representing me. A fast-talking young man, he licked his lips a lot while his black eyes darted restlessly back and forth. His dark hair lay sleekly on his scalp and I couldn't tell if it was plastered in hair gel or just naturally greasy. Either way, it was unattractive. At our initial meeting he stared intently at my eyes as though trying to read my mind, as he jumped straight in with his questions.

'Let's not waste any time,' he said. 'Did you kill your husband?'

'No, I did not.'

His eyebrows rose ever so slightly. 'Let's do that again. Did you kill your husband?'

'I just told you I didn't.'

He looked sceptical. 'Give me one reason why I should believe you.'

'Oh please, aren't you supposed to be defending me?'

'I'm trying to, but it's not a question of whether or not *I* believe you, the point is you need to be convincing in court. You're going to be quizzed by a prosecuting barrister who'll pick up on every minuscule slip you make, and at the same time as you're dealing with all that pressure, you'll need to persuade a jury of your innocence. Alternatively, you can confess to the murder, claiming loss of control.'

'But I didn't do it! That's an outrageous suggestion!'

'Such a defence challenges the mens rea by establishing there was no premeditation,' he continued, ignoring my outburst. 'The defence is that the crime was committed while you were temporarily out of control due to your emotional distress. It's what's sometimes referred to as a crime of passion. Pleading loss of control could reduce your sentence to a conviction for manslaughter and that's an option we ought to consider.'

'But I didn't do it,' I insisted. 'Why would I confess to a crime I didn't commit?'

'That's what you say, but why should a jury take your word for it?'

I shrugged. 'They can't ask Paul, can they?'

Andrew shook his head disapprovingly. 'That sort of flippant comment isn't going to help you.'

'I'm sorry.'

'Don't apologise to me. I'm on your side, remember. It doesn't matter what you say to me, but you have to strike the right note in court. You were a devoted wife for nearly twenty years, dedicated to raising a son who has cerebral palsy. A jury is bound to take that into account. All things considered, confessing to a crime of passion and expressing heartfelt regret for what you did, might be the best defence we can offer.'

'You're not listening to me. Why would I confess to a murder I didn't commit? I told you I'm innocent.'

'And so are many people who are convicted of crimes they didn't commit. How exactly are you intending to persuade the jury you're innocent when all the evidence points to you being guilty?'

I hesitated. 'I can tell them I loved my husband-'

'So, you want to plead temporary loss of control when you discovered he was having an affair?'

'What? No, I want to say I couldn't have killed him because I loved him. I'm not saying I necessarily *did* love him, not anymore, but that would be a reason for being unable to kill him, wouldn't it? If I loved him?'

My lawyer made it clear he wasn't interested in my actual feelings, only in what might stand up in court. According to him, it was fine to fabricate our own truth if the jury believed it. And who can say what the truth is, where our emotions are concerned? Perhaps I really had loved Paul right to the end, despite his betrayal. It seemed that no one cared whether the truth was told in court, but how could I be sure I hadn't been lying to myself all along?

Andrew shook his head, and his black hair glistened under the harsh lighting. 'The police know that you discovered your husband was having an affair. It would be understandable for a woman in love to have an extreme reaction to such news.'

'By killing her husband?'

'It wouldn't be the first time.'

I gazed at him for a moment, stumped. 'What do you suggest then?' I asked him. 'Granted, the police arrested me at Bella's flat, but they can't be sure that I knew she was sleeping with Paul. She could have been a friend of mine. In fact,' I went on, warming to my idea, 'why would I have gone to see her if I had known about her and Paul?'

He nodded. 'Why indeed? And yet you did. The police seem convinced you had discovered the affair. Had you told anyone about it?'

I remembered Katie asking me how I could have killed him. I hadn't seen her since then. She could have told the police that I had discovered Paul's adultery. I had nothing to lose, so I told Andrew about it.

He looked solemn. 'The police may have questioned your friend- your former friend- and found out that you made the discovery your husband was having an affair one week before he was murdered. So, I'm going to ask you again: how are you going to convince a jury that you didn't kill your husband?'

'By finding out who *did* kill him,' I replied. 'There's no other way out of this mess, as far as I can see. But I can't do anything while I'm stuck in here. Can you get me out on bail?'

'That's not going to be easy if you're up on a murder charge, but if we can get that reduced to manslaughter due to loss of control.'

'I'm not going to confess to something I didn't do. Once I admit I killed him- which I didn't- there'll be no going back, will there? There must be another way. There just must be. I can't have my son believing I killed his father. It would destroy him. I need to get out of here to find out what really happened to Paul. And I want to see my son.'

I could hear my voice rising in agitation and forced myself to calm down, breathing deeply. We faced one another in silence for a moment. Then Andrew gave a curt nod and walked over to the door.

'Where are you going?' I asked, with a sudden rush of fear that he had decided to abandon me as a hopeless cause.

'I'm going to see what I can do to get you out of here. Those were your instructions, weren't they?'

After he had gone, I struggled against a growing sense of despair. My friends didn't believe my protestations of innocence, and my own lawyer was trying to persuade me to plead guilty. It was almost impossible to cling to the hope that I would ever walk away from a prison sentence. More than ever, I felt a burning hatred for Paul who had brought all this trouble crashing down on me.

Chapter 15

I barely had the energy to protest at being moved from the police cells to a remand prison to await trial. On hearing that I had a visitor, I expected to see my lawyer back again. Hoping it was a good sign that he had returned so soon, I was disappointed to discover who had come to see me.

'Nina! What are you doing here?'

While I did my best to conceal my dismay, she made no attempt to hide hers. I was shocked at the change in her. It was only two weeks since I had last seen her, but she looked gaunt and wan, and twitchier then ever.

'You look terrible, Nina. Are you ill?'

'No.' She sat down.

'Is something wrong? You would tell me, wouldn't you?'

'There's nothing wrong. But why are we talking about me? You're the one who's here. How are you? How are they treating you? What the hell, Julie? Is there anything I can do?'

'Get me out of here?' I replied with a twisted smile.

The next day I was informed that I had another visitor. When I asked who it was, the sergeant told me my brother wanted to see me. On the point of telling him that I don't have a brother, I stopped. It was obviously a mistake but seeing anyone would alleviate the tedium of my day and get me out of my cell for a short time at least. Having assumed that I had seen the last of my jewellery, I was surprised to see Ackerman seated at the table waiting for me. He looked up with a smile as I approached.

'Hi,' he called out, as though we had known one another all our lives, 'are they treating you, all right?'

'What made you say you're my brother?' I hissed as I sat down opposite him.

'It makes it easier for me to gain access to you. Like this, no one asks any questions.'

'Why couldn't you just say you're my friend?'

He shrugged. 'We're no more friends than we're brother and sister, so what difference does it make which lie I choose to tell? I'm here, aren't I? Now, shall we crack on?'

I was pleased he hadn't abandoned me, but amazed. For his part, he seemed equally taken aback when I told him I hadn't expected to see him again.

'You've hardly had your money's worth out of me yet,' he replied. 'There is such a thing as professional integrity. Now, we don't have very long,' he went on, suddenly businesslike. 'The police know you were in contact with your husband's mistress. You made several phone calls to her from two different mobile phones, which makes it look as though you might have been concerned to hide your approaches to her, and they have CCTV film of the two of you having coffee together at King's Cross station. And then of course they apprehended you at her flat after she tipped them off that you had arranged to go there.'

'She must have called them as soon as we hung up. I remember she seemed shocked that I got there so quickly. She must have expected the police to be there by the time I arrived.'

'If she believed you killed Paul, she might well have been frightened to be alone in her flat with you.'

'Do you think that means she knows I didn't kill him? If that's the case, then she must have killed him herself.'

He shook his head. 'It means she thought the police would be waiting at her flat to arrest you when you arrived. In any case, if she had killed him, the police would have found traces of her DNA in your house. Now let's focus on your movements. Added to your crude attempts to hide your phone calls to your husband's mistress, the police have found nothing to indicate you ever contacted her before you discovered she was having an affair with your husband.

All of which serves to substantiate what your friend- your former friend- Katie told them about how you discovered your husband's adultery shortly before he was murdered.' Ackerman shook his head again. 'It's not looking good. You found out your husband was having an affair and a week later he's killed in bed with you. But don't look so downhearted. If you discovered the affair, someone else could have discovered it too. I've not been idle since our last meeting. I've been looking into Bella's circumstances and found there was an ex. He's proving difficult to track down, but I'll find him.'

'What do you know about him so far?' I asked.

Ackerman was proving invaluable.

He shook his head again. 'I'd like to say he has a history of violence and was obsessed with her and had been heard threatening to kill any man who laid a finger on her, but from what I've picked up so far, there's nothing about him that sounds even remotely helpful. He's working abroad, but I'll keep you posted if and when I hear anything to suggest he's back here.'

'Have you asked her about it?'

'Not yet.'

'If you could get me out of here, I could go and see her,' I suggested.

The truth was, I was desperate to be let out, so I could arrange to go and see Dan. I was afraid he might believe the dreadful accusation that had been levelled against me, and I had to make sure he understood it was a terrible mistake. I was allowed to talk to my father-in-law on the phone, but Dan refused to speak to me.

'He's feeling very confused right now,' Mark told me. 'But he's doing all right. You don't have to worry about Dan.'

'Is he eating?'

'Oh yes, in fact he's put on a bit of weight since he arrived. You know what Stella's like in the kitchen.'

I did. But I also knew what my son was like, and I wasn't sure I believed what Mark was telling me. The frustration of being locked up, unable to see my son, was like a physical ache.

I called my parents-in-law daily, but the news was always the same. Dan was coping, but he didn't want to speak to me.

After a few days, Mark suggested it might be best if I stopped calling.

'It distresses Dan,' he explained.

'Please let me speak to him,' I begged.

'We feel that has to be his decision, and he's not ready yet.'

'Not ready? What do you mean, he's not ready?'

'I'm sorry, Julie, but we feel we need to protect him from any further upset.'

'Protect him?' I burst out, repeating his words stupidly. 'Protect him from what? I'm his mother!'

But Mark remained adamant. There was nothing I could say to change his mind. In his place I would probably have done the same thing.

'I'm sorry for you, Julie, really I am, but Dan is our priority. It's best if you don't call us again for a while.'

'A while? What does that mean?'

'Call back in a week and maybe he'll be ready to speak to you then.' Mark hesitated. 'He's seeing a counsellor and she agrees it's best he has no contact with you for the time being, while he's dealing with the trauma of what happened.'

Mark didn't accuse me of having murdered his son, but I knew what he must be thinking.

'Mark, you know I didn't do it. You know I would never do anything to hurt Paul. You can't let a stranger dictate when I can speak to my own son.' I stifled a sob. 'Dan needs me. He can't lose both his parents. It's too cruel.'

'I'm sorry, Julie, but it's for the best. Goodbye.'

If he was trying to punish me for killing his son, he couldn't have found a better way of doing it. This was all Paul's fault. When I thought of how he had ruined my life, and that of our son, I shook with rage. But I knew I had to keep my emotions in check if I was to have any hope of being given bail.

Another advantage of being moved to a remand prison was that I was allowed more frequent visitors, although so far Ackerman was the only person who had taken advantage of that.

'You'll have to leave this to me,' he said. 'You have to trust me.'

'Yes, yes, I will leave it to you, and I do trust you. Thank you. Thank you very much. I'm very grateful to you.'

He interrupted me. 'I'm on the clock.'

I guessed that meant he expected to be paid for his time, but there was nothing I could do about that as long as I was locked in a cell.

'Until they let me out, I won't have access to my bank account,' I said. 'But if you can get me out of here, I'll pay you whatever you want.'

'Your lawyer's working on that.'

'You know about him?'

'Andrew? Yes. We've worked together before. He's no pushover. But this is no time for chitchat about mutual acquaintances. We have a lot of ground to cover and very little time. You know I'm trying to track down Bella's ex-boyfriend, but there's more.'

Speaking in a low voice, he told me that he had uncovered some interesting evidence in the police records of my case.

'How did you get to see the records?'

He shrugged. 'It's my job to find out information.'

The news he gave me was perplexing: the drug flunitrazepam had been mentioned in Paul's toxicology report.

'Fluni what?'

'The street name is roofies,' he replied. Seeing I still looked puzzled, he went on, 'You may have heard it called Rohypnol.'

'The date rape drug?'

'That's the one.'

'Sorry, you've lost me. What's that got to do with Paul? Are you saying he was drugged the night he was killed?'

'You know that added to a drink the drug causes confusion, followed by unconsciousness, and then loss of memory?'

'Yes.'

'Evidence of this drug was found in your husband's blood stream. Although it's untraceable in the blood of a living person after just a few hours, it remains detectable where a victim dies shortly after the drug is administered. It's the breakdown product not the drug itself that remains, and that's what was present in your husband's body.'

I could hardly believe what I was hearing. 'So, Paul was given Rohypnol on the night he was killed?'

Ackerman glanced around to check that no one else was listening to our conversation. 'Exactly.'

I frowned. 'But surely that proves I didn't do it. Where would *I* get hold of Rohypnol?'

'That's what the police are looking into. Obviously, it would tie up the case nicely for them if they found evidence you *had* acquired it, but it's not necessary for them to come up with that proof, because Rohypnol's not difficult to get hold of. Anyone can source it from a drug dealer, and it's available online. So, I need you to tell me, did you get hold of Rohypnol with the intention of giving it to your husband?'

'No!'

'I thought not.'

'How come you're convinced I'm innocent when no one else believes it?'

He smiled. 'No one else is paid to believe it.'

There were a lot more questions I wanted to ask him, but it was time for him to leave.

'When will you come back?' I asked as he stood up.

'As soon as I have any more news for you.'

Watching him stride from the room, I wished I *did* have a brother like Ackerman. I wouldn't have been left wondering whether I would ever see him again.

Chapter 16

While Ackerman's news hadn't exactly improved my situation, my interviews with the police were even less encouraging. Detective Inspector James Morgan stared at me, scarcely blinking, his eyes cold. For all the warmth he evinced, he might as well have been the victim in one of the murders he investigated. The only sign of life about him was his quick intelligence, which made me feel under constant threat of slipping up and saying something that would later be held against me. I suppose he was only doing his job, but he was damn good at making me feel insecure.

'So, your husband was dead when you woke up,' he asked me, yet again.

'Yes, that is no, I mean I don't know.' At my side I heard my lawyer stir, but he didn't come to my rescue, so I ploughed on. 'What I mean to say is, if he was already dead when I woke up, I didn't notice, because I got up straight away to take my son to school.'

'Your husband was lying in bed beside you, dead, and you didn't notice?' The inspector's sceptical tone challenged my assertion.

'My client has already answered that question,' Andrew responded for me.

Without blinking, the inspector switched tack. 'Your husband was killed one week after you discovered he was having an affair.'

It was a statement, not a question, so I stayed silent. This was a dangerous game and I was only dimly aware of the rules. Every time I spoke I risked incriminating myself in some way.

'You discovered his affair, and a week later you told your friends about it.'

I nodded.

'For the purpose of the tape, the defendant is nodding.'

Without knowing exactly what Katie and Nina had told the police, I was on shaky ground. If either of them had said something that I denied, I might expose myself as a liar. I could almost hear Andrew warning me that a blunder like that wouldn't help convince a jury to believe anything else I said. Staring into the inspector's inscrutable grey eyes, I wracked my brains to recall what I had said to Katie and Nina the last time we were all together, but we were drinking that evening and my memory was hazy.

'Honestly, I can't remember what I told my friends,' I admitted. 'We were drinking a lot, and I don't suppose they can recall much of what was said either. I wouldn't imagine any statements they gave you would be reliable.'

The Deteceive Inspector nodded. 'We only need one witness to remember what you said,' he pointed out softly.

'Anyone could be mistaken, especially after drinking so much,' I insisted.

Without knowing what Katie or Nina had told the police, I had to be circumspect.

'But if she's prepared to swear to it under oath, I daresay it will go against you.'

The inspector gave a rare smile that barely reached his eyes. I remembered Andrew warning me never to allow my interrogators to rile me and I looked down at the table. But I could feel myself shaking.

'Is there any point in harassing my client like this?' Andrew intervened. 'She has already told you she can't remember what happened that night, and she can't tell you what she can't remember.'

'Is that her defence?' Morgan turned back to me. 'Do you deny that you discovered your husband was unfaithful?'

I shook my head. 'No, I've never denied that.'

'And you told us you kept quiet about it so as not to upset your son.'

'He was doing exams.'

'So, you held back from challenging your husband about his affair, because you wanted to avoid a row? What was going through your mind at that point, I wonder? You discover your husband of twenty years is having an affair, and you say nothing and do nothing.'

'I was going to confront him about it once Dan's exams were finished.'

'So, you were prepared to upset your son then?'

'He was going to stay with his grandparents in Edinburgh as soon as his exams were over. It was arranged months ago. I thought that would be the ideal time to talk things over with Paul.'

'Things?'

'Yes. I was going to tell him I wanted a divorce.'

The Detective Inspector's eyebrows rose slightly. I glanced at Andrew, but he was staring at the table and did nothing to help me.

'Why would I want to stay married to a man who was cheating on me?'

'So, you were angry? At the same time as you were still living together as man and wife, and he was having sex with another woman.'

I took my time thinking how to answer him.

'Oh, come on, Julie, it's not a difficult question. You must remember how you were feeling.'

'I felt let down, and flat.'

'Flat?'

'Yes, flat. Empty. After nearly twenty years, it was hard to believe. I was sad, very sad, for Dan as much as for myself. But I wasn't angry. If anything, I felt numb about the whole thing. Any romance between Paul and me had fizzled out a long time ago. I felt very sad that it was ending like that, but mainly I just felt... uninvolved.' I looked directly at the inspector. 'You can understand feeling emotionally detached from a situation, can't you?' I lowered my gaze. 'Anyway, I decided quickly that we had to separate because, after a betrayal like that, I'd never be able to trust him again. And without trust, marriage becomes meaningless.'

'For better or worse,' the Detective Inspector said.

'But only when forsaking all others,' I replied, and he had the grace to smile.

'No sooner had you discovered the affair, than your husband's phone disappeared. Presumably you destroyed it? You did a good job of that, I must say. We haven't been able to find even a trace of it.'

I didn't respond.

'But no matter. We found Bella's number on your new phone.'

'Paul must have used it.'

'After he was dead? Somehow I doubt it.'

I bit my lip, cursing my stupidity.

'My client contacted her husband's mistress to let her know her lover was dead,' Andrew said. 'She reasoned that Bella had no other way of discovering what had happened and she felt the other woman had a right to know he was dead.'

'A right to know?' The Detective Inspector picked up on the lawyer's words. 'Why would a betrayed wife think her husband's mistress had any rights in this matter?'

'Because she had a relationship with Paul,' I replied. 'For all I knew she didn't even know he was married. I couldn't imagine what she must have been going through, when he suddenly stopped seeing her and didn't get in touch. I mean, she might have been in love with him. I couldn't just pretend she didn't exist.'

'Very noble, I'm sure.' The inspector's tone didn't sound impressed. 'Now, let's return to the facts. You recently took a job at a medical centre.'

'How is that relevant?' Andrew asked, but he looked worried.

'That gave you access to medical information, and enabled you to research sources for Rohypnol, a drug that was detected in your husband's body-'

'That's not true!' I cried out. 'I had nothing to do with any drugs!'

My lawyer put a restraining hand on my arm to remind me to stay calm.

'Can you explain why, after seventeen years at home, you suddenly sought out a job in a medical centre? Why now, Julie? And why that particular job?'

The room suddenly felt chilly. Everything I had ever done was going to be investigated and used against me. I turned to Andrew.

The Detective Inspector's voice was remorseless. 'Just answer the question, Julie.'

Stammering, I explained how supporting my son had taken up all of my time when he was a child. Now that he had become more independent, at Paul's insistence, I had accepted it would be best for both me and Dan if I were to find myself occupation.

Andrew spoke up. 'My client cannot be held responsible for the post becoming vacant just at the time she had decided to look for a job. Any other suggestion is merely circumstantial.'

The Detective Inspector didn't bother to reply. Clearly the police were resolved to find me guilty. Their net was closing in around me. My one hope now seemed to lie in the regular visits from my supposed brother, Ackerman.

'Tell me why you're persisting with me,' I said to him.

'Because you're my client.'

'What happens when the deposit runs out?'

He didn't answer.

'Do you think I should plead loss of control? My lawyer's recommending I do. He thinks I should confess.'

'That's your call.'

'I know. But what do you think? Please, I'm only after for your opinion. There's no one else I can ask.'

He looked thoughtful for a moment, before answering. 'I can't see you have anything to lose. If you're convicted, a confession and admission that you're tormented by guilt, and you really loved your husband and couldn't bear to think of him in another woman's bed, and so on, all that is bound to go down well with a jury, and you'll receive a relatively light sentence. And if we do manage to find out that someone else murdered your husband, the fact that you made a confession won't affect your acquittal.'

'Wouldn't there be consequences for making a false statement?'

'You would have to explain that you were advised to make a false statement to reduce your sentence, advice you deeply regret having followed.'

I was horrified that Ackerman agreed with my lawyer's recommendation. No one seemed to understand I stood to lose everything if Dan were to believe I had killed his father.

'But won't it mean the police will stop trying to find out who *did* kill Paul?'

He shrugged again. We both knew the police were satisfied they already had the culprit in custody.

'Nothing about this seems real,' I said.

'Real?' Ackerman replied, smiling as though I had said something amusing.

Lying on my bunk that night, I thought about what he had said, and how little I knew about him. Ackerman was obviously a name he had made up from the initials AKA man, as though he wanted me to know it was an alias. Under any other circumstances I wouldn't have trusted him for an instant yet so far, he had turned out to be reliable. When he could have simply pocketed the cash from the sale of my jewellery and walked away, he had chosen to stay and work on my behalf. Ironically, I had been betrayed by the one man I trusted absolutely, while a stranger had kept his word.

Chapter 17

It soon felt as though I had been living in my cell all my life, but I didn't feel as though I was in prison. For a start, I could wear my own clothes, as I hadn't yet been convicted of a crime. Nina had been a real support, bringing in a case of my things. Since then she hadn't been back to see me, but I hadn't bothered to call her. I guessed she was busy, and the prison wasn't that easy for her to get to. In any case, I had lost interest in the world outside the confines of the institution where I now lived.

When I thought about it, I felt dazed by how quickly the outside world had faded away. In the prison we had a reasonably well stocked library, and a gym, and we were fed three times a day. Admittedly there was very limited choice, and no alcohol, but the food wasn't bad. If I hadn't been confined to a cell for hours at a time, in conditions that were scarcely luxurious, I could almost have persuaded myself that I was on holiday in retreat, where I was free of all responsibilities. It was like being a child again and I could have settled quite contentedly into my new way of life, had I not been tormented by the separation from my son.

Andrew seemed confident he would be able to get bail for me, as he said we had a good case for claiming I wouldn't be a danger to anyone else. I wondered if my proposed false confession was part of a deal, although he assured me the police didn't operate like that, outside of films. I was no longer sure what to believe, but I never thought he would succeed in getting me out on bail, so I just stared at him in surprise when he brought me the news.

'I thought you'd be at least a little pleased,' he said. 'It wasn't easy, I can tell you. And we've been a tad lucky. Not every judge would have been so sympathetic. Not that I think you don't deserve it,' he added quickly. 'We put up a very strong case. Now, your bail comes with conditions. Do you understand what I'm saying?'

I nodded, still dumbfounded by the news that I was going to be released, at least temporarily.

'It's taken a while to prepare the application for bail, but it had to be done properly since, in view of the seriousness of the crime you're accused of we're only going to have one chance to apply. I had to make sure the application contained all the supporting documentation, including the deeds of your freehold as surety.'

'My house? But what will happen to my son if they take my house away?'

'No one's going to confiscate your house, as long as you obey the conditions of your bail. You had to agree to put up your property as surety or the application wouldn't have succeeded. Now, you'll be staying in your own house, as we agreed. The forensic team have finished their search-'

'Did they find anything I don't know about?'

'I'm not quite sure. I'm waiting to see the reports. I'll be in touch soon.'

Again, I nodded. I didn't say anything, but my brain was working overtime. Andrew went rapidly through but the conditions of my bail, and I had to concentrate to follow what he was telling me.

'You need to go along to your local police station every twenty-four hours, so you won't be able to travel far. But you *will* be at home,' he said, smiling at me. 'Now, you need to read this and sign it before you go.'

'How soon can I leave?'

'You'll be escorted out of here tomorrow morning.'

'Tomorrow?'

'Yes.'

It didn't give me long to make my arrangements. As soon as Andrew left, I ran to phone Ackerman. To my relief, he answered his mobile at once.

'Julie, I was just thinking about you-'

I interrupted his greeting to tell him my news and ask him to bring me some money before the morning.

'Tell you what,' he replied. 'Why don't I come and pick you up tomorrow? What time are they letting you out?'

I gave him the details.

'All right, I'll be outside waiting for you.'

'And the money?'

'Don't worry. I'll bring it. Are you going to tell me what you want it for?'

I glanced around. There was no one standing close enough to hear what I was saying, but I wasn't sure if the prison phones were secure.

'I'll tell you all about it tomorrow,' I replied.

I hardly slept for excitement that night, knowing that what I was planning was risky, stupid even. But nothing was going to change my mind. I was up and ready early the next morning and at ten o'clock a prison officer escorted me out of the prison. In some ways that return to the outside was every bit as frightening as my journey in to the prison had been, each a shift into a different world with its own challenges and dangers, as well as its own comforts and recompenses.

The gates clanged shut behind me and I was free, within the restrictions of my bail conditions.

True to his word, Ackerman was waiting for me. I climbed into his old car, and he nodded at me as he pulled away from the kerb.

'Home?'

'No.'

'Where then?'

Quickly I explained my plan to him. He slowed down and turned to me, whistling between his uneven teeth.

'Are you sure?'

'Positive.'

'You're aware of the consequences of such a rash course of action?'

'I know what I'm doing.'

'I doubt that very much.'

'Please, I just need to talk to him.'

'And if he refuses to see you, what then? You'll have broken your bail and lost any chance of any further leniency, for nothing.' He sounded quite angry with me.

'Say what you like, this is my decision. I'm fully aware of the risk I'm taking-'

'I don't think you are.'

'I'm going to Edinburgh, with or without your help. So, are you going to take me to the station or not?'

Ackerman shrugged. 'You're the client. I'm only protecting my own interest in trying to keep you out of jail. But if you're determined to get yourself banged up, I can't physically stop you, can I? Here, you'd better take these.' He reached into the side pocket of his door and took out a pair of gold-rimmed sunglasses. 'At least you can try to avoid being apprehended before you even get to Edinburgh.'

Pocketing the sunglasses, I thanked him. 'I know it's probably stupid,' I added.

'There's no probably about it.'

'But I have to try. I don't mind going back to prison to wait for my trial, but I must see Dan and tell him I didn't kill his father. How can I leave him struggling to cope with that terrible idea? I must convince him I'm innocent. Even if I'm convicted, he must go on believing I didn't do it. How could he live with himself otherwise, believing his father's a liar and a cheat, and his mother's a killer? What's that going to do for his self-image?'

Ackerman shrugged again. 'It's your freedom you should be worried about, not your teenage son's self-image. I'd say having a mother who skips bail isn't going to do much to help him.'

I stared out of the window and didn't answer. I knew what I had to do.

Drawing up near King's Cross station, Ackerman reached over his shoulder and grabbed an old oilskin from the back seat.

'You might need this in Scotland.'

He handed it to me together with an envelope. I didn't stop to count the money but jumped out of the car, slipping on his sunglasses as my feet hit the pavement. By the time I turned to thank him, his car had vanished into the London traffic. Apart from being too warm, I thought the jacket might look conspicuous on a sunny day, so I held it over my arm. Hoping Ackerman's sunglasses would be mask enough, I crossed the road and entered the mainline station.

There was a train straight through to Edinburgh departing at midday. The queue at the machine was short and I completed my transaction as quickly as possible. Ackerman had given me a thousand pounds in ten and twenty-pound notes, and a one-way ticket to Edinburgh cost me just under seventy pounds. It would have made sense to buy a return ticket while I was there but, surrounded by security cameras, I was too nervous to think clearly. It didn't matter. I could take my time buying a return ticket at the station in Edinburgh. No one would be looking for me there.

I had twenty minutes to spare which I spent buying a less cumbersome raincoat, one that fitted me. Leaving Ackerman's oilskin on a hanger at the back of the shop, I paid cash and left.

'Sorry, Ackerman,' I muttered as I hurried away.

With what I had already paid him, he could afford to buy himself a new coat. By the time I had completed my disguise with a new scarf wound around my head and red lipstick, which I never wore, it was time to make my way to the platform.

Feeling like Richard Hannay in the film *The Thirty-Nine Steps*, I boarded the train and found an unreserved seat. Before the day was over, I would be reunited with my son.

Chapter 18

The train journey was just under four and a half hours. For a long time, I sat staring out of the window at a world I had almost forgotten. I was still wearing my sunglasses and scarf but had removed my new coat which lay folded neatly across my lap. I didn't dare look around in case anyone recognised me.

The carriage wasn't full, but at Leeds a number of passengers joined the train and a man took the aisle seat next to me. Although we were strangers, his presence felt like a buffer between me and the guard who came around checking our tickets. I held mine up, taking care to keep my face averted. I knew my paranoia was needless. No one would be looking for me out of London. But for a long time, I couldn't relax.

Eventually I must have fallen asleep, lulled by the steady rhythm of the train rumbling along the track. I woke with a start, but we were only in Newcastle, with about an hour and a half left before we reached Edinburgh. The passenger beside me was asleep and snoring gently. I dozed fitfully after that, my excitement increasing along with my apprehension as we raced north. By the time the train drew into the platform I was nearly crying with anticipation. Soon I would be seeing my son for the first time in weeks.

Before leaving the train, I pulled my new coat on over the clothes I had been wearing when I left prison that morning. It felt like a lifetime ago. No doubt the police would contact my in-laws should they discover I had broken the terms of my bail and gone missing, but there were nearly eighteen hours to go before I missed my deadline to check in at my local police station. That was more than enough time to see my son and hopefully return to London without breaking my bail conditions. There was no reason why

Mark and Stella would contact the police, but even so I couldn't afford to waste any time. Having established which train I would need to catch back to London, and with my return ticket safely stowed in my purse, I walked out of the station and took a taxi to my in-laws' house.

Stella gaped, and her arm jerked as though she was about to slam the door, but I stepped forward and put one foot over the threshold, so she couldn't close it.

'Julie!' she gasped, her eyes wide and staring. 'What are you doing here?'

'I've come to see Dan.'

'Go away or I'll call the police!' she hissed at me.

'No, no, you don't understand,' I protested.

She really didn't understand. One of the conditions of my bail was that I had to remain close to my home, yet here I was, over four hundred miles away from there. By no measure could that be considered "close".

'I've been released,' I lied. 'So, you know I'm innocent. And now I want to speak to my son.'

'Come back in the morning,' she said. 'You have to give us time to prepare him for this. You know he struggles with anything spontaneous, and this is a huge deal for him. Why on earth didn't you phone us before coming here?'

I shook my head. 'It's complicated. But I can't come back in the morning. I have to return to London tonight.'

'Tonight? Why?' She glared suspiciously at me. 'What's going on, Julie? Tell me the truth.'

I had to admit that they had only let me out on bail. 'I'm not supposed to go too far away from my home, and I have to check in at my local police station every twenty-four hours. So, I have to get back to London tonight. That's why I have to see Dan right now.'

'Go away, Julie. Leave him alone.'

'How can I? He's my son.'

'And Paul was my son.' She spat the words at me. 'If you don't leave right now, I'll call the police.'

With an unexpected burst of vigour, she thrust my leg aside and slammed the door. I was trembling so much I could barely stand, but I managed to stagger back to the pavement. Leaning against the low wall outside my in-law's house, I tried to think. My reason for travelling there was innocent, and I fully intended to return to London by the morning and report to my local police station within twenty-four hours, but no one was going to believe my story if I was picked up by the police so far from my home. Even now Stella might be on the phone, summoning them. I had to get away from there and make sure I caught my train back to London in time.

Having come all this way to see my son, I considered trying to attract his attention without anyone else knowing. If I knew which room he was sleeping in, I could chuck some gravel up at his window and call to him. But he would be confused by something so unusual, and I had no idea how he might react if he discovered me outside the house. He had been staying with his grandparents for nearly three weeks. Stella was convinced I had killed Paul, and presumably Mark shared her opinion. They were decent people, but if they believed I had murdered their son, no one could blame them for turning Dan against me. After all my efforts to get there, I couldn't risk trying to see him.

Devastated, I walked in what I thought was the direction of the centre of town and was soon lost. I was worried that I might end up missing my train, but at last I found a main road where I managed to hail a taxi back to Edinburgh Waverley station. It was still only six o'clock when I arrived back there. So far from home, it wouldn't have occurred to me that the police might be looking for me had it not been for Stella's threats. As it was, I put my scarf on, kept my head down, and walked quickly. With nearly six hours before my train was due, I rushed along the street outside the station, trying to look as though I had somewhere to go.

Passing a café, I remembered that I hadn't eaten since my breakfast in prison, so I stopped for a pizza in a small restaurant in a side turning off Market Street. The service was fast, and I was soon finished.

Having eaten, I felt more alert and set off again. Wandering along the street, I resisted going into a bar for a drink. I hadn't touched alcohol since my arrest, and although I was tempted, it was better to keep a clear head, given the risk I was running by having come to Edinburgh. There were still almost five hours to go until I was due to leave the city. Tired of waiting, I considered trying to find out whether it was possible to exchange my ticket for a seat on an earlier train. Entering the brightly lit station, I slipped on my sunglasses, and pulled my scarf more tightly around my head. As I traversed the busy walkway, I decided against trying to exchange my ticket. The fewer railway staff I spoke to, the better. Instead I bought a newspaper, made myself as comfortable as I could on a bench, and settled down to wait.

Chapter 19

Careful to hide my face from any security cameras, I scurried to the platform and boarded my train without a hitch, and at last we were speeding on our way towards London. Although it was late, I slept less on the way back to London than I had done during the day on the way to Edinburgh. In addition to the anguish of leaving without even having seen my son, I was worried in case the train was delayed. If I missed my appointment at the police station the next morning I would return to prison, and this time I wouldn't be allowed bail. The prospect of never seeing my son again almost paralysed me with fear. He was only seventeen. Stella and Mark were in their seventies. Dan was a capable boy, but his cerebral palsy meant he might need more support than many other teenagers as he progressed from school to college, and on into more independent living. What long-term security could his grandparents offer him? I had to extricate myself from the trouble Paul had caused me.

The train drew into King's Cross early the following morning. Donning my sunglasses and winding my scarf around my head, I put on my new coat and stepped out onto the platform, half expecting the police to surround me and drag me back to prison. But I left Kings Cross unchallenged, jumped into a taxi, and an hour later was back in my own house on the outskirts of Harrow. As the front door closed behind me, I burst into tears. Forcing myself to stop crying, I made a mug of tea, and went upstairs for a shower.

Paul's toothbrush and shaver were beside the sink in our bathroom, as though he was going to walk in at any moment. His old blue towelling dressing gown hung on the bathroom door, and his shampoo had fallen over on the shower tray, relics of a dead man.

In the bedroom, his wardrobe was crammed with his shirts, his jumpers, his trousers, his smell. I couldn't bear it. Fetching a black bin liner, I threw all his toiletries away, including the half-used toilet roll which he would have touched. Then I scrubbed the sink, and the floor, and the toilet, anything that might still retain vestiges of his skin and sweat. I wanted every trace of him out of my life.

At last, I jumped in the shower and tried to wash away all my memories of him. Of course, it was a futile gesture, but I needed a shower anyway and felt better for it. Taking my new scarf and coat with me in a carrier bag, I set about getting rid of them in case I had been spotted on a security camera while travelling out of London. The best way to dispose of them was to surreptitiously leave them hanging on a rail in a charity shop. It wasn't difficult, and I was soon on my way to the police station in South Harrow, wearing my own familiar clothes. This time there was no problem using public transport without a disguise. The police could trace my movements and welcome. I was only travelling to fulfil the conditions of my bail.

There was no one else waiting for the sergeant's attention, so I went straight up to the desk and explained why I was there. As I signed the register, he explained the procedure. It didn't take long, and I was soon out of there, walking along the street like anyone else, breathing fresh air, able to go wherever I chose for the next twenty-four hours. For a while at least I could pretend I was at liberty, and nothing terrible had happened to ruin my life. But that was never going to be true again.

After stopping off at Waitrose, I went home. I had nowhere else to go. Having put away my few bits of shopping, I could no longer resist my longing to go into Dan's room. I just wanted to feel close to him. I should never have gone in there. It was torture seeing all his things, knowing he was so far away from me. He might as well have been dead, like his father. With tears streaming down my cheeks, I reached up and touched his posters, one by one. He had stuck them up on the wall himself and I had chastised him too late for having used blue tack on the wallpaper.

'What am I supposed to do?' he had retorted, with an aggrieved expression. 'Do you want me to take them all down again? I thought you said this was my room and I was free to do whatever I wanted in here.'

That feeling of liberty was so precious, and so rare. The posters had stayed.

I sat on his bed, remembering and crying, until my head was pounding. At last I gathered myself together, washed my face and went downstairs to make a cup of tea. The rest of the day stretched out in front of me, empty. All I could do was visit the police station each morning and wait for the justice system to crawl to a conclusion. For now, this was my life. I felt I ought to be doing something, but the health centre where I had worked part-time as a receptionist had let me go and I couldn't be bothered to contest their decision. Compared to my other problems, that was insignificant.

With the demands Dan had placed on my time when he was younger, I had never gone back to a full-time job after he was born, and I wasn't sure I could find another post when all this nightmare was over. But that didn't matter. There were always jobs to do around the house. One day I might find the energy to redecorate the living room. For now, I couldn't even be bothered to weed the garden or mow the grass which had grown an incredible amount in the month since it had last been cut.

That evening, I was seriously tempted to open a bottle of wine, but I thought it might not be wise to drink alone, in my present desperate circumstances. Instead, I stuck to tea.

Just as the kettle boiled, the doorbell rang.

'I heard you were back,' Nina said, flinging her arms around me. She smelled strongly of perfume. 'But, how are you?' She drew back and gazed earnestly at me. 'You look bloody awful. You've been crying, haven't you?'

I shook my head and burst into tears.

'Oh, you poor thing,' she said, giving me another hug.

'Everything's gone,' I wailed. 'Everything. My life is over. And I don't know what to do. I don't know what to do.'

'Let's go in and sit down, and you can tell me all about it,' she said, patting me sympathetically on the back. 'Sometimes it helps to talk.'

Over a glass of wine, I told her about Dan. 'Stella wouldn't even let me see him. When I tried to insist, she threatened to call the police.'

'You should have gone in anyway.'

'I couldn't, not without physically shoving her out of the way. And she said it was best for Dan not to see me.' I burst into tears again.

'That's horrible. But don't worry, he'll be back home once this is all over. It can't be much longer until it all gets sorted out. And in the meantime, you know he's in good hands. It's not as if he's with strangers, is it? They might hate you right now, but you know they love Dan. Everything will be fine in the end, you'll see. The police will get to the bottom of it. That's their job.'

She was trying to be nice, but it didn't help. Still sobbing, I offered her another glass of wine.

'I can't stay long,' she said. 'I'm going out tonight.'

I nodded. 'That's okay. It was nice of you to come over. I appreciate it, really I do.'

'You know you can be honest with me.' She paused. 'Tell me, *did* you kill Paul? I mean, I'd understand if you did, after the way he behaved.'

I looked at her. 'No. I didn't kill him. How could you even ask that?'

Nina shrugged. 'I felt like killing Eddy when I found out he was seeing someone else. I mean, it wasn't just a brief fling for Paul, was it? They'd been seeing each other for years, hadn't they? That makes a difference, doesn't it? All the lies he must have told you.' She shook her head and glanced at her watch. 'I really ought to go. Are you sure you'll be okay on your own?'

I grunted. 'I'm going to have to get used to it, aren't I?'

After she left, I switched the television on and sat gazing miserably at the opened bottle of wine on the table in front of me. It was only half empty. Or half full. Two versions of the same truth.

Chapter 20

The house was eerily empty after Nina left. Evenings were going to be the worst time. I had often been on my own during the day, but Dan and Paul had always come home by supper time. Now the silence was painful, so I kept the television on as background noise. Even the voices of strangers were preferable to nothing at all. I slept little and was almost glad when it was time to go and report to the police station again. At least it gave me something to do. This time when I went back to the police station, the desk sergeant asked me to take a seat and wait for a moment.

'But I'm only here to check in with you,' I told him. I lowered my voice. 'I've been let out on bail and need to report here every twenty-four hours. I've done that now, so can I go home?'

'Just one moment,' he replied stolidly, 'we need you to sign the register. Take a seat please.'

He picked up his phone, indicating our conversation was concluded, so I went and sat down. It was annoying, but I wasn't going to make a fuss. I would just have to get used to the process. In the meantime, I would be home again soon enough.

After a few minutes, a female officer in uniform emerged through an internal door and headed straight for me. I glanced around but there was no one else sitting waiting.

'Julie Barrett.' It wasn't a question. 'Please come with me.'

'I hope this isn't going to take long,' I grumbled as I followed her through the door. 'I thought I just had to sign a register.'

She led me along a grey corridor and into a small room furnished with grey chairs and a low table.

'Wait here please,' she said.

'What's this about?'

She left the room without answering and returned a few moments later. Instructing me to follow her, she escorted me outside where a police car was waiting with the back-passenger door open.

'Where are you taking me?'

'Mind your head please.'

I grunted. I knew the drill. This wasn't the first time I had been in a police car.

My resistance was short lived. 'What's going on? I demand to know where you're taking me.'

She pushed me firmly into the car and slammed the door. Doing my best to reassure myself that we don't live in a police state, and I was in safe hands, I leaned back in my seat and resigned myself to this journey to an unknown destination.

Only our destination wasn't unfamiliar. I recognised the Hendon police compound as soon as we drove into the car park, and it was no surprise when Detective Inspector Morgan entered the interview room where I had been taken.

'No,' I cried out, scowling at him as he sat down opposite me, 'this isn't fair. You know perfectly well I was released on bail. There was a court order, signed by a judge. You can't bring me back here. You have to let me go home.'

Ignoring my protests, he spoke quietly. 'Where were you between five and six a.m. yesterday?'

'I don't know what you're talking about. You can't keep me here!'

'Can you answer the question, please?'

'Not until you tell me what I'm doing here.'

I wasn't going to say anything until I knew what was going on.

'We just want to ask you a few questions, Julie. I'm surprised that you would refuse to co-operate with us.'

He was trying to unnerve me, to force me into making an admission I would later regret, but I had the presence of mind to tell him that I refused to say anything without my lawyer in the room.

Apart from anything else, I needed time to decide how to respond to his question. Someone must have spotted me on the train, but Morgan was very specific about the time, and between five and six I had been in my seat. It was trick. Morgan was hoping to catch me out, but I couldn't fathom what he was up to.

I was led back to a cell, protesting loudly all the way. Andrew joined me after a while.

'What's going on?' he asked me, his narrow features twisted in perplexity.

'Why are you asking me that? You're the lawyer. You're the one who's supposed to know what's happening.'

'Okay, calm down. Getting yourself, all worked up isn't going to help. Now,' he lowered his voice even though there was no one else there, 'your friend Ackerman told me about your trip up north.'

'Yes, I know, but I swear no one saw me, and I was back in time to report to the police station in Harrow by ten thirty yesterday morning.'

'That's good.'

'So, what's going on? Why have I been brought back here?'

'They're still trying to nail you for your husband's murder. They're probably just trying to put pressure on you, to make you break down and confess.'

'Can they do that?'

He shrugged. 'That's up to you, whether you let them get to you or not. But I can't see you caving in to pressure. There's nothing they can do, really, expect play these stupid games to unsettle you. That's all it is, Julie, I'm sure of it. Now, stand firm and you'll be back home in no time. Admit nothing, say nothing. They can't keep you here.'

We reconvened, but this time I had Andrew at my side, his assurances that the police couldn't hold me ringing in my ears. Morgan's expression gave nothing away, and I met his gaze with what I hoped was similar inscrutability. Andrew had told me this was all a game. I was ready to play.

'Where were you between five and six a.m. yesterday?' Morgan asked again, as though the interview hadn't been interrupted.

'I was at home.'

Morgan was trying it on, but I was confident no one could prove I had travelled further than the terms of my bail allowed. Miserable though it was in my empty house, I wasn't going to lose my bail privileges without a fight.

'Can I go home now?'

'I'm afraid not.'

'You can't stop me leaving.'

'My client fulfilled the conditions of her bail,' Andrew interrupted quickly, no doubt intending to remind me to keep my mouth shut. 'She was released on bail by the court and you can't keep her here without good reason.'

'I'll ask you once again, where were you between the hours of five and six a.m. yesterday?'

'Like I just told you, I was at home. My memory hasn't altered in the last two seconds.'

'Was anyone else at home with you?'

'What? No, of course not. A friend came around later, but no one was there at that time.'

'A friend?' he repeated.

Wondering if they were suggesting I had also been having an affair, I found it difficult to hide my indignation and glared at him.

'So, no one can vouch for you being at home in the early hours of yesterday morning?'

'What? No.'

'You have no alibi for that time?'

I turned to Andrew for support, but he was looking at the inspector with a faintly uneasy expression.

'Alibi?' he repeated, frowning. 'What is the significance of this line of questioning? What happened yesterday morning that could have any relevance to my client's status?'

Morgan stared straight at me as he answered Andrew's question. 'Bella Foster is dead. She was murdered in her bed early yesterday morning. But I expect you already knew that, didn't you, Julie?'

For a moment no one spoke. Morgan's question hung in the space between us like an invisible web.

'Where were you between five and six a.m. yesterday?' he asked again, very softly.

Andrew answered. 'I need to consult with my client.'

Simultaneously I shouted over him in my terror at this new implied accusation. 'So, Bella's dead? What's that got to do with me? You can't think I had anything to do with it.' I could feel myself shaking. 'I wasn't even in London!'

Morgan's features remained impassive, his voice devoid of expression. 'You weren't in London? Meaning what, precisely?'

'I was in Scotland. No, I was on a train coming back from Edinburgh at that time. I'd gone to see my son. I knew I had to come back, so I could report to the police station at ten thirty.' I was babbling, almost incoherent in my shock. 'I didn't want to do anything to jeopardise my bail. I did what you wanted. I've done nothing wrong.'

'My client's distressed. We would like to take a break.'

Ignoring Andrew's intervention, Morgan pressed on. 'You were in Scotland? No, you were on a train? But you also just told us you were at home. Which is it, Julie? Which of your differing accounts are you asking us to believe?'

'It's the truth. I'm not making this up. I was on the train.'

'Why did you tell us you were at home?'

'I lied.'

Morgan grunted.

'I need to confer with my client,' Andrew interrupted me urgently.

But I felt compelled to explain. 'I was afraid to admit I'd broken the conditions of my bail by travelling to Edinburgh to see my son. That's the only reason I said I was at home, where I should have been.'

'At what time did you see your son?'

'I didn't see him. They wouldn't even let me talk to him. But I saw my mother-in-law. Ask her. She'll tell you I was there. Ask Stella. She saw me.'

Morgan sat forward in his chair. 'Will she be prepared to swear in court that you were with her between five and six yesterday morning?'

'It would take five hours to get back to London,' his colleague pointed out.

Morgan nodded and amended his question. 'Will your mother-in-law swear in court that she was with you in Edinburgh at any time after midnight last night?'

I was finding it difficult to speak. 'No.' I cast a desperate glance at Andrew. 'I saw her at about five o'clock in the afternoon, on the day of my release. I went straight there, but I didn't come back to London right away. I was booked on the eleven forty train which got in at seven twenty-seven yesterday morning. So, you see, I was on the train all the time.'

'Let's hope for your sake that we can find evidence you boarded the train. Sergeant, get onto it straight away.'

Back in a cell I struggled to take in what had just happened. While I had been busy covering my tracks travelling to Scotland and back, another murder had been committed. CCTV film couldn't prove my whereabouts because I had disguised my appearance, and there wasn't even any proof I had bought a train ticket because I had paid in cash. Ackerman had dropped me at King's Cross station in the evening, but he hadn't seen me board the train. Stella had seen me about twelve hours before the murder, and the train took under six hours, leaving me more than enough time to return to London and kill Bella. In my determination not to risk being discovered breaking the terms of my bail, I had left myself without an alibi for the time of the murder. And this time the victim was my husband's mistress, the woman who had stolen my husband and wrecked my life.

Chapter 21

I felt numb when they led me back to a cell, my brief spell of restricted liberty over. Accused of murdering my husband, and suspected of killing his mistress, there was no way I would be granted bail again. I was aware of that yet felt nothing. My anger was spent. Feeling as though there was no longer anything to fight for, I slept well that night. The following day I was informed that my friend, Nina, had come to visit me. I refused to see her. There was no point. She could do nothing to help me, and her sympathy would only unsettle me. I had shed enough tears. I didn't want to cry any more. All I wanted to do was repair my relationship with my son. Somehow, together, we had to get past this. But first I needed to regain my freedom, and that seemed impossible.

'It's a pity your husband's mistress was murdered the morning after you were released,' Andrew said quietly at our next meeting.

'I know, but I didn't do it.'

'All the same you've got to admit it's a coincidence, isn't it?'

'I didn't do it. I couldn't have.'

He leaned forward, and I continued with my convoluted explanation.

'When she was being killed, I was on a train travelling back to London. I must have been somewhere around Doncaster, or Peterborough, I don't know where. Somewhere miles north of London anyway. So, unless I managed to kill her by some sort of remote telekinesis, I can't have done it.' I paused, trying to interpret his expression, but it was impossible to tell what was going through his mind. He had somehow closed off from me. 'I know it doesn't matter what *you* think. It's all about the jury. But you must believe me, otherwise you're not going to be so determined to prove my innocence. And you must get me out of here. My son is only seventeen.'

He nodded. 'Tell me everything that happened after you left the remand facility.'

Starting with Ackerman dropping me at King's Cross station, I went through it all. By the time I finished, he was frowning.

'It's just about plausible, I suppose,' was his response.

'You can go to the charity shop and find the coat and scarf I was wearing on the train, if they're still there.'

His face brightened. 'Did you hand them in to someone who might remember seeing you with them?'

'Actually, I slipped them onto a hanger when no one was looking. But I know where they are. Surely that proves I put them there.'

'No, it just proves that you saw them there.'

'But the coat could have been picked up on CCTV. How would I know about that?'

'What does it look like? Perhaps if it's distinctive we might be able to build a case.'

'It's not distinctive at all. Quite the opposite.'

He heaved a sigh.

'I was trying not to attract attention. It's just a black raincoat. I put it on a hanger with other black raincoats.'

We stared at one another as the implications of my actions sank in. I had been too successful in covering my tracks.

'Wouldn't the coat have my DNA on it? Surely you could persuade the police to check? This isn't some petty crime we're talking about. They want to charge me with another murder.'

'Traces of your DNA on a coat in a charity shop would only prove you'd worn it or had tried it on. It wouldn't provide evidence that you travelled to Scotland and back in it, returning too late to have killed Bella.' He paused. 'You could have gone into a charity shop after you killed her and tried a coat on with the intention of fabricating an alibi.' He shook his head. 'The coat proves nothing.' He gave me a curious look. 'Did you kill her? I'm beginning to wonder if you're actually an extremely cunning woman.'

'No. No, I didn't.'

He nodded. 'Our problem is that you have a motive for killing both your husband and his mistress, and we are unable to prove you didn't have the opportunity to commit both crimes. Jealousy and revenge are powerful emotions. I know you remain adamant you didn't kill them, but you wouldn't be the first if you had.'

He left after promising me he would do whatever he could to prove my innocence, but it was a very unsatisfactory meeting. Had it not been for my son, I would have been tempted to give up the fight altogether.

When I was told my brother had come to visit me, I stood up with alacrity. Ackerman was one of the few people who might be able to help me. Perhaps he was the only one. I needed to keep him on my side. Like Andrew, he insisted I tell him everything I had done since we'd parted at King's Cross station.

'And I mean everything,' he insisted. 'Don't leave out a single detail.'

He muttered something incomprehensible when I reached the part where I had discarded his oilskin jacket, but other than that he heard me out in silence, an expression of intense concentration on his face. I even went through my entire conversation with Andrew.

'So, finding the coat will prove nothing,' I concluded.

'Unless you left your train ticket in the pocket,' he said. 'Now, how would you have known it was there if you hadn't put it there yourself?'

'You're right. Although Andrew would point out that would only establish the fact that I bought a ticket. It wouldn't prove I actually travelled anywhere.'

'Yes, that's true. It could be a ruse to set up an alibi,' he agreed. 'Andrew's right. A prosecuting barrister would drive a coach and horses through a defence like that. Now, are you sure you've told me everything? You didn't speak to anyone on your journey back to London?'

'No. I was being careful not to leave any trace. I've told you everything I can remember, as accurately as I can.'

'Leave it with me then. I'll see what else I can find out. But first, there's something I have to do.'

He strode out of the room without a backward glance. The following day he was back, wearing a new coat.

'How are you today, sis?' He leaned forward. 'There's something I didn't tell you yesterday. Are you paying attention?' He lowered his voice to barely more than a whisper. 'I've seen the autopsy report. There was evidence your husband had ingested Rohypnol before he died.'

'I know. You already told me that. The police told me about it as well.'

'I had a word with one of the SOCOs on the forensic team. Did the police also mention that traces of the drug were found on *two* glasses in your home?'

'So?'

It was clear from his animated expression that he was telling me something significant. I just didn't know what.

'If you were slipping a roofie into someone's drink, would you drug yourself as well?' He paused, one eyebrow raised quizzically.

I thought about what he said. 'I was very groggy next morning,' I said, 'but I thought it was just a hangover.'

'Did you have a headache?'

'Yes. Yes, I did. But I don't remember drinking with him when I got home.'

'One of the effects of Rohypnol is that it induces a temporary amnesia. You might well not remember what happened afterwards.'

'I don't remember. I don't remember anything.'

'Which suggests you might have been given Rohypnol as well.'

'Would I have been able to smother my husband with a pillow if I'd been drugged?'

'No way. You'd have been unconscious.'

'Why didn't you tell me this yesterday?'

'It doesn't matter. If it were urgent I'd have told you straight away. But you might mention it to Andrew next time you see him, in case the police haven't shared the information with him either.'

'I will, but I still don't understand why you didn't tell me straight away.'

He shrugged. 'I was busy.'

'Busy? With what?'

'I had to get myself a coat.'

Chapter 22

When I heard that my son had come to see me, I felt as though I was suffocating. For a moment I couldn't say anything.

'Here?' I asked when I found my voice. 'My son's come here? To see me? Are you sure?'

I was impatient to see him but before going to the visitors' room I went to the bathroom and washed my face, although I had showered that morning and my face wasn't dirty. My hair was a mess, but I didn't have a brush or comb on me. All I could do was run my fingers through it and try to make it look tidy. Smoothing the creases in my shirt, I hurried along the corridor to the room where Dan was waiting.

My son was looking around with a surprised expression when I entered the room. My breath caught in my throat at the sight of him, he looked so small and helpless all on his own. Catching sight of me, his jaw dropped. Despite his apparent consternation, his hand rose in a tentative wave, but he didn't answer my smile as I approached.

'Why did you do it?' he blurted out as I took my seat. Close I could see he had been crying. 'Why did you kill him?'

His direct question shocked me, as did his evident distress. We stared at one another for a moment. After weeks of rehearsing what I was going to say to him, when we finally faced one another I was unable to utter a word. The silence between us grew awkward, and I was aware that we might not have long. I forced myself to speak.

'Dan...' I stammered, 'you can't believe I would ever do anything to hurt your father...'

'Tell me what happened to him.'

I shook my head. 'I wish I could answer that question, and believe me I'd tell you if I could, but I simply don't know. Even the police don't know, and they've been investigating his death ever since it happened. No one knows how he died. But they think someone killed him, and I promise you it wasn't me.'

'So why are you here? First Nana Stella said you were in prison because you went crazy when you were drunk and killed him in a fight, then she said they let you out of prison because you didn't do it, then she said you were back in prison because it was you all along.'

'I didn't do it.'

'So why are you here now?'

Having regained my composure sufficiently to be able to talk coherently, I tried to explain that I was being punished for having disobeyed an order to stay in London.

'Why weren't you allowed to leave London?'

'It's just something that happens when the police are carrying out an investigation. They wanted me to stay around in case they needed to ask me anything. They think what I have to say could be important because I knew your dad, and the house. And they think I might be able to help them because I know everyone your dad knew.'

That wasn't the case while Paul was alive, but it might be true since.

Dan nodded. 'So, the police want you to stay around. I think I get that. But why did you leave London then? If you weren't allowed to?'

'I went to Edinburgh to see you. Didn't Nana Stella tell you? I've missed you so much.'

'But I never saw you in Edinburgh,' he replied, looking puzzled.

'No. I went all the way there on the train.' It crossed my mind to ask him whether he would tell the police he had seen me in Edinburgh at around midnight, but I couldn't ask him to lie for me. It was simpler to stick to the truth. Or a version of it, anyway.

'When I arrived your grandmother and I decided you might find it confusing to see me, so I went straight back to London. We didn't want to upset you. We only did what we thought was best for you.'

He shook his head. 'Nana Stella didn't tell me that. She doesn't tell me everything.' He paused and lowered his voice to a conspiratorial tone. 'She didn't want me to come here. She said you're in prison and it's not a nice place, and I shouldn't come here. But I told her I was going to see you and she couldn't stop me. So, she came to London with me. She's waiting for me outside. She didn't want to come in.'

I reached across the table and took his hand. 'I'm very pleased you came,' I said. 'Far more pleased than I can possibly put into words.'

'It's difficult, isn't it?' he agreed. 'To say what you mean.'

I remembered his childhood struggles to speak clearly, and the exercises I used to help him do for the speech therapist, but that wasn't what he meant.

'Yes, it can be very difficult,' I said. 'Sometimes it's hard to find the right words, and sometimes it seems impossible to even work out what it is we want to say.'

'But why are you in prison?' he asked, reverting to his earlier question. 'Nana Stella said they let you out because you didn't do it, and you're telling me you didn't do it. So, I don't understand why you're still here. Why can't we go home?'

'The police haven't finished their investigation,' I replied. 'They want to find out how your father died, and we need to know that too. The police think someone killed him, and until they find out who it was, we can't go home.'

Dan stared at me. 'What do you mean?' he stammered. 'I don't understand. Why can't we go home now? Why?'

His face had turned even paler and he was writhing in his chair, a physical sign of his agitation.

I spoke firmly. 'Dan, you need to stay calm. Breathe slowly. Close your eyes and concentrate on your breathing.'

'But he was murdered!'

'Yes, that's what they think. It would have been very quick, Dan. The doctor said he wouldn't have suffered at all. Anyway, the police still want to talk to me, to see if I can help them find out who killed him, and how it happened. They even thought at first that I might have been responsible. But of course, I wasn't. You know I would never do anything to hurt your father. I... I loved him very much.'

Dan's face creased in a wretched smile. 'I know you did, Mum. I love him too. And I love you.'

I could no longer control my tears.

'Wait... there's more...' I stammered, wondering how to explain that I had only been allowed out on bail. 'It's complicated, but I'm not completely free, not yet. The police are still looking into what happened. Basically, until they conclude their investigation, they're going to want to know where I am, all the time. So, I can't go away anywhere for now. It's because they don't trust me not to come to Scotland again, to see you.'

He nodded. 'I always knew you didn't do it.'

My spirits rose. Dan believed I was innocent, and in that moment, nothing else mattered.

'What about me?' he asked.

'You're okay staying with Nana and Granddad for now, aren't you?'

'Can't I come home with you, Mum?'

I hadn't anticipated that question. 'Of course, you'll be coming home with me, but not just yet.'

'Why not?'

I glanced helplessly at him.

'Apart from anything else, it wouldn't be fair on Nana and Granddad to take you away from them so soon. They love having you staying with them, and you know your visit is really helping them to cope with losing your dad. In any case, I've just explained to you that I can't go home just yet. The police haven't finished their enquiries.'

He paused. 'They searched me when I came in,' he said. 'I had to walk through a huge metal door and they shut that behind me before they opened another huge metal door and then they shut that one behind me. And then they asked me to empty out my pockets and I had to walk through a metal detector. I asked them if they were looking for a gun. It's like-' He paused, searching for the words to describe what he meant.

'Like a prison?' I suggested softly.

'Like a space-ship. I was going to say it's like a space-ship.'

I smiled.

'But why can't we go home, Mum?'

'I told you, the police are still busy looking into it all. Until they finish, they can't let us go home.'

'Why not? Are they still searching the house for clues? Like in CSI?' he asked, his eyes suddenly alight with understanding.

'Yes, that's exactly what it's like.'

That wasn't true. Apart from the fact that the forensic examination of my house had been completed, compared to the glamorised forensic science of the glossy American television series, the real-life search seemed to have been protracted, rigorous and professional, involving a lot of tedious sample gathering and testing of various fragments of different materials, all resulting in very little as far as I could tell. But the comparison seemed to make him happy. At any rate he nodded, apparently satisfied.

'Okay, then,' he said. 'Now I get what you're doing here.'

And just like that, it seemed his questions had all been answered. I had finally come up with a reason he understood to explain his continuing stay at his grandparents' house. It *was* true that I wasn't allowed to return home at the moment, but that was only because I was a suspect in a double murder investigation. It was also true that the police were still searching for clues, although no longer in my house. So, although what I had told Dan wasn't strictly true, I hadn't lied to him either.

Telling lies is easy. The truth is rarely simple.

Chapter 23

Slowly I settled back into my life in prison. There was no point in fighting against my situation and it wasn't that bad, once I got used to it. There were getting on for a thousand of us at the facility which had originally been designed to hold seven hundred prisoners, so many of the women had to share cells. That caused problems, mainly when someone was kept awake by her cell-mate snoring.

I was lucky to have a cell to myself, and was allowed to keep photos of Dan on the shelf beside my bed. In fact, the management actively encouraged prisoners to stay in close contact with their families on the outside and allowed unrestricted phone calls and regular weekly visits. I had even been permitted to give my son a hug and a kiss when he had visited me. The memory of that kept me buoyed up for days afterwards. Of course, I wasn't a convicted criminal, but innocent until proven guilty, along with around twenty per cent of the prisoners who were also there on remand, awaiting trial. We were treated more leniently than those serving a sentence, but even those who had been convicted seemed resigned to their circumstances, and generally content. Their attitude surprised me when I first arrived, because of course none of us were at liberty. We were safe and well cared for within the confines of the prison, but we couldn't leave and at night we were locked in our cramped cells for a twelve-hour stretch.

Almost as restricting as the loss of freedom was the daily routine which forced us out of bed at seven o'clock every morning and had us back in our cells at seven every evening. That was when it really hit me that I was being held in a prison. My bed was comfortable enough, once I grew accustomed to it, but I resented being subjected to such an early lock-up time. Conversely, it was difficult getting up so early every morning with a dreary day stretching ahead in seemingly endless boredom. This was real loss of control, daily, grinding me down. I tried not to let it get to me, but it was a struggle not to succumb to depression.

For the first few days, I avoided the company of my fellow prisoners, members of an intimidating criminal class with whom I had nothing in common. Afraid of being bullied, I had heard prison described as a training ground for villains and feared for my future. But as day followed day in a monotonous routine, I became cautiously acquainted with a few of the other women. Like me, Tracey was also awaiting trial, but she had been arrested for fraud. Tall and slim, with neatly cut greying hair, she held herself very upright. She never told me the details of her alleged criminal activities, only that her ex-boss deserved to lose everything.

'He's the one who should be locked up, not me,' she said, slagging him off in some of the foulest language I had ever heard.

When she wasn't talking about her boss, she was well spoken and personable, so I avoided enquiring into her background and we became friends, after a fashion. We both knew that we would never see one another again once we left the prison. In the meantime, it was comforting to feel I had a friend in there, and I hoped she felt the same. We walked together in the garden, a path barely wide enough to allow two people to walk side by side, bordered by narrow flower-beds tended by prisoners.

Polly was the only convicted prisoner to befriend me. She told me she was nineteen although she looked at least thirty, and she was serving a sentence for repeated shoplifting.

'It's all right for them,' she told me.

She never clarified who 'they' were but appeared to hold a grudge against anyone who wasn't in prison. Listening to Polly complaining, I tried not to think about the clothes I had stolen to disguise myself and couldn't help wondering if I had just been luckier than her. But she was going to be released in a few months' time. If I went down, it would be for life. I couldn't imagine spending the rest of my life locked in that small place with nothing to do but eat and sleep, walk and read. When it rained, I couldn't even go outside. I was offered work in the kitchens but declined. Once I was out of there I would be a wealthy woman, in possession of a house and a small fortune. I didn't need to do menial work for a pittance. But afterwards I regretted having turned down the offer. It would have helped to pass the time.

During the day I entertained myself tolerably well, walking around the small garden gazing at the neatly arranged flowers, and sitting in the library. I read a lot, words sliding across my mind occasionally distracting me from my thoughts. Alone in my cell at night there was nothing to take my mind off my situation and I lay in bed, wondering what Dan was doing and picturing him in Edinburgh, chatting to his grandparents, growing steadily closer to them. We spoke every evening, but our stilted conversations were a poor substitute for his company. I missed his cheeky grin so much it felt like a physical ache. In a way it would have been easier if I had stopped all contact with him and tried to shut him out of my mind completely.

One afternoon I was crouching down in a corner, studying the spines of books, trying to find something that might help occupy my thoughts, when a prisoner accosted me. Serving a long sentence for offences including drug dealing, soliciting, and aggravated robbery, Layla was the sort of prisoner I was keen to avoid. We came, as the expression goes, from different sides of the track. More than anything else, her reputation for violence terrified me. But on this occasion, I was unaware of her approach. Too late to effect an escape, I avoided her gaze and tried to conceal my fear without provoking her by appearing defiant. Layla's dark hair was scraped back off her face in a high pony-tail, accentuating her sharp features and bulging eyes, and, as she squatted down beside me, I caught a whiff of her stale sweat.

'Want to score?' she hissed, her blue eyes glittering with a strange fervour.

Caught off guard, I stumbled backwards in surprise, hitting my head on the shelf behind me. As a couple of books landed on the floor, Layla let out a low laugh, amused at my discomfiture. Edging forward, she trapped me in the corner.

'Spice?' she hissed. 'I got some good shit.'

My eyes flicked to a poster on the library wall warning of severe penalties for drug dealing. Hardly daring to look at her, I backed away and knocked another book on the floor. It was impossible to remain oblivious of the prison authorities' battle against drugs, with signs and posters displayed in every room discouraging the use of illicit substances.

'No...' I stammered. 'No... thank you. I don't... I never have done. It's not for me.'

'Fucking rookie,' she snarled.

Mesmerised by a tiny trickle of saliva sliding down the side of her chin, I prayed that my silence wouldn't be interpreted as provocative.

'You'll be begging for it soon enough, rookie.'

Snapping her fingers in my face, she spun round and darted away leaving me trembling in the corner. After a few moments, I grabbed one of the books that had fallen on the floor and hurried to join a few prisoners who were sitting around a table reading. No one glanced at me as I sat staring at a pristine copy of Jane Eyre. I must have been the first prisoner to remove it from the shelf.

'How do they get hold of drugs in here?' I asked Tracey the next time we went outside for a walk in the garden.

'Why? Are you looking for ways to numb the pain of existence?'

I wasn't sure if her question was serious or not. 'I just wondered how they did it, that's all. No reason. I mean, why doesn't anyone stop them? It seems ironic that they're allowed to break the law in here, when the whole purpose of the place is to punish people for doing just that. It doesn't make sense.'

'Some prisoners ask their visitors to bring in whatever they want.'

'I thought visitors were searched when they arrive?'

She grunted. 'They are. So what? They still smuggle stuff in. Everyone knows it goes on, but they can't seem to stop it. And then there are prison staff who aren't as clean as they should be, and a few of them bring stuff in for the prisoners. It's a problem. Some of the women here are stoned a lot of the time, and they keep the doctor busy with their adverse reactions to the shit they shove into themselves. If you ask me, they should just let them pass out and leave them to it. Let them rot. Doctors shouldn't be wasting their time saving the lives of drug-crazed criminals.'

'They're entitled to medical care when they're ill.'

'Not if they bring it on themselves.'

'What about alcoholics?'

She shrugged. 'Alcohol's a different matter. For a start it's not illegal.'

I didn't want to argue with my only friend in the prison, so I let the matter drop. It hadn't occurred to me that many of the prisoners were using drugs. In my naïveté I had assumed the prisoners were mainly docile because, worn down by the system, they had come to accept their condition. Tracey told me some of the prisoners had violent outbursts, which she said were drug induced, although I couldn't help wondering if some prisoners were only quiet when they *were* under the influence of drugs. Possibly the truth was that the authorities tolerated the abuse in order to maintain the peace. When I raised the question of drugs being available in the prison with one of the older officers, she told me the situation had deteriorated when a raft of senior officers had all left within the space of a few months, resulting in a high proportion of inexperienced officers running the facility.

'Why weren't they replaced with experienced staff?'

She sniffed. 'Budgets. Government cuts are making it impossible for us to do our job properly. We're already understaffed, and the prison population keeps growing, and we're expected to carry on improving the service. Lack of funding is putting a real strain on the system. But it all goes on behind locked doors, literally, and so everyone turns a blind eye.'

'It doesn't help if prison officers are smuggling in drugs,' I said.

She gave me a disapproving frown. 'Where on earth did you get that from? You don't want to believe everything you hear in this place.'

Observing the erratic behaviour of a few of the prisoners, I was inclined to believe what Tracey had told me. My experience of prison life was growing increasingly uncomfortable as time went on. In addition to my separation from Dan, my loss of liberty, and the endless boredom, I now had Layla to worry about. Whatever else happened, I would have to make sure I never found myself alone with her again.

Chapter 24

I stared in genuine disbelief. It seemed like a miracle, although Andrew assured me it wasn't unusual.

'Family concerns always get court sympathy,' he said. 'And quite rightly so. The fact that you broke the terms of your bail to go and see your son definitely counted in your favour. We couldn't have swung it without your mother-in-law's statement confirming she saw you in Edinburgh on the afternoon of your release. Pity you didn't see her later that night,' he added with a shake of his head. 'The police are doing everything they can to implicate you in the death of your husband's mistress, but they haven't come up with any concrete evidence yet. And without anything that proves you were there, it's all speculation. They won't find evidence to place you anywhere near the scene of the second murder, will they?'

'No. They haven't found any evidence, because I wasn't there. I mean, I have been to her flat but they already know that. They arrested me there.'

'Which means any traces of your DNA found in her flat will be useless.' He smiled at me.

'If I hadn't gone to see her that evening, there wouldn't *be* any of my DNA there. I've only been to her flat that one time, and I was hardly there five minutes before the police turned up.'

I broke off, feeling churlish. Andrew had just arrived to inform me that he had succeeded in renewing my bail and instead of thanking him, I was complaining.

'Anyway,' I said brightly, 'this is wonderful news. I really can't tell you how grateful I am. So, what happens now?'

'You pack your bag and walk out of here. Go straight home. The same conditions apply as before but this time you won't need to report to your local police station. Instead you'll be subject to electronic monitoring with a six o'clock curfew which means you have to stay in your house after six o'clock every day. At some point this evening, a supplier will arrive to install the monitoring equipment at your home. There's no need to look so worried. It's a very straightforward system. You might have heard it called tagging. You'll be fitted with a transmitter device around your ankle, and if you remain at home after six in the evening, the receiver device fitted in your home will send radio messages to the monitoring unit. If you leave the curfew address, the signal from the tag automatically stops and an alert sounds at the monitoring centre within a minute of your departure and, basically, the police will turn up before you have a chance to go anywhere. It's just a way of keeping tabs on you, and it saves you having to go along to the police station every day. You're free to go out and about during the day and, under trousers, no one will even see you're wearing a tag.'

'What if I take it off?'

'The short answer to that is you can't, not without damaging the tag and that will set off the alarm. This is serious, Julie. You can't afford to mess up again. Next time the courts won't be lenient. They'll leave you languishing in prison until your trial comes up. To be honest, you wouldn't have been released at all if they weren't desperate to get people out on bail to relieve the pressure on overcrowded prisons.'

I promised to obey the conditions. In a way it was like still being in prison except I had to be back inside by six instead of seven, and I would have to feed myself from now on. But my comfortable home was vastly preferable to my prison cell, and I wouldn't have to worry about bumping into Layla again. Dan might even come home. I cried with relief as I packed my bag. It only remained to say goodbye to my few friends in the prison.

Tracey said she was pleased to see the back of me. I knew what she meant. Neither of us wanted to stay in prison any longer than we had to. We shook hands and then hugged, and she wished me luck.

'The same to you,' I replied.

She nodded. Her case was due to come up in court soon and then she would know the length of her sentence.

'I could come and visit you,' I said.

We both knew that was never going to happen.

'I don't intend to be here long enough to have visitors,' she answered.

Without such bravado, our stay in prison would have been unbearable.

'See you on the dark side,' she smiled.

The only other person I would have said goodbye to was Polly, but I couldn't see her anywhere. She must have been in the gym, working in the kitchen, or perhaps at the doctor's. I didn't want to hang around, so I left. I don't suppose she would have cared, one way or the other. People were constantly arriving and departing, and once they had gone they were quickly forgotten.

It felt strange and wonderful to be walking back into my house. The place had a dusty in feel to it, as though it had been uninhabited for years. I switched on the television to people the silence. Grabbing a black bin liner, I emptied the contents of my fridge: a half litre of milk which had been turning sour for weeks, a pot of mouldy yoghurt, a portion of cooked chicken which smelled disgusting, half a loaf of bread which had turned green, and other bits and pieces at various stages of decay. It was only four o'clock, so I went out to Sainsbury's.

My credit card didn't work. I tried three times before I realised what had happened.

'Shit!'

The cashier smiled wearily at me. 'Have you got another card?'

I shook my head. If the police had stopped one of my cards, they must have stopped all of them.

'Are you paying cash then?'

I checked my purse. 'Yes, but I'll just have to put a few things back.'

Mortified, I glanced apologetically at the customers waiting behind me as I manoeuvred my way past them back into the store. Only one woman grumbled at me as I pushed by her.

'Oh piss off,' I growled, and she fell back, scowling.

'How rude,' someone else said, loudly enough for everyone in the queue to hear. 'Some people have no manners.'

I stalked off to replace my most expensive items, taking a puerile pleasure in putting them on the wrong shelves. Jars of olives, artichokes, and sun-dried tomatoes from the deli counter found their way to the dairy section, a welcome home present of a bottle of Champagne appeared on the bottom cheese shelf, to be substituted with a cheap Pinot Grigio, until my trolley contained less than a basket's worth of bargains. After all that hassle, I barely made it home by six.

While I was unpacking my shopping, a fitter arrived to install my monitoring equipment. She assured me the box would leave no unsightly marks, and I had no choice but to accept her word. The unit was much smaller than I had anticipated and once she set it up in a corner of the living room, out of sight behind the television cabinet, it wouldn't really have mattered if it did leave any traces. Next, she handed me a chunky grey plastic bracelet and instructed me to fit it around my ankle. Once it was on I could twist it around, but it wouldn't come off unless I physically cut through the band holding it in place.

'What happens if it gets wet?'

She assured me there was no need to worry about that as it was waterproof, and she handed me a booklet which she said ought to answer any queries I had. There was a number to call if I had any trouble with it, although she assured me that thousands of people had been fitted with these devices without any problems.

'That's it,' she said. 'You're all set.'

She had only been in my house for a short time, but she left me wearing a constant reminder of my status, as though I had been branded with a hot iron. Crying with self-pity, I opened my cheap bottle of Pinot Grigio. This was all Paul's fault. I wished he were still alive, just so I could tell him what I thought of him. I was overcome with fury, but it didn't matter. There was no one to see me punching the sofa. No one to hear my howls of rage.

Chapter 25

My head ached after my crying fit, but somehow I felt better for having given voice to my anger, and ready to focus on practical problems again.

That evening I called Ackerman to ask him for more money, but there was no answer. With my purse empty, and no more expensive jewellery to sell, I had to find a way of raising some cash. First I raided my bedroom and found a string of pearls and a pair of pearl and diamond earrings that had belonged to my mother. They wouldn't raise much, but anything was going to be useful to help tide me over until I could access my bank account again. I blessed my mother's hankering after expensive jewellery.

Next, I came across an old watch which had belonged to my father. It looked as though it was gold, which could fetch a few pounds. But my find of the evening was an old bank book from a savings account I had opened years earlier, before I was married. It was hidden down the back of a drawer where I had kept it concealed from Paul, just in case I ever needed it. I had forgotten about it. The fact that the book was still in its hiding place in my bedroom raised my hopes that the police hadn't stumbled on it. They had been looking for evidence of murder, not old bank books. There was a chance they didn't know about the account which had over three thousand pounds in it the last time the book had been updated. With interest accrued over the years, there might be considerably more in there by now. The only problem was getting hold of it without my driving licence which the police had retained. I could hardly ask them to return it. Once again, I would have to ask for Ackerman's help.

Having fixed myself a supper of toast and baked beans, quick, nourishing and cheap, I switched on the television and settled down with my bottle of Pinot for company. I must admit, I wasn't unhappy, despite my situation. There could be few women as well off as I now was who were reduced to eating on next to nothing, but that was a temporary cash flow problem. As soon as Ackerman returned my calls, he would sort out my finances. With luck, there might even be sufficient funds in my savings account to keep me going until this whole sorry business was over and I could access the rest of my money again.

When I still hadn't heard from Ackerman by ten o'clock, I decided to try his number one last time before turning in. His failure to answer his phone or respond to my increasingly frantic messages was beginning to worry me. If anything happened to him, I would be in trouble. With no money at my disposal, it wouldn't be easy to replace him.

By the time he picked up his phone, I had drunk nearly the whole bottle of wine. Not having touched a drop for over a month, I was almost incapable of stringing two sentences together.

'Where have you been?' I demanded.

'You sound drunk.'

'I had a drink, yes. So what? Wouldn't you if you were me? Wouldn't you have a drink? If you were me, wouldn't you have a drink?'

'Probably not,' he replied. 'I think I'd be careful to keep my wits about me.'

'What's that supposed to mean? Do you think I've lost it? Do you think I've lost my wits?'

'Never mind. There's no call to get angry. I'm on your side, remember? So, have you been calling me for a reason?'

'Too right I have. Calling and calling.'

'How much have you had to drink?'

'Never mind. Do you know they've tagged me?'

'Yes, I heard. So no more trips to Scotland for a while.'

'That's not the point.'

'What is the point?' he asked.

I gesticulated fiercely, forgetting that he couldn't see me. 'I've run out of cash. Purse is empty. And I had to put nearly everything back. Even the tomatoes.'

'Are you calling to ask me to bring you some tomatoes?' He sounded as though he was laughing.

'I'm celebrating my homecoming with a cheap bottle of wine and one tin of baked beans,' I told him.

'Are you drinking alone?'

'I'm not inviting you round to share it, if that's what you're after.' I picked up the bottle. 'This is mine.'

'I most certainly am not interested in joining you.' He sounded indignant.

'There's no need to be like that. I'm an attractive woman. I'm...' I struggled to find the right word. 'I'm a woman.'

'I was referring to the wine,' he said. 'I wouldn't go out for a bottle of cheap plonk, however attractive the person issuing the invitation was.'

'I didn't issue an invitation.' It was like a tongue twister. 'To anyone. Not to you.'

'Julie, before you pass out, can you just tell me why you rang. Was there a reason for your call?'

'I just told you. I'm broke. No money. Nothing. But I've got a bank book. It's an old account so I think we might be able to get the money out. Only I haven't got my passport or driving licence. They took them away and I haven't got them back.'

'How much is in there?' he asked, somehow managing to grasp my meaning even though I was virtually incoherent. 'Wait,' he added, 'we might need to act quickly. I'm coming over, so listen out for the bell. Julie, can you understand what I'm saying? You mustn't go to sleep before I get there. I don't want a wasted journey. Make yourself a strong cup of coffee and be careful not to scald yourself. Have you got that?'

'You don't have to treat me like an idiot,' I replied. 'I may be pissed but I'm not a moron.'

'Just make sure you stay awake,' he said.

He hung up, so I went downstairs to make my coffee. Despite what Ackerman thought, I knew how to keep my wits about me. Still, regardless of my efforts to stay awake, I dozed off in front of the television. Something woke me. Apart from the flickering light from the television screen, I was sitting in darkness. For a moment I was too confused to recollect exactly where I was. Only as I came to, did I remember that I was no longer in prison, but back in my own home, a wealthy but penniless widow. It came again, a sharp tapping at the window. Although I was befuddled with alcohol, fear made me instantly alert. Someone was outside. Slowly I slid off the settee and crawled across the carpet towards the phone. Reaching the table, I thought better of my initial impulse. The last people I wanted to contact right now were the police. If they discovered I had been drinking, they might take steps to prevent Dan from coming home. As I hesitated, undecided, I heard someone calling my name. With a shuddering breath of relief, I realised that Ackerman was outside, tapping on the window for me to let him in.

'Why didn't you answer when I rang the bell?' he demanded as he came inside.

'I didn't hear it with the TV on. I wasn't asleep,' I added.

He grunted, one eyebrow raised sceptically. 'Come on, then, let's take a look at this savings account.'

He went into the living room and sat down while I went upstairs to fetch the book. Studying it, he nodded and looked at me with a grin.

'Nice,' he said, pocketing the book. 'I'll get these funds out first thing tomorrow.'

'Are you sure you can do that?'

He tapped the side of his nose. 'I know a man who can.'

'And then you'll bring me the money?'

He gazed at me, eyes narrowed as though he was calculating. 'What say you we go halves this time?'

'Halves?'

'Jesus woman, are you a parrot? Yes, halves. Half for you, and half for me. To recompense me for my trouble and for taking the risk of extracting the funds. If I'm caught, I could be locked up. At any rate, the police wouldn't be best pleased with me if they ever learned I'd helped you outmanoeuvre them. And that could make my life very difficult. Still, it's not like we're talking about a vast fortune, is it? Just enough to keep us both afloat for another month, if we're careful.'

'A month?' I repeated, momentarily forgetting his jibe about me repeating everything he said. 'How much longer is all this going to carry on?' I raised my trouser leg to reveal the ugly grey tag around my ankle.

Ackerman shrugged. 'One step at a time. Now, is there any of that wine left over or have you downed the lot?'

Chapter 26

Late the following afternoon a brown envelope was posted through my door. It had been secured with wide sticky parcel tape which made it difficult to tear open. Ripping the end of the envelope carefully I drew out five twenty-pound notes. I counted them several times and tore open the envelope. He had sent me only a hundred pounds. Besides that, I still had my mother's pearls and earrings, and my father's watch. My memories of the previous evening were hazy, but as far as I could remember I hadn't mentioned the additional jewellery to Ackerman. Every time I moved, my head pounded, and I felt sick. I was on bail, and hungover, and I was virtually broke.

It was too late to go out to the shops that day and be home for six, but I decided against spending any of my meagre funds on a takeaway, instead settling for another supper of beans on toast. Hopefully money would no longer be a problem very soon, but it was as well to be thrifty with my cash, just in case it took time for me to get my hands on the small fortune Paul had left me. The legal system could proceed painfully slowly, and there was nothing I could do to expedite matters, however frustrating it was.

By about eight o'clock, I couldn't restrain my irritation any longer and called Ackerman, but he didn't answer, nor did he call me back. I had spent the day alone, more isolated than a prisoner behind bars. My husband had cheated on me, and now Ackerman had conned me out of my few thousand pounds and I couldn't even report the theft to the police. Tired and dispirited, I had an early night, resolving to go out in the morning, even if just for a walk. And on my way home, I would pop into Marks and Spencer's for a chicken and a bag of potatoes that would keep me in dinners for a few days. But this time, I would skip the wine.

I went to bed early but couldn't sleep. Everything that had happened to me lately kept going round and round inside my head, until I was crying with anger and exhaustion. It had all started with Paul being unable to keep his dick in his trousers. I could have forgiven his infidelity. If we hadn't been able to resolve our differences, we could have split up, even divorced. It was hardly unusual for a marriage to fail. What I couldn't stomach was knowing he had persistently lied to me, deliberately and resolutely, for two years.

The next day it rained steadily, but I went out anyway, after calling Ackerman without managing to get hold of him. I was going stir crazy sitting at home on my own. Much as I hated prison, at least there were other people around in there to help pass the time. Apart from my frightening encounter with Layla, my fellow prisoners had given me no trouble, and they had been company of a sort. Now I was on my own, my only visitor a private investigator who was supposed to be working to prove my innocence. He hadn't done too well so far. As I walked I could feel the tag around my ankle. It wasn't uncomfortable, not tight or anything, but I was aware of it. Maybe that was the intention of its clunky design. I glanced at my phone. It was ten o'clock in the morning. In eight hours' time, I would be stuck at home with my tag sending regular messages to an unknown monitoring centre where anonymous operators would be checking up on me.

The interim was mine.

I did my shopping, taking my time and choosing food I would really enjoy. After two nights of beans on toast, I deserved something scrumptious. After that I bought a pair of cheap jeans in Sainsbury's.

Taking my shopping home, I luxuriated in the shower. It was a waste of the time I could have spent out and about, considering I would be imprisoned at home all evening and would have plenty of time to shower then, and nothing much else to do, but I had missed the privacy of my own shower while I was in prison. I couldn't resist it.

By the time I had finished shopping and washing my hair, it was nearly midday. Only six hours to go. Time, which had passed so slowly in prison, was now racing by.

With my hair washed and dry, and wearing new jeans, I went into Harrow for a sandwich and a coffee. The company of strangers was preferable to spending yet more time on my own. The shopping centre in Harrow is arranged in two covered malls: St Anne's and St George's which was added on after the first site was established. Connecting the two shopping areas is an outdoor walkway lined with shops, with a large pub on the corner. I walked along between the two, enjoying the fresh breeze, and entered St George's.

Sitting in Starbucks, I was anonymous. No one could see my tag. For a few hours I could pretend my life was back to normal. Paul wasn't dead, and Dan would be home from school soon. With a toasted sandwich and a coffee, I sat facing the large picture window that looked out on the shoppers walking past. It was striking how few bright colours people wore. Most were dressed in sombre grey or black, peppered with dark blues and only an occasional flash of a bright red jacket or orange shirt. At liberty to wear whatever colour they wanted, hardly anyone seemed to take advantage of their freedom. Most people probably weren't even aware of it.

While I was sitting there, watching the shoppers go by, my phone rang, and Nina's number came up on the screen display.

'Hi, how are you?'

'Fine. I've been calling you every day to see if you'd got your phone back yet. What's happening?'

I told her I had been released. 'I'm in Starbucks, in Harrow.'

'Oh my God, I don't believe it! Why didn't you call and let me know? I'm on my way. I'll be there in twenty minutes.

Only a short while earlier I had been feeling sorry for myself because I was at home by myself. Now I was out in a café, and a friend wanted to see me. Smiling, I put my phone back in my bag. When Nina called me again, I hoped she wasn't going to say she couldn't join me after all.

'What's up?'

'Listen,' she said breathlessly.

'Are you okay? Are you running?'

'No, well, yes, I was. The thing is, Katie called me. She's broken up from school and she suggested we get together, so I had to tell her I couldn't because I'd arranged to meet you, and she said that was fine and she would join us. I couldn't very well say no. I mean, she caught me on the hop. So I said that would be great. But I thought I ought to call you and check that's okay with you. I mean, is it okay with you?'

I assured her it was fine. As I hung up I realised that I was quite excited about seeing Katie again. If she wanted to see me, that must mean she no longer believed I was guilty. Although I knew my friends would easily find me, I kept glancing up at the door every few minutes, impatient to see them again, glad I had washed my hair and put on new clothes. Until then I hadn't realised quite how desperately lonely I had been.

Nina came in first. Looking around the room, she caught sight of me waving at her and came over. Soon after we had greeted one another, Katie joined us.

'I've been wanting to apologise to you,' she said straight away. 'What I said to you was unforgivable.'

'It was understandable,' I told her.

'I thought... we all thought... ' She sat down.

'I didn't kill him,' I said quietly.

The whole café didn't need to know that I had been suspected of murdering my husband.

'No. I realise that now. They wouldn't have let you go if they still thought you were guilty.'

Involuntarily I glanced down at my ankle to check my tag wasn't visible. If necessary, I would launch into an explanation of my current circumstances, but for now, I just wanted to relax with my friends. It was quite busy in Starbucks, so Nina and Katie went up to the counter while I kept the table. When we were all finally settled with our coffees, Katie asked me how I was.

'I mean, really, how are you? It must have been so hard for you. I can't imagine. Still, you're better off without him. I mean, I hate to speak ill of the dead and all that, but you are my friend and honestly, he brought it on himself. Not that I'm saying I'm pleased about what happened to him, no one deserves that, but I'm just saying you're better off without him. If I ever found out Tony was cheating on me, he'd be out of my house faster than you can say Jack Rabbit.'

'Jack Rabbit?' Nina laughed. 'Who the hell is that?'

'It's just an expression. But the point is, Paul was playing away from home. You can't say he didn't deserve what he got.'

'I don't know about that,' I said, slightly taken aback by her vehemence. It wasn't *her* husband who had been unfaithful.

'You told us he was having an affair,' she said.

'Of course. I know all about his mistress. I met her.'

Katie's eyebrows shot up. 'You *met* her? What was she like?'

'Nothing special. She was about ten years younger than us. Blonde. She was quite nice. If it hadn't been for the situation, I would probably have quite liked her.'

'You thought she was *nice?*' Nina repeated, looking amazed. 'Julie, how can you say that? She was screwing your husband!'

'Blonde?' Katie seemed surprised. 'Oh well, I guess Tony got it wrong, as usual. He told me he saw Paul getting into a car with a dark-haired woman. He said that's how he knew she wasn't you, Julie. He was sure there was something going on between them, but it looks like he got the wrong end of the stick.' She gave an embarrassed laugh. 'That's so typical of Tony. Men are the worst gossips.'

'Oh for goodness sake, Katie,' Nina replied. 'Just drop it, will you? Whatever he did or didn't do, Paul's dead, and he *was* Julie's husband. She doesn't want to listen to speculation about what he may or may not have been getting up to.'

'That's okay,' I said. 'You're right. I'm better off without him. This is nice, isn't it?' I added, looking at them both and forcing a smile.

I was grateful for Nina's intervention. She was right. Although I had implied I was fine with Katie's comment, it had upset me more than I cared to admit, but I was determined to hide my feelings. At one time meeting two girl friends for coffee would have been a missable event. In the context of my life for the past month, it felt like an exciting social gathering. I didn't want to spoil it.

'It's like old times,' Nina said, picking up on my attitude.

To all outward appearances, she was right. But my husband's body was lying frozen in the mortuary, my son was living four hundred miles away from home, and I was hiding a hideous plastic bracelet on my ankle. I struggled to understand how my well-ordered life had so rapidly deteriorated into chaos. Thinking about the bottle of wine cooling in my fridge, I felt an unexpected affinity with Layla, who had relied on mind-altering chemicals to shield her from life. We weren't so very different. I had more in common with a violent drug addict than with my old friends who were blithely sipping lattes, blinkered by their fragile veneer of respectability.

Chapter 27

By half past five I was back home, in time for the start of my curfew, and shortly after six I called my mother-in-law to find out how Dan was getting on. She was pleased to hear that I had been released on bail again.

'That is good news, well done,' she said, as though it was a personal achievement to be let out of prison.

'But I won't be able to come up to see you just yet,' I added.

It might have been possible for me to get to Edinburgh and back without breaking my curfew. I could try to find out. But it would be cutting it very fine to cram about eleven hours of travelling from my house and back again, within my twelve-hour allocation. It would make more sense for Dan to come to see me. I didn't want to risk being held up by any delay on the trains. I suggested to Stella that Dan come to London. Although she agreed, in principle, she was evasive about fixing a date.

'We've got a lot planned for the next couple of weeks,' she explained. 'Lots of outings. And Mark has promised to take him fishing, of all things. But after that, of course he must come and stay with you.'

She made it sound as though he would be paying me a visit, not coming home, but I let that go. We would sort out the arrangements for his return once the police confirmed that I was home for good. In the meantime he was enjoying his stay in Edinburgh.

When Dan came on the line he was excited about the excursions his grandparents had been taking him on since I last saw him. He also told me he had joined a youth club that met every week in the local church hall. I wasn't sure it was a good idea for him to start making friends of his own age in Edinburgh, since he would be coming home soon, but I didn't mention my reservations to him. I would take that up with Stella at the appropriate time. For now, my position was weak.

'A youth club?' I said. 'What do you get up to there?'

'Table tennis mostly,' he told me. 'And they show us films. It's a bit churchy, you know, but I like it there.'

I wondered if it was an evangelical church community trying to welcome him into the fold and determined to bring him back home as soon as I could.

'And Nana and Granddad took me to St Mary's Close,' he babbled eagerly.

'What's St Mary's Close?' I wondered if that was another kind of church community.

'It's this place underground. It's a very old street where people used to live that's been preserved because it was built on top of. At least, I think that's what happened. I think it was discovered when they were excavating, or digging foundations, or something. But it might always have just been there. Anyway, a lot of people lived there in medieval times, when they had the plague in Edinburgh. Almost everyone died of the plague in those days, even children and babies. They only got rid of it in the end because they burned rats to get rid of them. They didn't know it was the rats that were spreading the plague in the first place. Well, it wasn't the rats exactly, but the fleas that lived on the rats that bit the people and infected them with the plague which the rats carried. It was horrible,' he added cheerfully. 'They lived squashed together in tiny cellars, without any light at all, well, maybe one candle, and every day they emptied their buckets of sewage into the street and if anyone was outside, they were covered in poo! Really, Mum, you should go there. It's awesome. Only a few people were immune to the plague and recovered from it, but I don't think anyone knows why they survived. Life wasn't easy in those days.'

'I'll call you tomorrow,' I said when we were about to hang up.

'Oh not tomorrow,' he replied. 'Nan and Granddad are taking me to the cinema. But I'll speak to you soon. 'Bye, Mum.'

Although I was glad he was settled and having a good time, I was jealous, knowing he was happy without me. I had devoted so many years of my life to nurturing his development, helping him with his physical exercises and talking him through the bullying and isolation he had encountered as a child, selflessly dedicating my life to his welfare. Not that I regretted it for a moment. I would willingly do it again. Dan had given meaning to my life in a way that no one else ever could. But now that he had grown into an articulate and caring young adult, I resented the fact that his grandparents were the ones enjoying the results of my efforts. Still, he would soon be home again. In the meantime, I knew I ought to be pleased he was happy in Scotland. And, after all, his grandparents were good people who had lost *their* son. It would be selfish to begrudge them their transient pleasure.

The rest of the evening passed slowly. I was in limbo, waiting to hear from Ackerman, waiting to hear from Andrew, and waiting to hear from the police. It was the feeling of helplessness that was hardest to bear.

The next morning I went to the supermarket and stocked up on cleaning materials and bed linen. The house was dusty and had an empty feel to it, even though I had moved back in. I spent the afternoon wiping and scrubbing, dusting and polishing, and pushing the hoover around. I even took down the curtains in my bedroom and washed them. As soon as I could get my hands on my money, I was going to replace the bed Paul and I had shared for nearly a quarter of a century. He was history. I was going to start again. I might even move to a new house.

I flicked aimlessly through the television channels. There were any number of programmes, but none of them appealed to me. My attention was caught by a promotion aimed at people who had problems sleeping. It was nothing more than an advert for a brand of bed claiming to be so popular that the price had been reduced in an offer that had to end on Sunday. It wasn't going to help me get to sleep that night, but it might be worth following up later. I made a note of the name but until I could access my funds, it was pointless. With a curse, I screwed up the slip of paper and tossed it away.

There was a film on television that evening. For the first time since Paul's death, I lost myself in another story in which a man died in a war leaving his pregnant wife to the care of his best friend who had always loved her. It was a daft story, really, but I shed a few tears at the end of it, because her baby would never know his father. After that I watched a film where a woman married a man only to discover he was a violent maniac who punished her if she didn't arrange the kitchen cupboards neatly or hang the towels in tidy rows in the bathroom. They lived in a house overlooking the ocean, so she managed to escape by pretending to drown but of course the mad husband discovered her ruse and came looking for her. After she ran away she met a gentle, fun-loving man but the husband tracked her down. I sighed with relief when she shot her husband and cried when the man who had been kind to her turned out to be alive after appearing to die. But of course it was fiction, so when the heroine left her husband, she could somehow afford to live in her own beautiful house although she hardly had any money of her own, and the villain died in the end. If only life was that generous and fair to people acting out their stories in the real world.

Chapter 28

The police called me the following morning to say they had finished with our computers and other devices, and I was free to collect them. At least it meant they hadn't forgotten about me, stuck at home with a tag round my ankle, like a fettered animal. After the officer rang off I wondered whether I ought to contact my lawyer, but collecting my computers hardly constituted a formal interview, and besides, I wasn't obliged to say anything if I didn't feel comfortable talking to the police.

Arriving at the police station, I was dismayed when Detective Inspector Morgan appeared. I should have known he would want to see me and kicked myself for my naïveté. He towered over me as he greeted me. I had forgotten how tall he was. He must have been about six feet four and solid without being overweight, carrying his bulk well on account of his height. It gave me a childish satisfaction to think he would probably grow fat in his old age, but for now he looked like a man in his prime, physically robust, mentally sharp, and generally satisfied with his own competence. Only a month earlier, I might have found his confidence reassuring. Now, he intimidated me. No doubt he boasted a hundred per cent conviction rate and was keen to see me sent down so as not to leave a blot on his so far unblemished record, like a sexual predator chasing another notch on his bed post, except that Morgan got his kicks out of locking people up. Apart from valuing my freedom, I wanted to wipe the smug look off his face.

He turned up with the same female Detective Sergeant in tow. If anything, I was even less pleased to see her than the Detective Inspector. Also tall and well built, she was dwarfed by Morgan. I hadn't taken to her on our first meeting, and I liked her even less this time. Her voice was soft and low, and sounded gentle, but her features were hard, and her eyes glittered coldly at me. All the time the Detective Inspector was talking, she kept her lips pressed together as though she disapproved of me. I was sorry I had allowed my enemies to lure me into their lair on my own.

When we were all seated in a small room, with the three laptops on the table between us, the Detective Sergeant spoke first. Her voice was pleasant, but her eyes were hard. She had missed her vocation as a nurse caring for blind patients.

'We found evidence your husband was drugged before he was killed.'

'I wasn't aware my husband took drugs.'

'The drug in question was Rohypnol, also known as a date rape drug. We don't believe your husband took it knowingly. We believe it was given to him without his consent.'

Ackerman had already told me about that, but I feigned surprise. 'That's terrible. Poor Paul. Do you know who did that to him? Was he drugged to make it easier to kill him? The killer must have been strong, to lift his body onto the bed after he was knocked out, before he was suffocated with his pillow.'

They looked at me, their expressions blank.

'Either that, or he went to bed because he was feeling faint and dizzy, either of which can be initial reactions to Rohypnol,' the Detective Sergeant replied.

'There were no bruises or marks indicating he had been manhandled onto the bed, and he undressed before he was killed by a pillow pressed over his face,' the Detective Inspector said.

I nodded, uncertain whether they knew how much of that information had already been shared with me. It could have been one of them, or Ackerman or Andrew, who had told me how Paul had been killed. So many people had been informing me and questioning me about his death for so long, it was hardly surprising I was confused and didn't know how I ought to react on hearing exactly what had happened.

'Did he... would he have known about it?' I stammered.

It seemed a natural question to ask. A loving wife would have been concerned to know her dying husband hadn't suffered. There was no need for the police to know how much I hated him for his betrayal.

'He would have been unconscious when he died,' the Detective Sergeant replied. 'He was drugged.'

'You said. I'm sorry-'

I covered my face with my hands, as though talking about Paul's death distressed me. Which of course it did, only not for the reasons the police might imagine. My overwhelming feeling was rage, not sadness. His death, and his activities leading up to it, had wrecked my life. The detectives waited in respectful silence for a moment. Working with murder cases as they did, they must have understood better than most people that grief is a private emotion. But I couldn't sit like that interminably, knowing they were there, watching me and analysing every word I uttered, hoping to trip me up.

They carried on casting around for leads, waiting for me to say something incriminating that would make life easy for them. Under a guise of nonchalance, they were constantly observing my reactions and twisting my words to imply I had something to hide, but I knew what they were doing and remained alert, claiming ignorance when I didn't know how to respond. I reminded myself constantly that they were just doing their job and doing it thoroughly. It wouldn't help my cause if I allowed myself to become agitated. I was really thankful they hadn't turned up the previous evening, when I had been drinking.

'That's not what you said last time we spoke to you,' the Detective Inspector told me at one point, his eyes a shade more animated than usual.

'Isn't it? To be honest, much as I want to help you, I really can't remember exactly. It might have been eleven or eleven thirty when I got home. I didn't look at the time. It could have been earlier or later than that. The restaurant might be able to tell you what time we left, or at least when we paid the bill, and you can probably make a reasonable estimate from that.'

'We don't do "earlier or later",' the Detective Sergeant said shortly. 'And we don't work with "more or less" either. A matter of a few minutes can result in a conviction.' She gave a rare tight smile.

'Or in an accusation being disproved,' I pointed out.

If they hadn't taken me in a police car, I don't know how I would have found my way home afterwards, I was so stressed. After struggling to appear calm while I was out, I burst into tears as soon as my front door closed behind me.

Still sobbing, I took Dan's laptop up to his bedroom and placed it gently on the landing outside his room. Going into his room would make me cry even more, because he wouldn't be sleeping there that night. I put Paul's laptop in a black bag and shoved it in the bin outside, where every trace of him belonged.

Back in the house, I showered and changed my clothes, trying to eliminate every trace of my excursion. Then I opened all the windows in the living room and dusted and cleaned the hard surfaces and hoovered the furniture and carpet.

When I had finished cleaning up, I flopped down on my sofa and tried to rest. I had just about calmed down, when Nina called me.

'Have you seen the paper?' she asked.

'What paper?'

'You're in the *Times*. Well, Paul is.'

'What?'

'Just look it up, go on. And then call me back.'

With a sense of foreboding, I googled the site but couldn't find any mention of Paul, so I hurried down to the shops and bought a print copy of the paper and went straight home to study it carefully. Whatever it was, it couldn't be good news.

But, when I finally found the article Nina had been talking about, it wasn't that bad. My name didn't appear, and Paul was only mentioned once, in an article about Bella. It was a short paragraph.

"A woman is helping police with their enquiries following the unlawful killing of Isabella Foster who was found dead in her

Hampstead home last week. Miss Foster was an acclaimed local artist whose work has been exhibited at the Royal Academy. 'She was a lovely woman, and a wonderful artist,' her neighbour, Anita Masters told us. 'We're all going to miss her.' Miss Foster's death has been linked to the murder of her lover, Harrow resident Paul Barrett, whose body was discovered at his home, where he lived with his wife and teenage son."

That was all it said, but it was enough to give me an idea.

Chapter 29

The next day being Saturday, I figured there was a reasonable chance Anita Masters would be at home if I called round early in the morning. After a quick breakfast I set off for the converted Victorian house in Lindfield Gardens, off the main Finchley Road, where Bella had lived. I didn't know whether Anita lived in the same building, but my journey would hopefully not be wasted even if I didn't manage to track her down, as there might be other neighbours who could help me.

Reaching the building I checked the names written up beside the numbered bells and quickly spotted A. Masters, in flat number 2. I had to ring the bell a couple of times before the intercom buzzed and a voice enquired who was calling.

Anita looked under thirty, with long curly hair and a friendly smile. She let me in, after I had assured her that I wasn't a journalist but a friend of her former neighbour. As I climbed the stairs to the second floor, it occurred to me that Anita would have no inkling that I was the widow of Bella's murdered lover and there was no need to let her know my relationship with the dead woman.

'You weren't really her friend, were you?' Anita asked me as she opened the door.

I stared at her in dismay.

'You're from the police, aren't you? Do you know how long your forensic team are going to be traipsing up and down, looking for clues?'

I shook my head, trying not to smile with relief that she didn't know who I was. It was obvious really that the police would still be there, subjecting Bella's flat to a forensic search. With her death only just over a week earlier, the last thing I wanted was to be seen loitering around near her home.

'I told you, I was her friend.'

'What did you say your name was?'

I have no idea why the name Laura Burnley popped into my head. 'Can I come in?'

Her front door opened into a poky hallway which led to a living room which appeared smaller than it was because there was more furniture crammed in there than the space could easily accommodate. Apart from a gap for the door, every inch of wall was covered by a sofa or armchair, all squashed up against each other. Two of the armchairs matched one of the sofas, but the rest were a miscellaneous collection of seats.

'Take a seat, Laura,' Anita said.

'You must have a lot of people here,' I said, looking around at all the seats.

'Yes, I do.'

She didn't expand on her answer. I guessed she ran some kind of alternative therapy group, but I didn't enquire. The less inquisitive I was, the fewer questions she might feel able to ask me, and it was already going to be difficult enough to maintain my pretence of having known her neighbour.

'Tell me about Bella,' I said.

'I thought you said you were a friend of hers?'

'Yes, we were friends.'

Like her, I didn't add any information, wary of exposing my subterfuge. The less I said, the more likely I was to succeed in concealing the fact that I barely knew Bella.

'Thank you for agreeing to see me.' I smiled as warmly as I could. 'It's really very kind of you.'

She shrugged. Somehow, I had to keep control of the conversation to stop her asking me too many unanswerable questions.

'The thing is, I really want to know what happened to her. How did she die? I just can't stop thinking about her. I know the police said she was murdered, but why? I'm guessing it must have been an intruder. I mean, no one would want to hurt Bella. Or do you think her killer could have mistaken her for someone else? What do you think happened to her? Please, tell me everything you know.'

I did my best to sound upset.

Anita frowned. 'You're right that no one would want to hurt her. Unless they were unhinged, that is. It's frightening to think we could be passing maniacs like that on the streets every day.'

'I know,' I agreed. 'The same thought has been bothering me ever since I heard what happened.'

'I hope the police catch whoever it was soon.'

'Is there any chance it might not have been a random attack by a lunatic?' I asked. 'Perhaps she had a violent ex-boyfriend she never talked about? Did you ever see any suspicious-looking strangers visiting her?'

She rose to her feet and paced up and down the restricted space between the chairs and sofas. Pausing in mid stride, she spun round to face me.

'You do know she was seeing someone?'

Her eyes searched my face as though she was trying to discover how much I knew.

I nodded. 'She told me she'd met a married man. Do you think he-'

'No, not him,' she interrupted me. 'It was his wife.'

'His wife? What about her?'

'She was madly jealous of Bella.'

I raised my eyebrows. 'She told me she never met his wife.'

'No, but he warned Bella about her.'

'Warned her about what?'

'According to this man she was seeing, his wife was a dangerous woman. He was afraid to leave her. He would have divorced his wife and married Bella, if he could have done. I met him once,' she added.

I tried to sound merely curious, but I could hear my voice shaking. 'What was he like?'

'He seemed nice. Kind of old.' She glanced at me. 'Older than you, I mean. Not that you're old.'

'And he was going to leave his wife for Bella?'

'He wanted to, but he was afraid his wife would go crazy. He told Bella his wife ought to be locked up for her own protection because she was insane.'

'Insane? How was she insane? It sounds to me as though he was inventing reasons for not leaving his wife. I know it's a cliché, but I warned Bella it's never a good idea to get involved with a married man. Someone always ends up getting hurt.'

'You know her boyfriend was murdered?'

For a second, I didn't realise she was talking about Paul. It was strange hearing him referred to as someone else's boyfriend. He was a forty-six-year-old married man, father of a teenager.

'You'll never guess what happened to Bella after he was killed.'

'What?'

'It was about a month ago, and only a few days after his death.'

'She was very cut up about it,' I said.

'Who wouldn't be?'

'So, you were saying something happened to her?'

Anita nodded. 'Guess who went to see her.'

I shook my head. 'Who?'

'The crazy wife.'

'The boyfriend's wife?'

Anita nodded again.

'She never told me that,' I said. 'I had a couple of missed calls from her, but to be honest I was up to my eyes at work, and then my mother had a fall and I had to go and stay with her for a couple of weeks, and by the time I got back home, Bella was dead. I wish I'd returned her calls while I was away. I never spoke to her again.'

'That's a pity, but you shouldn't feel bad about it. You weren't to know. Is your mother all right now?'

'What? Oh yes. She's fine, thank you, much better. But you were telling me what happened when Bella's boyfriend's wife went to see her? Please tell me Bella didn't let her in. She didn't, did she?'

Anita smiled. 'Bella knew the police were looking for the wife, who'd done a runner after she killed her husband. The police had already contacted Bella to see if she had any idea where the killer had gone. They thought her boyfriend might have mentioned a hiding place his wife might be using, you know, that sort of thing, and they'd asked her to let them know if she heard anything.'

I was puzzled. 'How did the police have her number?'

'It must have been on his phone. So, anyway, when the crazy wife called and asked to meet her, Bella arranged for the woman to go to her flat.'

'What? Why?'

Anita grinned. 'Because then she called the cops on her.'

'Wow!'

'She was gutsy.'

'She certainly was. I remember- '

I broke off and put my head in my hands, as though overcome with emotion at some memory of my friend, Bella.

'I'll go and put the kettle on,' Anita said gently. 'And then you can tell me all about it.'

Anita had told me as much as I wanted to hear. She clearly believed Paul's jealous wife had killed him and then come for his mistress. I needed to get out of there before I let something incriminating slip. It would be ironic if she were to call the police on me as well. I was tempted to leave while she was busy in the kitchen but didn't want to risk alerting her suspicions. Instead, I texted Nina and asked her to wait five minutes and then call me back.

Anita returned with two mugs of tea. She set them down on the table and took a seat opposite me.

'Thank you.'

'Now, tell me all about Bella,' she said. 'You probably knew her better than I did, even though she lived directly above me. How did you meet her?'

I hesitated. 'We were at school together.'

That couldn't be a risky claim, surely. Everyone went to school. But Anita looked puzzled. Too late, I remembered that Bella had been a good ten years younger than me. I could have kicked myself for making such a stupid blunder.

'But then we lost touch for a while. It's not as if we were close at school. I mean, she was quite a bit younger than me.'

Even being as vague as possible, I was beginning to tie myself up in knots. Just as I was panicking that Nina might have missed my message, my phone rang.

'Sorry, I ought to get this.' I listened to Nina asking me what was up. 'Don't worry,' I told her, 'I'll be there soon.'

I hung up.

Before I could say anything to Anita, she stood up. 'Is it your mother?'

'Yes, yes.'

My phone rang again. Gabbling to a bemused Nina that I was on my way, I raised a hand in farewell and left. I ran all the way down the stairs and along the street to the station.

Chapter 30

After a disturbed night worrying about how I was going to manage with less than a hundred pounds in my purse, I woke up to a message notifying me that I was eligible to withdraw a weekly allowance to cover my living expenses. Listening, I remembered being told something similar before leaving the prison, but I had been too agitated to take it all in.

I hurried straight down to my nearest ATM to withdraw two hundred pounds and was pleased, out of all proportion to the amount I received, when the cash appeared. Until then, I had never had any serious worries about money. Paul earned enough for all our needs and most of our luxuries as well. His firm had even offered us private health cover for myself and Dan at a reduced rate, which had been a godsend when Dan was small. I wasn't sure what would happen to that now Paul was no longer working there. Money assumed a significance it had never had for me before. Grabbing the cash, I slipped it into my purse and started walking back home. On the way, my phone rang. Glancing at the number, I fumbled to answer before he could hang up.

'Sorry, I meant to get back to you yesterday, but I was busy- ' Ackerman began.

'You only sent me a hundred pounds!' I blurted out, not caring that someone might hear me. 'What's that about?'

'You got the cash all right then? Good.'

'Yes, a hundred pounds. What happened to the rest of it?'

A young woman jogged past me, pony-tail bouncing behind her, and I lowered my voice.

'There must have been getting on for four thousand pounds in that account, if not more,' I grumbled.

'Four thousand four hundred and fifty-seven.'

'You only sent me a hundred. What about the rest of it? That's more than four thousand pounds you owe me. Where is it, Ackerman? I want my money.'

I had arrived home and was standing on the doorstep, fishing around in my bag for my key.

'They only let me take out two fifty without notice,' he said, his calmness provoking me even further.

'Two and a half thousand pounds? Then-'

'Two hundred and fifty,' he corrected me.

I went into the living room and flopped down on the sofa, shaking with disappointment. 'You still only sent me a hundred of the two hundred and fifty,' I pointed out.

'You owe me a lot more than that.'

'How am I supposed to pay you if I haven't got any money? I can barely afford to feed myself.'

'All right, all right, I'm working on it. Banks aren't that easy to hoodwink.'

'I'm not expecting you to hoodwink them. This is my money we're talking about. It belongs to me.'

'All the same, we don't want to do anything to attract attention and risk that account being frozen along with the rest of your assets.' He sighed. 'Life must have been so much easier when everyone kept their money hidden under the mattress. But you must be getting a weekly allowance through the court?'

'No one ever kept their money hidden under the mattress,' I told him. He was really annoying me. 'And yes, you're right, I *am* getting a stingy weekly allowance, but it's not even enough to live on. I certainly can't afford to give any of it to you. I do have to eat.'

'And so do I,' he told me.

I hesitated. 'I've got a few more bits of jewellery.'

At once, he offered to come over and take a look, adding, 'We did all right with the last haul, even after Martin took his share.'

'Don't expect so much this time,' I warned him. 'It's only a few bits and pieces, and they're probably worthless.' But he had already rung off.

I called him back, but he didn't answer, so I went and put the kettle on, put my feet up and tried to relax, but I was too wound up to be idle. Having gulped down my tea, I ran upstairs to fetch the earrings, pearls and watch that I wanted to show Ackerman. Putting them down on my bed, I scrabbled around in all the drawers, mine and Paul's, hoping to come across anything else that might fetch some serious money, but found nothing that looked even vaguely valuable. Paul's bedside table was tidy enough, with his radio, keys and water bottle all within reach. Only his new mobile phone was missing, because the police had taken it. Lifting out the drawer I tipped the contents onto the bed. A jumble of miscellaneous items fell out, keys and odd socks, European plug converters, a couple of old wallets that were both disappointingly empty, boxes of pills and lotions, most of them out of date, and all sorts of papers, tubes of toothpaste, a spare toothbrush and random other toiletries.

I hesitated about going through Dan's belongings, but it was possible his grandparents had given him something worth selling that he would never miss. He had been given some trinkets on his birthdays that he hoarded, probably without even remembering what was there. It was worth a quick look.

With a tremor of apprehension, I pushed open his door and went into his room. If I did find anything worth selling, I probably wouldn't risk my theft being discovered, but that wasn't really the point. My trespass was driven by curiosity rather than cupidity.

It was more than a year since Dan had banned me from entering his bedroom. He even made a show of hoovering in there himself, albeit rarely.

Paul had fully supported Dan's wishes. 'Our son's entitled to some privacy. He's not a child anymore.'

Still, the house no longer belonged to Paul. It was mine, and no one could stop me from going into any of the rooms any time I liked. No one else was even living there, although Dan's absence was only temporary. Admittedly he hadn't given me permission to go through his belongings, but he would never need to know. I took a deep breath and went in.

The room was a mess, clothes strewn all over the floor, and on the chair. He evidently hadn't hoovered in there for a long time but must have just run the motor behind the closed door to fool me. I had to smile at his shenanigans, remembering how earnestly he had assured me there was no need for me to clean his room because he was taking care of it. Ignoring his clothes, I picked my way over to his wardrobe. Pulling open his drawers, I searched through them but they were stuffed with underwear and pyjamas, nothing of any use, or any interest, to me.

I turned my attention to the small untidy desk which Paul and I had bought seven years earlier when Dan was about to start senior school. He had outgrown it, but we hadn't yet got around to replacing it. His printer was there, surrounded by papers and books, mostly revision guides, and the surface was littered with pieces of a broken model airplane, a few mugs cultivating green mould, empty crisp packets, and different coloured pens and scraps of paper, receipts and notes. The top drawer was locked but the key wasn't difficult to find, tucked away out of sight in the middle drawer. Feeling a flush of shame, I fitted the key in the lock and prepared to turn it carefully. If by some awful mischance the key broke in the lock, Dan would know I had been snooping around in his room. He would never forgive me.

I went to my room and bolstered my courage with a couple of slugs from the whisky bottle I had taken to keeping beside my bed. Less wound up, I returned to Dan's room, telling myself he would never know I had been in there. The locked drawer opened easily.

Inside was an old phone charger, various souvenirs from our holidays, and other miscellaneous junk he had collected. Taking a few of the pieces out, I sifted through them, trying to recall when we had bought them. Throughout his childhood he had been absorbed by a succession of fads. At one time he had collected comics, another time foreign coins, then bottle tops and the like. No one craze had held his interest for long. There was also an assortment of broken bits of toy cars, wheels, spokes, and tiny brightly coloured doors. Hidden away at the back of the drawer, I found a thick brown envelope. Feeling guilty, I pulled it out and withdrew a bundle of photographs.

It was predictable that Dan had been secretly hoarding pictures of his dead father. I stared at images of Dan and Paul together, smiling and messing about in the garden, with Dan at different ages from when he was a baby. Dan had always idolised his father. I remembered taking some of the photos, at birthday parties and Christmases, and on our family holidays.

Trembling, I put his laptop on the desk and opened it up. His password wasn't difficult to guess. An entire photo album was dedicated to his father. There were no images of me. The room was filled with reminders of Paul, but I had been airbrushed out of his life. Sitting on my son's bed, I gazed at a photo of Dan and Paul laughing together, and wept uncontrollably for the love we had lost.

Chapter 31

Awash with regrets and drowning in self-pity, and more than a little drunk, I had forgotten that Ackerman was on his way until the front door bell disturbed my miserable solitude. I hurried from the room, wiping my eyes while I went downstairs. It wouldn't have required any investigative skills to detect I had been crying, but Ackerman made no comment on my appearance as he followed me into the living room. Once we were both seated, he asked what I had brought him, eyeing the laptop I was still clutching.

'No,' I replied, 'this isn't for sale.'

'That's a shame. It looks new.' He took it from me and turned it over. 'This must be worth a few hundred quid.'

Paul had paid over a thousand pounds for it.

'It might fetch up to a grand, in the right hands.'

'Maybe, but it's not for sale. It's my son's.'

'So what else have you got? You mentioned some more jewellery?'

I went upstairs and fetched the pearls and earrings, and the gold watch, and he examined them all carefully.

'I should think we can get a decent price for these.'

After that, we discussed how he was getting on with looking into Paul's murder. He didn't seem to be making any progress so far. When I told him about my visit to Bella's neighbour, he looked surprised.

'I didn't find out very much,' I admitted.

'She told me you murdered your husband and his mistress,' he said.

'She can't possibly have any proof because it never happened,' I replied sharply.

'It was just her impression from what Bella had told her and of course she could have been lying, or your husband could have lied to her about you. None of this proves anything.'

'Why didn't you tell me you'd been to see her?'

He shook his head. 'I didn't think you'd be very happy to hear what she told me.'

'And presumably she told the same thing to the police as well.'

'If it's what she told me and you, I'd say that's a reasonable assumption.'

'But it doesn't prove anything.'

'No. It's all hearsay about what a dead man told a dead woman. It can't be investigated.'

'And they can't use it in court, can they?'

'No. Although the prosecuting council doubtless will. The jury will be instructed to discount it, but if they hear any of it, they might be influenced despite the judge's instruction.'

'How can we stop her spreading her lies?'

'I don't think she's lying. If anyone played hard and fast with the truth, I'd say it was your husband. But we can't gag her if the case goes to court.'

'Then we have to make sure it never gets that far.' I stared at him in consternation. 'And the only way to do that is to find out who killed my husband. I can't be convicted for a crime I didn't commit. And what about my son? How is he going to cope if he's told I really did kill his father after all?'

With assurances that he would continue working to prove my innocence, Ackerman left. After he had gone, I realised Dan's laptop wasn't in the living room. I hunted everywhere, but it had vanished. There was only one possible explanation: Ackerman must have taken it with him. In a panic, I called him, but he didn't answer his phone. I kept trying, without success.

A couple of days later, Dan called to say he was bored of Edinburgh, fed up with his grandparents, and missing me. I was thrilled. The only problem was that I hadn't yet recovered the laptop from Ackerman who had proved impossible to get hold of since our last meeting. I kept trying but either his phone was switched off, or he didn't want to talk to me. Checking Dan's room, I was confident nothing else was missing and he wouldn't be able to see where anything else had been disturbed. Even the brown envelope of photos was back in place, all but concealed beneath a confused mess of broken toy car parts. Leaving a few coffee cups cultivating green and white mould as evidence that I hadn't entered the room, I took a last look around and left, closing the door behind me. Apart from the absent laptop, Dan would never know I had been in there.

Frantically, I called Ackerman's number and left another message for him to contact me urgently, telling him that I needed my son's laptop back immediately, but he remained silent. I didn't know where I could get in touch with his contact Martin and had no idea where we had gone to meet him. All I could remember was that Ackerman had driven me to some kind of industrial estate and taken me to the back of a warehouse. It could have been anywhere. I could hardly drive around every industrial estate I could find, searching for him. As a last resort, I called my lawyer, but I hung up before anyone answered. I couldn't ask him if he could trace a man whose name I didn't even know.

I considered trying to pass another laptop off as Dan's, but there was really no point because his data, including his photos, would be missing. He wouldn't believe all his data had been wiped out in a power cut, or by the police. In any case, I didn't have enough money to buy a new one. So, I waited anxiously for Dan to come home, cursing Paul for causing me so much trouble. I still couldn't believe he had done this. We had been happily married once, happy enough to want to have a child together, and he had thrown it all away to sleep with a younger woman. Even if he had fallen in love with her, had it been worth destroying everything we had built together and wrecking our family in pursuit of his selfish desires? It was infuriating that I would never be able to challenge him to answer that question. Just thinking about him made me angry. This whole situation was so unnecessary. All Paul had needed to do was consider the happiness of the two people who loved him and tolerate his reasonably contented life, and none of this would have happened.

Dan arrived early one evening. Irritable from travelling, he was annoyed with me for not picking him up at the station. Reluctant to admit that a curfew had been imposed on me, I didn't say anything. Of course he would find out soon enough, but it didn't seem like a good idea to tell him when he was tired and hungry. I insisted he sit down and eat before going upstairs.

'I want to check my emails,' he told me. 'Nana wanted me to write to her as soon as I got back.'

'You can phone her. I'm sure she'd like to speak to you. Why don't you give her a quick call while I'm dishing up?'

'I said I'd write.'

'It can wait until after supper.'

'Because I'm so slow you think it'll take me ages to send an email?'

I tried to laugh as though his suggestion was absurd. 'No, because dinner's ready.'

'How can it be ready? You didn't know when I'd be home.'

'I had a pretty good idea. Now come on, let's eat.'

He brightened up once we sat down together. I had gone out earlier and bought pizza and chips and chocolate ice cream, all his favourites. I even made him a shandy. It was going well, until he went upstairs.

'Mum! I can't find my laptop!'

He raced into the kitchen where I had just finished loading the dishwasher.

I straightened up, a puzzled frown on my face. 'Did you leave it at your nan's?'

He shook his head, his face taut with worry. 'I didn't take it with me. Don't you remember? The police took it away. But you said they'd brought it back.'

'They must have taken it up to your room.'

'It's not there.'

'The police must still have it then.'

'The police?'

'Yes.'

'They can't keep it!'

'No, of course they can't. We'll go along there first thing in the morning and get it back. Now, why don't you go and call Nana and tell her you're home and you can write to her tomorrow.'

With an unhappy nod, he went into the living room to make the call. When I followed him, he left the room and I heard him going upstairs, still talking on the phone. I wondered what he was saying that he didn't want me to hear.

'Don't forget to put the phone back when you come down or the battery will run out,' I called up the stairs.

But he didn't come down again.

When I tapped on his door on my way to bed, he didn't answer. Quietly I opened the door just enough to peer inside. He was lying on the bed, still fully dressed, asleep, clutching the phone in his hand. I thought better of disturbing him. Recharging the phone battery could wait until the morning. It was hardly the joyful homecoming I had hoped for, and we still had the problem of the missing laptop to resolve. I called Ackerman again several times before I went to sleep, but he didn't answer.

Chapter 32

Before breakfast the next morning, I phoned Ackerman. All set to leave another message, I was surprised to hear his voice.

'I didn't think you'd answer.'

'Why not? You called my phone, didn't you? What is it?'

'I've been trying to get hold of you for days.'

'Yes, well, I've been busy, but I'm here now. So, what is it?'

'Listen, I need my son's laptop back. I need it now. No, I need it yesterday. He's home and he wants his laptop. How soon can you get it here?'

My fears were realised when he told me he had already sold it. He sounded pleased, telling me he had managed to get more for it than it was worth second hand.

'Don't stress about it,' he concluded, 'I made sure the memory was wiped before I parted with it. There was nothing on it.'

All Dan's precious photos of his father had been deleted by a stranger, and Ackerman was telling me not to feel stressed. I felt sick. When Dan came downstairs, he was impatient to head off to the police station straight away, but I insisted we have breakfast first. I didn't tell him that the visit was going to end in disappointment and he might deal with it better on a full stomach. It seemed I was right, because he was cheerful and relaxed on the way to the police station, almost as though his father had never died. The trip to Scotland had clearly done him good. He chatted about his visit to Edinburgh.

'So, tell me about this youth club,' I said.

'It was okay,' he muttered.

'What were the other young people like?'

'You mean girls, don't you?' He gave an embarrassed laugh but didn't answer.

'Come on, Dan, how was it?'

'It was okay,' was all he would say about it. 'So, what are we going to do today, after we get my laptop?'

'What would you like to do this afternoon?'

'We could go out for lunch first?'

'OK.'

'Can we go for pizza? And this evening to the cinema.'

My only option was to pretend to be ill later, but the situation was becoming tricky in ways I hadn't foreseen. I wouldn't be able to hide the truth for much longer. All the way to the police station my mind was working overtime, planning what I was going to say to the police, and afterwards to Dan to convince him it wasn't my fault his laptop had gone missing. The desk sergeant quickly grasped what we wanted and summoned a colleague to help us. She went off to track down Dan's laptop for us. I did my best to appear surprised when she came back and told us that everything had already been returned to us.

'They're all listed here, all accounted for,' she smiled. 'Three laptops, one PC and two mobile phones.'

Dan pounced on what she said. 'Thee laptops? That includes mine then?'

The sergeant read out the descriptions of the computers. 'All the electronic equipment was handed to you,' she told us.

They both looked at me, the sergeant's eyes impassive, Dan's accusing.

'Where did you put it?' he demanded. 'She said they gave it back. Where is it?'

'I don't think that can be right- ' I said, doing my best to sound both self-assured and puzzled at the same time.

'You signed for each of the items.'

'I must have been confused. My husband had just died.'

'It's down here in black and white. There's really no possibility we could be mistaken, Madam. They were signed out of the station and signed for on delivery. Here.'

She held out a scanned copy of a delivery note, the itemised details clear, as was my signature.

'One of the laptops was missing,' I insisted.

'That's not possible. They were checked off on the delivery and you signed for everything:- three laptops and a PC. Can you remember what you did with the computers when they were returned to you?'

'I didn't do anything with them.'

'They must be at your house then.'

It was clear I could say nothing to persuade her to investigate it any further, so we left, but not until I had assured her that the matter wouldn't end there.

Dan and I stopped off at Sainsbury's on the way home. Dan pulled a face when I steered him away from the DVDs.

'Let's stick to what we need, shall we?'

'Oh please, Mum.'

'Until the probate is sorted, we need to be careful with money,' I told him.

'What's that?'

'I don't want you to worry. We don't have any problems in the long term, but the legal process to sort out your father's estate is complicated and it's going to take a while- '

'Estate? Do you mean his will?'

'Yes.'

'His money?'

'Exactly. And until everything's sorted out, we can't get hold of any of it.'

'Are you saying we're broke?'

'We'll have enough to live on, but that's all for now. So we're not getting any new DVDs now. I'm sorry, but that's how it is.'

He frowned. 'Okay. No DVDs then. That's why we're not going to the cinema, isn't it?'

'Yes,' I lied, relieved at the reprieve, 'but it's only for a while. Once the probate's over and done with, you'll be able to buy as many DVDs as you want, and go to the cinema every day if you like. You can have anything you want. That's how it's going to be, Dan.'

He smiled and I had a feeling everything was going to turn out all right in the end. It was just going to take a while, exactly as I had told him.

Back at home, we sat down for lunch. As I was opening the fridge, the bottom of my trousers caught on my bag. It was bound to happen sooner or later, but I had hoped to have more time to prepare my speech about it.

'What's that on your leg?'

Turning around, I saw Dan staring at my ankle. The mug in my hand smashed. In the silence that followed the crash, I watched splinters of china floating in a puddle of tea oozing across the floor. For the next few moments I was preoccupied with cleaning up the wet mess without cutting myself. When I finally sat down, Dan repeated his question. Although I would have to tell him the truth at some point, it was hard having the confession forced on me before I had decided what to say. Still, the longer I lied about it, the angrier he would be when he finally heard the truth.

'The police let me out on bail. You know what that means?'

He nodded.

'One of the conditions of my bail was that I don't go out after six in the evening. It's called a curfew.'

'You mean you're grounded?'

'Yes, exactly.'

'I don't understand. How can they do that to someone as old as you?'

'It's just so they know where I am, in case they need to speak to me.'

'Why can't they just phone you if they want to speak to you? Why do you have to stay at home? It's like you're still in prison.'

'Not really. I can go out all day if I want to. The curfew is only from six.'

'But what if they need to speak to you earlier? And how can it be every day? That means you never get to go out in the evening.'

His eyes narrowed in suspicion. 'Why didn't you tell me straight away?'

'That's a good question. The thing is, I was so excited to see you, I forgot all about it. And then we were busy looking for your missing laptop.'

He scowled and went upstairs without another word. A few moments later he came down again, demanding to know where his father's laptop was.

I hesitated before answering. 'I threw your father's computers away.'

That, at least, was true.

'And you threw mine away as well, didn't you?' His eyes were blazing with unfamiliar rage. 'Didn't you?'

'No, no. Of course not.'

'You're lying, like you lied about your curfew. All you do is lie to me.'

'I'm not lying, Dan. I've never lied to you.'

'Why did you throw away all my photos of Dad? Did you lie about killing him too?'

'I didn't touch your photos. They're all there, in your drawer- '

'You went in my room!'

'Of course I didn't.'

'How do you know about the photos in my desk then? You went in there, didn't you?'

'No, I already told you I haven't been in there. You must have told me they were there, ages ago.'

'I didn't. I never told anyone about them. It was a secret.'

He ran out of the room and I heard him go upstairs. I was tempted to run after him, but decided it was best to leave him alone for a while. That turned out to be a mistake because less than an hour later I heard the front door slam.

'Dan? Dan!'

Grabbing my phone, I ran to the door. As I reached for the handle, I noticed the time. It was three minutes past six.

Chapter 33

Lately I seemed to be constantly frustrated by people refusing to answer their phones. First Ackerman had been impossible to get hold of, now it was Dan who wouldn't pick up. Frantic with worry, I left message after message, begging him to at least call and let me know he was all right. My teeth were chattering uncontrollably and my whole face seemed to tense up until I could barely move my jaw to speak.

'You don't have to call me back, just send me a text, so I know nothing's happened to you.'

'Where are you?'

'Please let me know you're okay.'

'I'm worried about you. Please get in touch.'

'Dan, please, call me. Please.'

'Just tell me you're all right.'

I must have left about twenty messages and sent even more texts, imagining all kinds of dreadful accidents that could be preventing him from answering his phone. If I had known where to look for him, I would have broken the conditions of my bail to go after him. It was two hours before my phone finally rang. It felt like two days.

My hands shook as I answered. 'Dan? Is that you? Dan?'

It was Stella calling to tell me he was safe. She explained that Mark was on a train to London where he had arranged to meet Dan, and they planned to travel back to Edinburgh together in the morning.

'No, he can't go,' I protested, struggling to speak calmly, although she must have heard my stifled sobs. 'Not without seeing me first. I need to tell him it wasn't me. It wasn't me.'

'I'm not going to discuss any of this with you,' she replied curtly. 'Mark and I agreed it wasn't fair to let you worry about Dan, and that's the only reason I called. There's nothing more to say. I'll call you tomorrow to let you know they've arrived back here safely. We just didn't think it was right to leave you in the dark.'

Tears choked my words when I tried to tell her that without Dan I would be permanently in the dark. She hung up. I kept trying his number, but he didn't answer.

That night I barely slept. I tried to take comfort from knowing that Dan was safe, and Mark would be there to take care of him, but I was tormented by the thought that my son hated me so much he wouldn't even speak to me. First Paul, now Dan, had abandoned me.

I was alone in a hostile universe.

True to her word, Stella rang me the next day. 'I promised to let you know when Dan got back. He's here with us now, and he's welcome to stay here as long as he likes. He doesn't want to go back to London.'

'He can't stay there. He's got a place at college,' I said.

It was a stupid objection.

'We're getting in touch with all the local colleges here. We'll find him a place. Mark has already been in contact with the support services for disabled students and explained the situation to them, and they understand why he can't return to London.'

She made it sound so final, I felt myself shaking with anger. How could they have stepped in and reorganised our entire lives without even consulting me?

'What do you mean, he can't return to London? This is where he lives. It's his home. I'm his mother!'

'He found the experience of going back to London very traumatic. We can't let him be distressed like that again. Mark and I have talked it over with him and we all agree this is the best thing for him right now.'

'What are you talking about? How could he be traumatised by coming home and seeing his own mother? Where is he? I need to speak to him.'

'I'm calling you now because he's not here.'

'What do you mean? Where is he?'

'There's no need to become hysterical, Julie. Dan's fine. He's perfectly safe. Mark's taken him into town to get a new laptop. He was very upset about losing his pictures, but Mark's confident that all the data can be restored from the cloud. They just need to work around a few things.'

'What things?'

'Oh, I don't know, passwords and things like that. Mark understands it all better than I do. But hopefully he'll get everything back.' She paused. 'You know Dan had photos of Paul on there?' Her voice dropped to a whisper. 'How could you have hated him so much?'

'What? No, no, I didn't hate Paul. That's not true. I never hated him. I loved him. You mustn't tell those lies in front of Dan. And I didn't throw out Dan's laptop. It was the police. I'm going to lodge a complaint. They lost Dan's laptop. It wasn't me. You have to tell him. Tell him I'm going to make sure it's found.'

'Oh, they're back. I have to go.'

'Stella, let me speak to him, please-'

I was still begging to speak to my son when she hung up.

I called her number again, but no one answered.

At my third attempt, she picked up.

'Mark's taken Dan up to his room to check his new laptop's working,' she muttered. 'If you try and contact us again we'll report your number as a nuisance caller and get it blocked.'

'You can't do that. I want to speak to Dan. He's my son.'

'I'm sorry, Julie, Dan doesn't want to talk to you right now. He'll be in touch when he's ready. But for now, you need to leave him alone. It's going to take time for him to settle into his new life here with us.'

She rang off without giving me a chance to respond. When I redialled, the line was engaged. She had left the phone off the hook, or perhaps she was already reporting my number as she had threatened. I didn't know what to do. It was hard to believe that my in-laws were trying to steal my son. I wasn't going to accept this without a fight.

Dismissing the temptation to open a bottle of wine, I washed my face and made myself a pot of coffee. At a time like this I needed to think clearly. Searching through my bag I found the card from Andrew, my lawyer and called the number. A woman's voice answered.

'I need to speak to Andrew. Please, this is really urgent.'

'Who shall I say is calling?'

'Tell him it's a client.'

'And your name?'

'Julie Barrett.'

As clearly as I could, I explained the situation to Andrew. 'You have to help me. I can't lose my son as well as my husband. Surely you understand that. Please say you'll help me. I don't know who else to turn to.'

When I stopped speaking there was a long pause, although I knew from background noises that he was still on the line.

'I can't let them take him away,' I insisted. 'It's a lie to say my son is better off without me. I brought him up. I devoted myself to caring for him while he was growing up. They can't just take him like this. It can't be in his interests. Don't you see, they're just doing it to punish me. They don't really love Dan, not like I do. They think I killed their son so they're taking my son away from me. You can't let them get away with it.'

At last Andrew spoke. 'What does your son say about all this? He's how old?'

'Seventeen.'

'And what's his view on his living arrangements?'

'I don't know. They won't let me speak to him. God only knows what lies they're telling him about me. You have to stop them. There must be a law to stop them. They've kidnapped him. He's a child- '

'He's seventeen.'

'But he's not... he has cerebral palsy.'

'And from what I've gathered, he's a bright capable young man, thanks to all the care you've lavished on him.'

'Which is why he belongs here, with me. You can't let them take him away, you can't. There must be a law to protect him.'

'Are you saying he was taken against his will?' he asked, his languor gone.

'Yes, well, no, not exactly.'

Miserably I explained that Dan and I had argued, and he had walked out.

'Do you have reasonable grounds to suspect he's in any way at risk from his grandparents?'

'At risk? What do you mean?'

'Is living with them likely to cause him any harm?'

'No, of course not. It's nothing like that. They take good care of him. But it's not the same. He should be here, with me. I'm his mother. It's just that we had an argument and he's gone running back to them.'

'So he contacted his grandparents himself, asking them to take him back?'

I hesitated.

'If the family court questions him, is that what he'll say? That he left you of his own volition?'

'I suppose so.'

'Then I'm sorry, Julie, but there's really nothing I can do to help you. In law, your son is free to make his own decision about where he wants to live. No law has been broken, and so this is not a legal issue. I'm sorry.'

'So what can I do?'

'If you want my advice, speak to your son and request that he meet you to discuss your relationship and heal the rift between you.'

I shook my head. Dan was my son, my flesh and blood. There could be no rift between us.

Chapter 34

Assuming Stella was right, Dan had a new laptop giving him access to the internet. I spent the rest of the morning drafting an email to him, telling him how much I loved and missed him, just as I still loved and missed his father. I went on to tell Dan that the disappearance of his laptop had nothing to do with me. The police were responsible, and I had filed a complaint about their negligence.

With any luck, I told Dan, he would receive compensation for the loss of his old laptop in addition to his grandparents buying him a new one. I told him I had called the police station to enquire into the procedure for making a claim for property lost while confiscated by the police. That at least was true. I *had* been in contact with my local police station to lodge a complaint about my son's missing laptop.

Once they accepted responsibility, Dan would have to agree that it wasn't my fault his computer had gone missing. The police insisted my signature confirming receipt of the laptop was proof it had been returned to us, but I was adamant they should compensate Dan for his loss. Somehow, I had to persuade them to accept liability for the lost laptop or Dan might never absolve me of blame.

After working on that one short email for more than an hour, writing and rewriting it over and over again, I finally sent it off. It was one o'clock by the time I finished. The house seemed to be suffocating me, I had spent so much time there alone, so after a quick lunch, I checked my emails for the last time before going out. I couldn't stay at home interminably, waiting for Dan to respond. In any case, I could pick up any messages on my iPhone so there was no need for me to stay in. I was free to go out until

six, at any rate. I didn't know where I was going, only that I had
to get out of the house with all its painful memories.

My phone rang while I was walking to the station. With a
thrill of anticipation, I checked the screen, but it wasn't Dan. So
much had changed in my life since I had last seen Nina, that I
wasn't sure how to respond when she invited me over.

'It's been a while since we had a good chat, just the two of us,'
she said. 'We're in the same boat now and have to support each
other. I know what it's like.'

Her husband had left her for another woman a couple of years
earlier, but at least he hadn't skulked around hiding his affair from
her, and he hadn't died. She had been inconsolable at the time,
veering hysterically between rage and grief. Katie and I had both
spent hours counselling her to move on and Nina had finally
come to terms with her situation. The divorce settlement had been
generous, considering she was financially independent in her own
right. Even more important than the house was the fact that she
had no children who could be stolen away from her. She had no
idea of the torment I was experiencing. Even so, I agreed to see
her. I was desperate to see a friendly face.

As soon as we sat down, Nina reached out and put her hand
on my arm.

'Julie, you look terrible,' she said. 'How are you bearing up?
Have they found out who did it yet?'

I shook my head, momentarily unable to speak.

'It's all too awful,' I muttered.

'Let me get you a coffee and you can tell me everything,' she
said.

Alone, I gazed around her orderly living room. Magazines were
neatly stored in a rack on the floor in front of a row of shelves, each
one tidily arranged with books and ornaments. Everything looked
clean, and there were no finger marks on the table or smears on
the windows, as though the whole room had recently been dusted
and polished. I wondered if this was what my house was going
to look like now I lived alone with nothing to do all day but

clean and tidy. Nina's curtains looked as though they had just been laundered, her carpet was spotless and the glass ornaments on her shelves sparkled.

'It's not Paul,' I told her as she sat down. 'I mean, it is about him too, but he's dead and gone from my life now, whatever happens.'

'It must be so hard for you,' she sympathised. 'What have the police said? Have they got any idea who did it?'

I shook my head. 'If they have, they haven't told me.'

'Obviously it was an intruder, but how can they not have found any evidence yet?' She gave a wry smile. 'It's nothing like CSI in real life, is it?'

I shrugged. 'They're still investigating, and I suppose they'll let me know when they find out what happened.' I hesitated. 'I think they still think it was me.'

'That's terrible.'

'But the worst thing is that Dan's been taken away from me.'

I broke off, stunned by the enormity of what I had just said. Saying the words out loud to someone else seemed to give the situation a reality that had so far hovered in the realms of nightmare. But this was no bad dream. It was actually happening. My son had left me, and I might never see him again.

'Surely they can't do that!' Nina burst out, looking shocked. 'He's your son and he needs to be with you, especially at a time like this. Who's taken him? You've got to fight it. Get a lawyer onto it. Never mind *your* feelings, what about him? He needs to be with his mother, in a familiar environment, while he deals with what's happened. He's just lost his father. It doesn't matter what it costs. I've got money stashed away, from when Andy left. You can borrow as much as you need and pay it back whenever you can.'

Her kindness made me cry. I stammered my thanks.

'Now, get yourself a good lawyer, never mind the cost, and have Dan back home with you as soon as possible.'

I shook my head, sniffing back my tears. 'You don't understand. It's not that simple. The fact is, I spoke to a lawyer and there's nothing I can do about it because no crime's been committed.' I burst into tears again. 'Dan's grandparents have taken him in and offered him a home, and he's accepted. It's what he wants. He's chosen to go and live with them in Scotland. He doesn't want to be with me.' The last word came out in a long wail, broken by sobs.

'Dan's chosen to leave home? I don't believe that for a minute. Your in-laws have persuaded him to do it. Don't forget, they've just lost their son.'

I nodded, unable to speak. The same thought had occurred to me. Nina made tea, and did her best to comfort me, but her solicitude couldn't change what had happened. After a while, I pretended to feel a little better, embarrassed to admit that her kindness wasn't helping.

'I'm lucky to have a friend like you,' I told her.

But nothing she could say or do would bring Dan back.

'I might as well have died the night Paul was killed,' I said.

'Don't be so melodramatic. Dan will come around. He's bound to. Once he calms down, he'll come back to you. Remember, none of this was your fault. He's just venting his anger over his father's death, and taking it out on you, that's all.'

By five o'clock, I had to think about leaving. She tried to insist I stay for supper, saying she was happy to cook, or we could go out to eat. Tired of pretending everything was back to normal, I lifted my trouser leg to expose my tag. Her eyes widened in surprise.

'What the hell is that?'

I explained. 'So I have to get home by six.'

'Or what?' She gave a little laugh. 'They'll throw you back in jail?'

'This isn't a joke, Nina. Yes, they could do that.'

'Surely not. They can't treat you like a criminal. It's outrageous.'

'Not if they suspect I killed Paul.'

'But they can't prove it.'

'Of course not. They can't prove something that never happened,' I said. But I wasn't convinced that was true.

With Nina's assurances that she was always there for me ringing in my ears, I returned to my empty house.

Chapter 35

That night I hardly slept for worry. My plan to discover who had murdered my husband was going nowhere. Ackerman was useless. All he had done so far was take my belongings and disappear for days. Admittedly he had discovered that two glasses of wine had been spiked with Rohypnol, but the police already knew about that, so it hadn't led to any further investigation. Now it seemed I was losing my son as well.

It was time to start looking seriously into the cause of my husband's death. If no one else was going to do it, I would have to conduct my own investigation. Meeting Anita had been interesting. Maybe Bella's other neighbours could give me information about her affair with my husband. At any rate, it would do no harm to ask them.

Curious, but without high expectations, I set off for Hampstead early on Saturday morning. Bella must have been very successful to afford a flat there. Either that, or wealthy parents had been supporting her. For the first time, I wondered how many other lives had been ruined as a consequence of Paul's affair.

The sun came out as I left Finchley Road station, and I suddenly felt irrationally optimistic. All I had to do was find out what had happened to Bella, and my husband's murderer might be revealed. The pavement was crowded with people, mostly young, of diverse ethnicities, all staring straight ahead as they hurried along. Crossing at traffic lights, I left the busy thoroughfare behind me and walked up a wide side street. As the hill grew steeper, I turned into the side street where Bella had lived. At half past nine on Saturday morning, it was a reasonably safe bet that Bella's neighbours might still be at home. And there was no sign of any police presence. The forensic team must have finished examining her flat.

There was one other resident listed at the door, apart from Anita and Bella. The name on the third flat was Hallam, presumably a surname. Not quite decided yet what I was going to say, I rang the bell.

'Who is it?' a man's voice responded.

He sounded quite young, and sleepy. I had probably woken him up.

'I'm sorry to bother you,' I began.

'Who are you? Do you know what time it is?'

'I'm a friend of Bella's.'

'Who?'

'Bella Foster. She lived on the third floor.'

'Oh, yes, of course, Bella. The woman who died.'

He sounded embarrassed at not having realised at once who I was talking about. Having caught him on the back foot, I pressed on.

'I wanted to talk to you about her. Can I come in?'

'Hang on.'

I guessed he was throwing on some clothes.

A moment later he buzzed me in and I found his door ajar. Rapping as loudly as I could, I pushed it open and went in.

'Hi,' he greeted me with a cheery smile.

He didn't look much older than Dan, very young to be living in such an expensive area.

'I didn't really know her very well,' he said straight away. 'The woman who lived on the top floor. I mean, I know her name and we used to meet up to discuss maintenance issues. She seemed very nice,' he added lamely.

Of course, that meant nothing. Bella was dead, and I had told him she was my friend. He was hardly going to denigrate her.

'I'm trying to find out what happened to her,' I told him.

'She was murdered,' he answered solemnly. 'The police were all over the entry hall and in and out of her front door, in their white forensic suits, you know the kind of thing.'

'But they still don't seem to know who did it.'

He shrugged. 'I can't say I really have the foggiest idea about what they know or don't know. They haven't kept us informed and, to be honest, I haven't asked. Not that I don't care what happened to her,' he added quickly, 'but I've been busy. I work in the city and they keep us at it to all hours. So, can I offer you a coffee or something?'

Thanking him, I left as quickly as I could without being rude. There was nothing to be gained by staying any longer and while I was hanging around in his flat, other neighbours might be preparing to go out. Having spoken to both the other residents in Bella's block, I tried the building next door. This time there was no series of bells with names beside them, so I rang the main bell. The woman who came to the door was about twenty years older than me.

'Yes, dear?'

When she heard the same story that I had given to her neighbours in the next building, she shook her head.

'It was a terrible tragedy,' she said. 'The police were here for days. We thought they were never going to be finished.'

In her long-winded way, she told me the same as I had just heard from the young man living in Bella's building. She hadn't known the murdered woman and could tell me nothing I didn't already know.

The house on the other side of Bella's building had been converted into two flats.

'My friend Amelie might be able to tell you something,' the girl who opened the door on the ground floor flat said. 'She used to go out clubbing in Camden with Bella. If you'd like to wait a minute, I'll go and get her.'

She didn't invite me in, instead closing the door and leaving me outside. I waited impatiently to speak to her friend, hardly daring to hope I might actually learn something. A few moments later, another young woman came to the door and smiled uncertainly at me. She was very pretty, with blue eyes and long blonde hair. On closer inspection, she looked older than she had first appeared.

'What do you want?'

'You were friends with Bella who lived next door?'

Her features twisted in a faint scowl. 'We weren't exactly friends. I wouldn't say we were friends.'

I waited for her to go on, but she didn't say anything else.

'Your flatmate said you went clubbing with her?' I prompted her at last.

She nodded. 'That's right. We used to hang out at the World's End.'

'Is that a night club?'

She stared at me as though I were speaking a foreign language. 'Yes, that's what I just said.'

'So you were there with Bella?'

'Yes. That was before.'

'Before what?'

'Before we stopped being friends. Look, we used to be friends. That is, we used to hang out together. But then Bella got involved with a man.'

'Paul?'

She nodded. Knowing Bella only used to see Paul on Tuesdays, I wasn't quite sure how that relationship would have affected her other friendships, although Amelie seemed to be implying that once Bella met Paul she stopped going out clubbing and was no longer fun to hang out with.

'So what happened?' I asked her. 'What difference did that make? Was she too busy to see you once she had a boyfriend?' I knew that couldn't be true.

'No, no, it was nothing like that. It's just that...' She shrugged. 'Paul was, well...' Amelie glanced at me as though to figure out how I might react. 'Did you ever meet him?'

I shook my head.

'You wouldn't understand then. We never meant it to happen.'

'What do you mean? What happened? Please, I really want to know. Bella meant a lot to me.'

Amelie raised her blue eyes and stared straight at me, her expression inscrutable.

'Bella found out.'

'Found out what?'

She pulled a face. 'She saw him leaving my house one afternoon. He used to come and see me, when he could get time off work. It didn't happen often, because he couldn't get away much. Anyway, we were saying goodbye on the doorstep, and she caught us.'

'Caught you?'

'Yes. Oh Jesus, do I really have to spell it out for you? Bella saw us kissing. After that she never spoke to me again.'

I stared at her in surprise. 'You mean–' I wasn't sure what to say. 'Are you telling me you were having a relationship with him as well?'

'Yes. I just told you that. Although it wasn't exactly a relationship. It was very casual, and he stopped seeing me as soon as she found out. She kicked up a bit of a fuss. It's not as if I was the only one,' she added quickly.

I don't know how I kept my voice steady. 'What do you mean you weren't the only one? Was Paul sleeping with other women as well as Bella and you?'

'I expect so,' Amelie replied casually. 'That's why he went to the World's End. To meet girls. Paul and I agreed right from the start that we weren't going to be exclusive. And Bella wasn't either, because I heard he was married to someone else all the time she was in a relationship with him. And then she had the cheek to complain about him seeing me. Talk about hypocritical! Anyway, he stopped coming to see me after she found out, and she stopped talking to me. Next thing I heard, she'd been murdered.'

Just in time I remembered that I was pretending to be a friend of Bella's. 'How did she die?'

Amelie shook her head. 'I don't know.'

'Did she know her life was in danger?'

'I told you, we stopped seeing each other a few months ago. I've no idea what she knew or didn't know.'

'You stopped seeing her because of Paul, but she carried on seeing him?'

'Yes, he told me they had an open relationship and were both free to see other people if they wanted. It was all perfectly straightforward, or at least it should have been. But she made a fuss about it, so he told me he wouldn't see me anymore. And not long after that I heard she was dead.' She leaned forward and lowered her voice. 'If you ask me, he did it. He got fed up with her being so possessive and they had a row and he killed her. He probably didn't mean to kill her, but he did. That's what I think happened, anyway. I was sorry when I heard it, of course, because I liked Bella. She was a good friend before all this happened. But she never forgave me for sleeping with her boyfriend.'

'No,' I muttered. 'I don't suppose she did. What about his wife?'

'What about her?'

'Did she ever find out about Bella?'

'Not when I was seeing him. He told me his wife never suspected anything. He said he was too smart to be caught out, but Bella saw us together, so he wasn't that smart, was he? It wasn't his fault she came home early, just bad timing, but even so, he wasn't as clever as he thought he was.' She gave a sour laugh.

'What a shit,' I said.

'It wasn't his fault. He was a real goer, if you know what I mean, and for a man like that to be stuck with a frigid wife, well.' Amelie shrugged. 'He only did what any man worth his salt would have done.'

I nodded, momentarily too choked to speak.

'What did you say your name was?'

'I didn't.'

Chapter 36

There didn't seem to be much point in knocking on more doors to speak to other random people living nearby. In any case I was too sickened by what I had just heard to face anyone. In a daze, I caught the train back to Harrow, doing my best not to think about what Amelie had told me. I managed to control myself until my front door shut behind me, and then I burst out in a wail that seemed to erupt from my entire body. My legs shook, and my ears rang with my howls.

All this time I had been kidding myself that Paul had fallen in love with another woman. Difficult though that was to deal with, it was at least understandable. Such things happened. But learning that he had been a serial adulterer, sleeping with women younger and prettier than me, made me feel as though I had been punched in the head. For the best part of twenty years, I had been married to a man who was a stranger to me. I don't know how long I stood there, bawling, but at last I sank to the floor, exhausted, and lay whimpering into the carpet.

My snivelling was interrupted by my phone ringing. By the time I found it in my bag, it had stopped ringing. Checking, I saw Ackerman's number. The only person I wanted to speak to was Dan, but when Ackerman rang again a few minutes later, I answered his call.

'What?' I snapped.

'Hello to you too,' he said. 'I have some good news.'

My gasp must have been audible down the phone. 'Is Dan coming home?'

'What? No. It's nothing to do with your son, not directly anyway. I've got some money to give you, and I've been speaking to your insurers.'

'Who?'

'You didn't lose your son's laptop, and the police deny all responsibility, so we can only conclude your son lost it somewhere.'

'What? No, he didn't. You know perfectly well what- '

'You can make a claim,' he interrupted me. 'If you say your teenage son lost his laptop, your insurance company are willing to pay out a proportion of the replacement cost.'

'There's no point. His grandparents have already provided him with a new one.'

He sighed. 'You want the money, don't you?'

'Not like this. I've already profited from my son's laptop, as have you. And anyway, there's an excess of five hundred pounds on our policy. It's not worth claiming.'

'It's your choice.' He sounded rattled.

'Yes, it is. And can I remind you what you're being paid to do? You're supposed to be finding out who killed my husband, not grubbing around selling off my property so you can share the proceeds.'

There was a pause. 'You came to me,' he said curtly, going on to tell me that he had been working hard to look into what happened to my husband. 'And you've hardly been paying me.'

'What about the deposit?' I said. 'Anyway, let's get back to the reason we're talking to each other at all. What have you managed to find out? Was my husband seeing anyone else, apart from Bella?'

'What?'

'I'm asking what you've found out about my husband. Well?'

'I've found out that the police are still trying to pin these murders on you. The key point in your favour is that traces of the drug were found in two glasses in your house the morning after your husband was killed. They had been rinsed and were standing upended on the drainer, but forensics can detect the smallest trace and whoever washed the glasses didn't do a thorough enough job. Probably they were in a hurry.' He paused.

'I'm listening.'

'If it weren't for that, and the fact that you were nowhere near Bella at the time of her death, as far as they have been able to ascertain, all they have to go on is motive and the fact that you were in bed with your husband on the night he died. It's not quite enough which is why the court allowed you bail. You haven't been charged with Bella's murder. The police are still beavering away, searching for anything that can place you at the scene, but I'm fairly confident they won't find anything.'

'Because I wasn't there.'

'If there was any evidence, they would have come across it by now. The longer this goes on, the colder the trail becomes.'

'You're talking as though you think I killed her.'

'Not at all. But it's worrying that the police won't let it go. It's time they threw up another lead.'

'There was at least one other woman I know about,' I said.

'Another woman?'

Briefly I explained that my husband had been seeing Amelie, and possibly other young women as well. It seemed to me that any one of them might have been involved in one or both of the murders. At least it was worth considering.

Ackerman sounded impressed. 'You've been busy,' he said.

'The thing is, Amelie's flatmate told me they used to go to this club in Camden, so we could try to find out who else he met there, if he went there regularly, at least before he met Bella.' I paused, remembering the Friday nights he had been home late, bright eyed and reeking of alcohol, after a works outing. He used to complain about the amount of corporate entertaining he was expected to attend.

'It sounds like fun,' he used to tell me, 'all eating and drinking and making conversation, but when it's work it's... well, it's just work and bloody boring.'

Furious, I recalled how sympathetic I had been, while all the time the creep had been out picking up young women.

'Are you inviting me to go clubbing with you?' Ackerman gave a bark of laughter.

He knew very well I couldn't go anywhere after six o'clock. I think we were both relieved that he would have to visit the clubs on his own. It was way out of my comfort zone.

'You'll fit right in as a dirty old man,' I told him, and he laughed again.

'I can be discreet,' he said. 'No one will even know I'm there. And if they do, they'll think I'm a cop. I have that look about me.'

It was tempting to retort that he looked more like a tramp than a policeman, but this was no time to argue with him. He still had a job to do for me.

We agreed Ackerman would ask around in the club Paul had frequented, while I planned to visit Paul's office and find out how much evening work he had really been doing. It didn't matter, but I wanted to know all the same. Either Paul or Amelie had been lying to me, and they had both seemed very convincing. For my own satisfaction, I just wanted to establish the truth, whatever that might be, although I already knew the answer. There was no reason why Amelie would have lied to me.

Having spoken to Ackerman, I felt a lot better. At least we now had a concrete plan in place, and I was no longer casting around helplessly, looking for clues on my own.

As I was making myself some lunch, there was a ring at my bell. Hoping Dan had come back but fearing the police had returned to arrest me again, I opened the door. There was no point in pretending I wasn't home. If it were the police, they would simply return at six.

My hopes and fears were both confounded by my friend, Katie. Her ginger curls looked unkempt, and her face was unusually pale. She gaped at me for a few seconds, panting as though she had been running.

'Katie, what's up? You look terrible.'

'There's something I need to tell you,' she gabbled. 'I have to say it before I lose my nerve. Can I come in?'

Chapter 37

It was just like Katie to build things up to sound far more dramatic than they actually were, so I was curious rather than worried, expecting what she was about to tell me would be a distortion of the truth, whatever that was. Following me inside, she perched on a stool in the kitchen and sat there in silence, looking anxious. I was quiet too, waiting for her to say something, so neither of us spoke while the kettle boiled.

With the tea made, and still without exchanging a word, we went into the living room where we settled down in armchairs with a tray of tea and biscuits on the table between us. Finally, I nodded at her to begin, but she continued staring silently at the floor.

'You came here to tell me something,' I said at last, smiling to hide my impatience. 'What is it?'

She looked at the plate of biscuits and selected a chocolate one. I watched while she finished her mouthful and washed it down with a gulp of tea before she answered.

'This isn't going to be easy for either of us.'

'What are you talking about, Katie? What's not easy? What's going on?'

For the first time I suspected this could be something serious. It crossed my mind that she might be leaving her husband. I had only met him a few times, but he had struck me as a dull man, with virtually no conversation, and no sense of humour. Nearly as short and tubby as Katie herself, he wasn't even good looking. But she had just said this might be hard for me as well, and problems in her marriage would hardly affect me. I found her coyness irritating rather than intriguing and told her so.

'Okay, I'll come straight out with it.' She twisted her fingers together and I watched them writhing in her lap as she went on. 'Bella wasn't the only woman Paul was seeing.'

'By 'seeing', you mean...?'

'Yes, having sex with, if you want me to spell it out for you.'

This came as no surprise, and I couldn't understand why she was making such a big deal of it. Paul was dead. Why would Katie care that he had been sleeping around? I didn't.

'What makes you say that?' I asked.

She heaved a sigh. 'I don't just think it, I know. And you have a right to hear about it too.'

'But how come *you* know about it?'

'I saw them together and it was pretty obvious something was going on, so I asked her straight out, the next time I saw her, whether she was screwing him, and she told me she was. She didn't seem embarrassed or ashamed of what she was doing, but she made me promise not to tell you.' She reached across the table and put her hand on my arm. 'I'm so sorry. I should have told you before this. I should have said something straight away. Or maybe I shouldn't have told you at all. This must be so awful for you.' She was nearly crying. 'I didn't know what the best thing was to do.' I glanced down at her fingers lying on my arm like a row of fat worms.

'That's okay,' I lied, thinking how weird it was for *me* to be comforting *her* in this situation. 'This is nothing new. And even if it were, there's no need for *you* to apologise. You've done nothing wrong. This is all Paul's fault. He's the one who should be feeling guilty.'

'But I ought to have told you sooner.'

'It doesn't matter either way. He's dead now anyway.'

I would have liked to look him in the eye and challenge him about his behaviour, but instead there was only Katie. 'How could he have done it?' I burst out, suddenly losing my self-control and raising my voice. 'He lied to everyone. Our whole life together was a lie.'

'What he did was disgusting.'

'How long have you known about it?'

She shook her head and heaved another sigh. 'Since Christmas.'

'Christmas? That's over six months ago.'

'When I challenged her about what was going on, she didn't even try to deny it, although there was no way she could have pretended it was anything else. I've no idea how long it had been going on by the time I found out.'

'It stopped some time ago, because Bella found out and forced him to give her up,' I told her.

'Did Bella tell you that herself? Because it's not true. I guess Bella threatened to tell you, but he was still seeing both of them right up to the time he died. She said you'd never suspect her.' She looked at me sadly. 'She said you trust her because she's your friend. That's what makes it so despicable.'

This conversation was taking a very weird turn. Amelie was no friend of mine and I didn't understand how Katie had come across her in the first place.

'I don't get it. How did you meet her?' I asked.

Her eyebrows shot up. 'What do you mean, how did I meet her? We've been friends for years. We were all at school together.'

'Were we? I don't remember. She's so much younger than us. She can't be more than thirty.'

'What are you talking about?'

We stared at one another, simultaneously realising that we were talking at cross purposes.

'I'm talking about Amelie.'

'Who's Amelie?'

'One of Bella's neighbours.'

I explained how I had gone to question all of Bella's neighbours to see if they could tell me anything about Bella and Paul.

'I only wanted to find out anything that might help to establish who killed them,' I added, seeing her puzzled expression. 'I wasn't interested in hearing about his relationship with Bella. Only I found out more than I bargained for, because one of Bella's neighbours told me she'd also been sleeping with him. Anyway, her name's Amelie, and guess what? She's young, and she's pretty.'

I failed to conceal my resentment, but I didn't care.

Katie looked horrified. 'You can't be serious. Paul was sleeping with one of Bella's neighbours as well?'

'Yes. She met him at the same time as Bella did, in a club in Camden where he went to pick up young women.'

'No.' She let a strangled yelp of laughter, although her expression was troubled, and her face had gone almost white. 'I don't believe it. Who told you all that?'

'Amelie told me herself.'

'I don't believe it,' she repeated.

'Why would she lie about it?'

'You're telling me Paul was going to clubs to pick up young women? And you're seriously saying that he was conducting affairs with both these women? And all that while he was married to you?'

I shrugged. 'If he was sleeping with both of them it can't have been for long because Amelie told me Bella saw them together and forced him to stop seeing her. So after that he just continued his affair with Bella, until he was killed.'

Katie looked stricken. 'I wish that were true,' she whispered. 'But he was seeing someone else as well. That's what I came here to tell you.'

'Yes, you came here to tell me something. Whatever it is, it can't be worse than what I just told you.'

But from what she had told me, I thought I already knew the answer to my question. I recalled her telling me once that her husband had seen Paul with a dark-haired woman, and now she had as good as told me he had been seeing one of my friends. There was only really one person I could think of who might fit the description, the only friend who had always been there for me, a friend who had been incandescent with rage, and then inconsolable with grief, when her own husband had left her. I remembered how pleased Katie and I were when Nina had finally accepted being divorced, and how adamant she had been that she was finished with men for good.

'Was it Nina?' I whispered.

Katie nodded, her eyes shimmering with tears.

'It's okay,' I mumbled, 'I'm fine, really.'

But Katie could see that wasn't true. Shaking and tearful, I let her make me another cup of tea, and then she sat quietly with me, giving me time to digest the horrible news that I had lost not only my husband and my son, but my best friend as well.

'I'm sorry to have been the one to cause you so much distress,' she said at last. 'As if you haven't had enough to deal with lately.'

'How could she?' I hissed. 'My best friend. How could she have done that to me? She must have known I'd find out in the end.'

Katie shook her head and her ginger curls fluttered around her pale face. 'I guess some people get off on taking risks. The fear of being found out adds excitement to a relationship that would otherwise be dull and boring. Some people just seem to need that kind of thrill to liven up the monotony of their lives.'

Given that Paul was now dead, I would have preferred not to learn about Nina's betrayal at all, but I thanked Katie for doing what she believed was the right thing.

At last she left, apologising for having to go home to her husband and make his supper. She invited me to accompany her. For answer I rose to my feet and pulled up my trouser leg. When I explained what was around my ankle, she threw her arms around me, patting me on the back.

'That's horrible,' she mumbled. 'This is all so terrible. I can't believe they've done this to you.' She stared down at my tag. 'We have to get this hideous thing removed.'

'That's not possible. If I tamper with it, an alarm's set off at the monitoring centre. And the same happens if I break the curfew and don't get home by six. So, you see I can't come with you. Give my best wishes to Tony, won't you?'

'It's a relief to have told you,' she confessed as we walked along the hall to the front door. 'It's been a weight on my mind for so long, wondering what to do. I insisted Nina ought to tell you herself, but she flatly refused. She said he's dead and gone and it wouldn't make any difference to anyone now and so there was no reason to upset you over it. I just hope I did the right thing.'

'Definitely,' I lied.

Sometimes it's better not to know the truth.

Chapter 38

It was hard to believe Nina had the gall to behave as though nothing had happened between her and Paul. Really, it was impossible to fathom what people were thinking, and what appeared to be the truth so often turned out to be a tangle of lies. For months, Nina had seemed beyond reproach as a friend, going out and having a laugh, and then being sympathetic when Paul had died. She had always had my back, ever since we were at school together. And now this.

It made me feel physically sick even thinking about her. I wanted to slap her in the face and make sure she realised what she had lost. With his death, Paul had snatched from me the chance to tell him exactly what I thought of his infidelity. I wasn't going to miss a second opportunity to speak my mind. In some ways, Nina's betrayal was as bad as Paul's. She was my friend.

When I suggested visiting Nina for coffee the next morning, she insisted I join her for lunch. It didn't take me long to reach her apartment in Harrow, not far from where I lived. After her divorce, she had moved out of her house and bought a small maisonette on the top floor of a converted two-storey house. It was on a main road, but she said it gave her a sense of security to see buses going past, and there was a stop right outside her front door.

As I rang the bell, I still hadn't decided what to say to her. 'You were screwing my husband, you bitch,' was hardly subtle. I wasn't even sure whether to come out with it straight away or have lunch first. Either way it was going to be hard. We had been friends for a long time.

Still contemplating my options, I rang her bell.

It could have been my imagination, but I thought I detected something sly in her eyes when she opened the door and smiled at me. She went to hug me, but I drew back, pretending to sneeze. It didn't sound very convincing to me, but she made no comment, instead leading the way to the table at one end of her living room.

'I know it's all a bit compact compared to the house,' she had told us the first time she invited Katie and me over, 'but it's fine for me now I'm on my own, and there's no way I was going to stay in that house after everything that happened.' She screwed up her eyes as though to shut out an unpleasant sight. 'I don't even know if they did it there, in our bed.'

Taking my place at her table, I wondered where she and Paul had slept together. Suddenly I couldn't contain myself any longer.

'Did you do it here?' I asked.

'What?'

She looked surprised, more by my hostile tone of voice than the question which made little sense coming, as it did, out of context.

'I asked you whether you did it here, in your bedroom. Or did you meet in a hotel?'

She shook her head. 'What are you on about? Is this a joke, because I just don't get it?'

'You can stop pretending. I know all about you and Paul.'

'Me and Paul? What? You think I killed him? That's insane. What are you talking about? Why would I do that? Have you been drinking?'

'Do you really want to force me to say it? All right then. I know you were having an affair with Paul. You can lie about it all you want, but I know what's what.'

Nina gaped. 'What are you... What are you talking about?' she stammered. 'Me and Paul? You've got to be kidding... What are you thinking?' She shook her head. 'Jesus, Julie, what the hell gave you that idea? He was your husband. He's the last man- '

'Stop lying. I'm done with your lies. Admit the truth and tell me why you did it. I just want to know why.'

Somehow my anger had fizzled out leaving only a desperate urge to hear the truth from her lips. Nina stood up and paced to the other end of the room where she stood for a moment with her back to me, her shoulders bowed. At last she turned to face me.

'Julie, I don't know who told you this stupid lie, but I promise you there was nothing going on between me and Paul. I hardly ever saw him, and when I did, he was always with you.' Her voice, at first plaintive, hardened, and her eyes blazed. 'I can't believe you'd listen to such a vicious rumour, even for a second, let alone believe it.'

She came back to the table and sat down, gazing directly at me. I could tell she was struggling to control her anger.

'Julie, we've been friends for a long time. You know me. You know I'd never do that to you. Listen, you've been under a lot of stress recently. I know how hard it is when the man you're in love with turns out to be a cheat and a liar, and you realise you've thrown your life away on someone you never really knew. Your whole world falls apart. I know what that feels like. And I get it that you're all over the place at the moment. You think you can't trust anyone. But don't turn your anger against the people who are on your side. You won't help yourself get through this in one piece if you alienate your friends. It will send you over the edge. Believe me, I know what I'm talking about. So let's forget what you just said-'

'You'd like that, wouldn't you?' I interrupted her furiously. 'So how does this work for you, Nina? Let me see if I've got this right. You sleep with my husband and then I'm supposed to tell you that's all right and what's important is that we carry on being friends? Is that what you want? Right now, I want to- to throw something at you for betraying me.'

'Julie, it wasn't me that betrayed you. Can't you see what you're doing? You're fantasising, turning your rage against me when it wasn't me who hurt you. I'm your friend, and I'd never do anything like that. I just couldn't. You know me, Julie. Snap out of this, please.'

'Don't tell me I'm imagining it.'

'So, what makes you think I was having sex with him? Did you catch us at it?' She laughed, but her face twisted in disgust. 'Can't you see how stupid this is?'

'I didn't catch you, Katie did. She told me everything, and when she challenged you about what was going on, you didn't even try to deny it.'

Nina leapt to her feet, knocking her chair to the floor, her face stretched taut with astonishment.

Her voice came out in a strangled whisper. 'Katie never told you this.'

I nodded. 'She did. So you can stop denying it, because I know about it.'

'You know? You know?' Her voice rose to a shriek. 'You know only what Katie told you. What *I* want to know is why you immediately assumed she was telling you the truth. What makes you so sure *I'm* the one who's lying? Because I know I'm not.'

I stared at her, agitated by what she was saying. Someone was lying, that much was clear, but which of them was it?

'I don't see why Katie would have made it up,' I replied. 'And in any case, Tony saw Paul with a dark-haired woman.'

Nina raised her eyebrows. There was no need for her to point out that I had only heard that from Katie.

'Why would she lie about it?' I persisted. 'I can see why you might want to cover up an affair, if you *were* seeing Paul, but why would Katie make up something like that?'

'How should I know? You'll have to ask her. And it really never occurred to you until now this minute that she might be lying to you?'

I shrugged. 'It's so hard to know what the truth is.'

'I feel sorry for you, Julie, really I do. Do you know why? Because you're going to end up alone and friendless.' She stood up. 'I'd like you to leave now. As far as I'm concerned, I never want to see or hear from you, or Katie, ever again. I thought you were my friend, but it seems you're prepared to believe vicious gossip about me without a shred of proof. How could you? Now get out of my house.'

Chapter 39

Trembling, I made my way home. I would have to go and see Katie to find out what she was playing at, but the whole situation was so weird, I was afraid to tackle her. Nina had been very convincing, but I couldn't see what possible motive Katie could have for fabricating a story that Nina had been having an affair with my husband. It made no sense. On the other hand, if Paul *had* been unfaithful to me with my friend Nina, it was obvious she would deny it.

Whether or not Nina had been telling me the truth, our friendship could never be the same after this. One of us would never trust the other again. I didn't want to risk making the same mistake with Katie by rushing straight round to her house and calling *her* a liar. Of my various acquaintances, none had been in touch with me, beyond sending cards and emails of condolence for Paul's death. My circle tended to consist mainly of other married women, and I recalled how Nina used to complain that most of her women friends dropped her once she became single again.

Now that Nina had thrown me out, Katie was the only close friend I had left. Reluctant to challenge her for fear of losing her friendship too, I went home to plan my next move.

I had forgotten that Ackerman had arranged to come and see me that evening. Fortunately, I had showered and pulled myself together by the time he arrived.

'How was your day?' he asked as he came in. 'You're looking a lot better than the last time I saw you.'

I wasn't best pleased at the reminder that I had been drunk when we last met.

'It's not a sin to have a few drinks once in a while,' I replied coldly, turning away to hide my embarrassment.

'It is if you're a Muslim or a Sikh.'

'True. But I'm not. I'm an atheist.'

'No eternal hell fires for you then.'

'I like to think I'd be going to the other place, if there is an after-life.'

He laughed. 'I guess that's what everyone thinks. We all convince themselves we're justified in doing whatever it is we do. Even the bad guys fool themselves into thinking they can be saved. They were wronged, or they were doing God's work. Failing that, all they have to do is confess and repent, and they're off the hook. But mostly they delude themselves into believing they were right to do what they did, however egregious. We all twist the truth to suit ourselves.'

I scowled at him. 'Did you come here to lecture me, or do you want something?'

'A cold beer would be great or, failing that, a nice strong cup of tea might hit the spot.'

I suspected he knew perfectly well that wasn't what I meant, but I led him into the living room, so he could sit down in comfort while I made us some tea. My bottle of wine would have to remain unopened until later.

Sitting down opposite my visitor, with a tray of tea and biscuits on the low table between us, I repeated my question.

He took a moment to savour his tea, and bit into a shortbread biscuit. Then he lifted his cup and nodded appreciatively. 'This is good tea. Very good.'

'Tea always tastes better when it's made in a pot. So, are you here on a social visit?'

I had no idea where he lived, but he had complained before about having to travel such a long distance to my house. I guessed he might live somewhere in Kent since he had once mentioned Tunbridge Wells.

'Or perhaps you've come all this way to admire my new jewellery?'

I yanked up my trouser leg to display my tag, and he grunted.

'Well?' I asked him. 'Did you go to the World's End club last night?'

'Yes. Bloody hell, what a place. Talk about a meat market. Not to mention pretentious and overpriced. You know how much it cost just to get in?'

I shook my head. 'What was it like?'

'Loud. In every sense of the word. My ears were ringing for hours after I left.'

Listening to his description of the club, I was glad I hadn't been able to go although, as it turned out, I wouldn't have been out of place. According to Ackerman, there were a number of women my age there, several of whom tried to come on to him. In fact, if his account was true, there were women of all ages there, outnumbering the men by at least two to one, and he was kept busy fending off their advances.

'Why don't you start at the beginning?'

'I got there at ten and had to queue to get in.'

'What were the other people like?'

'They were mainly women.'

'What sort of women?'

'Most of them were young, and they were all dolled up with far too much make up. Even on such a mild evening, they must have been chilly in their short skirts and skimpy tops, but none of them complained about being kept waiting on the street. In fact, there was quite a festive atmosphere among them as we shuffled slowly forwards. At the entrance two bouncers were checking tickets and once we got inside, punters went through a kind of security check.' Ackerman's lips curled in a sneer. 'I could have got a Kalashnikov past those apes.'

'It wasn't an airport,' I said.

'No point in checking for weapons if you don't do a proper job of it,' he replied.

Inside, it had been almost impossible to find a space to stand without being knocked into by one of the dancers.

'I say they were dancing, but it was just a mass of sweaty bodies gyrating in such close proximity that they could scarcely move, and the whole place flickered with flashing neon lights and a giant glitter ball. It was an assault on the senses.'

Ackerman shuddered as he described it and I had to admit it sounded hideous. In the bar area the music was slightly less intrusive. Tables and chairs were packed together as closely as the space would allow, and most of the seats were taken by people either watching the show or shouting at their companions across the tables.

Ackerman's impression of the bar was dominated by his disdain for a drag artiste in a blonde wig and long silver robes and stilettos, who introduced a series of burlesque dancers, most of whom he found neither tasteful nor graceful. The stage was smoky, although not from cigarettes, and the whole space was illuminated by bright pink concealed lighting.

I doubted the place was quite as vulgar as he made it sound, his outrage compounded by the cost of a shot.

'What with paying for the entrance ticket, if I'd paid for one drink I'd have been set back the best part of a hundred quid.'

But he did confirm Amelie's view that it was a likely place to go to meet young women looking for a good time.

He had spent some time prowling around.

'I questioned the waitresses, showing them Paul's photo and telling them my brother's gone missing. I asked the bouncers and the manager, as well as the waiting staff, but no one admitted seeing him there, apart from one waitress who thought she recognised the photo, but that was no help as she couldn't remember seeing him with anyone. At around midnight, I was on the point of leaving when a brawl broke out between two of the male customers. Before the bouncers arrived to separate them, I stepped in and grabbed each of the combatants by the arm and pulled them apart.'

Once again, I wasn't sure whether to believe his account. If he was telling the truth, he had not only been a magnet for promiscuous women, but also a heroic peacekeeper, in his short time at the club. But whatever the truth of his exploits, they didn't alter the fact that he had made no progress with our investigation.

'I may have discovered something that will help us,' I said when he finished.

Ackerman listened attentively as I went over everything Katie had told me, and Nina's reaction when I had challenged her. He was inclined to agree with me that Nina had a clear motive for lying, whereas Katie didn't.

'But Nina was adamant it was a lie, and I kind of believed her. That is, I didn't not believe her.'

He frowned. 'I suggest we go together and see Nina and Katie tomorrow, and find out which of your friends knows a lot more than she's letting on. Leave the questioning to me. Someone knows what happened and has been hiding the truth from everyone.'

I nodded. He was right. One of them was lying. I just didn't know which one.

Chapter 40

The following afternoon I bumped into my neighbour who lived across road. I only knew her by sight. We exchanged greetings when we passed each other in the street but had never had a proper conversation. She was probably a few years older than me, although it was difficult to tell, one of those women who could be anything from her mid-thirties to her fifties with good genes. I guessed that she worked, because I had sometimes noticed her returning home on weekdays at around five o'clock, but I had never seen her go out in the morning, so assumed she usually left before I was up.

It occurred to me to ask her if she had seen anyone hanging around near my house in the days leading up to Paul's murder. If an intruder had broken in with the intention of killing him, they might have been there to check out the place beforehand. It was at least a possibility, and right now I was willing to consider anything.

'I hope you don't mind my asking, but have you seen anyone hanging around outside my house recently?'

She gave me a puzzled smile. 'No. Should I have done?'

'It's just that- ' I hesitated. This was a difficult subject to broach, but she gave me an encouraging smile, so I pressed on. 'You know my husband was murdered recently?'

My neighbour nodded solemnly. 'I was so sorry to hear that. I never met him, but I'm really sorry for your loss.'

'Thank you. The thing is, he was murdered, and I just wondered if you'd seen anyone hanging around outside on the night he was killed?'

She shook her head. 'No, I'm sorry. Only you and your friend.'

'My friend?'

'Yes. The woman who went into your house with you that night.'

'That night?'

'Yes. On the night your husband was killed.'

I wanted to question her more, but it was nearly six o'clock, so I thanked her and turned away. But as soon as I was inside, I called Ackerman and told him what my neighbour had said. If she was right, two glasses had been spiked with Rohypnol that night, but there had been three people in the house.

The following afternoon, at five, Ackerman rang my bell. I was ready. Together we crossed the road and marched up my neighbour's path, aware that this visit could be crucial for my future.

My neighbour smiled uncertainly when she saw us on her doorstep. 'Yes? Can I help you?'

'We wondered if you would be willing to answer a few questions?' Ackerman said. 'It would be very helpful.'

I was surprised to hear him speaking so gently and persuasively. He had never adopted that tone with me.

'I'd be really grateful,' I added.

'Of course,' she smiled at my companion. 'Come on in.'

We followed her into a living room that was of similar proportions to mine, but very differently furnished. Where my house was smart and contemporary, hers was quirky and full of interesting artefacts that looked as though they had been gathered while travelling: wooden carvings, small stone statues, highly decorated classical urns and other memorabilia. I regretted not having made her acquaintance properly. She appeared to be an interesting woman, and I could certainly have done with more local friends. That was one reason why I had found myself a part-time job close to home. But I hadn't been there long enough to have got further than recognising a few faces.

'This is lovely,' I said, with genuine enthusiasm.

She smiled, accepting the compliment graciously. 'Thank you. I think so. Now, you wanted to ask me something?'

'Julie's husband was murdered,' Ackerman said.

'Yes, I was sorry to hear that. And I heard that the police tried to blame you for what happened to him, when it was someone else all along?'

I nodded. Her sympathy made me feel like crying.

'So what did happen to him?'

I shook my head.

'He was smothered with a pillow while he was in bed,' Ackerman told her

. 'Oh my God.'

'I didn't do it,' I burst out. 'I would never have harmed him.'

'The police are still working on it,' Ackerman said. 'But while the investigation is ongoing, we're trying to see what we can do to establish what actually happened the night he was killed.'

'And you're looking for a witness who saw Julie coming home that night?' She nodded. 'Okay, I'm happy to go over what I saw. But first, let me fix you a drink. What can I get you? I've got a selection of herbal teas: camomile, peppermint, or jasmine, or I can make a pot of fresh mint tea. Or if you'd prefer something stronger, we could crack open a bottle of wine?'

'A glass of water is fine for me,' Ackerman said promptly.

I hesitated. My neighbour turned to me with a smile.

'I'll have whatever you're having,' I told her.

She left us, and I hoped she would return with two glasses of wine. But she came back after a few moments with a tray holding Ackerman's glass of water and a pot of tea with green leaves floating in it.

'I hope this is all right,' she said.

'That looks lovely,' I lied.

She poured the mint tea and I blew on my steaming cup. It was a long time since anyone had shown me such unprompted kindness. Blinking back tears of gratitude, I took a sip.

'Now,' she said. 'I'll tell you everything I saw. What I can remember, that is.' She gave an apologetic smile.

'Thank you, thank you,' I mumbled, and she smiled at me again.

'So it was about eleven, maybe half past. I can't be sure of the exact time, but I was going to bed. I heard a bit of a commotion in the street and glanced out of the window. A taxi had drawn up outside your house. A woman must have got out onto the pavement because I saw her walk around the vehicle and open the passenger door on the road-side. It looked as though she was struggling to drag someone else out, and then you fell onto the road and she grabbed you by the arm and pulled you to your feet. Together you staggered around the taxi onto the pavement. I couldn't see you for a few seconds but then the taxi drove off and I saw you both walking towards your front door. Except *you* weren't walking, exactly. One of your arms was around her neck, and she was holding it there with one hand and her other arm was wrapped around your waist, and she half carried you along the path to your front door.'

She paused and took a gulp of her tea. 'Is it all right?'

'Yes, it's lovely, thank you.'

I drank some tea and actually it was quite pleasant.

Ackerman leaned forward and thanked her. 'Was there anything else?'

She shook her head. 'No, that was about it. I wouldn't have seen anything if I hadn't happened to be going to bed and went to look out of my window because I heard voices outside.'

'Did you hear what they were saying?'

'No. I just remember hearing hysterical laughter, and a woman's voice urging you to 'Come on,' before she hauled you out of the taxi.'

Ackerman nodded, but I was impatient to know more.

'What did she look like?' I asked.

'I couldn't see. It was dark outside, and the only time she would have been clearly lit up by a street lamp, the taxi was blocking my view of her. After that you were draped across her shoulders, so I couldn't see the back of her head.'

'What about when we got to the house? You said I collapsed in a heap on the doorstep.'

She shook her head. 'Whoever she was, she was leaning over, rummaging in your bag for the key. Then, when she found it, she was bent down over the keyhole. Once the door was open, she grabbed you and dragged you inside, which meant you were shielding her again. There were no lights on inside the house until after she shut the door. Then I went to bed. And that's as much as I can say.'

'You must have seen something of her. The colour of her hair? Her shoes? Was she short, tall, thin?'

She shook her head. 'I'm really sorry. It was impossible to see anything in detail. It all happened so quickly, and I wasn't really paying that much attention. If you hadn't gone into your house, I wouldn't have known it was you, because I couldn't see you that well either.'

'But you're sure it was a woman who was helping me out of the car, and not a man? So you must be able to tell us something about her,' I insisted.

She nodded. 'I can't tell you how I know it was a woman.' She paused, as if struggling to recall what she had seen. 'No, I'm sorry. I think I assumed you were with a woman because of her voice when she was helping you out of the car.'

'Was she wearing trousers?' Ackerman asked.

'I don't know. I can't remember.'

'Is there anything else you can tell us? Anything at all?'

'She looked about the same height as you, although I didn't see her standing up straight.'

'What about her voice?' I asked. 'Can you tell us anything about that?'

She shook her head. 'I'm sorry, but I've told you everything I can remember.'

By now it was ten to six and I had to leave.

Thanking my neighbour again, we stood up. With assurances that her observations had been very helpful, we said goodbye. At least we now knew that I hadn't returned home alone. But while it was heartening to hear an honest statement in a world of shifting truths, it was depressing to realise that a stranger was the only person I could trust.

Chapter 41

The following morning, I took the tube to London to speak to Paul's former colleagues. Uncertain what I was hoping to learn, or even why I was really going there, my curiosity about my husband's affairs drove me on. Even though I already knew where he had been on the evenings when he was home late, part of me was still hoping to discover that Bella had been the only other woman in my husband's life. The number of women he had been sleeping with didn't alter the fact that he had been unfaithful to me, yet somehow one mistress seemed preferable to three. It would mean he hadn't lied to me quite so often.

Paul had worked for a large corporation based in an impressive office block not far from Euston station. On my arrival, a smartly dressed receptionist smiled an impersonal welcome and enquired whether I had an appointment.

'I'm Paul Barrett's widow. I'd like to speak to the senior partner here.'

I had nearly called myself his wife.

'But do you have an appointment? I'm afraid Mr Edwards' diary is full for the rest of this week,' she added without even glancing down at her screen.

'Please tell him I'm here. Tell him I'm Paul Barrett's widow. Please, just tell him.'

Raising one pencilled eyebrow, she asked me to wait. Then she picked up her phone and I heard her telling someone that a Mrs. Barrett was asking to see Mr Edwards. Listening to her, I regretted having travelled all the way into London. I didn't know what I was doing there and was tempted to turn and scurry out of the building. I had been reduced to begging to see Paul's boss, but what for? Apart from the fact that it was a humiliating waste of time, I didn't know what I was hoping to discover. But before I had a chance to slink away, the girl put her phone down and nodded at me.

'You can go up,' she said brightly, as though she hadn't just told me her boss was too busy to see me. 'Take the lift to the fifth floor.'

Mr Edwards' personal assistant was waiting for me as the lift door opened. She was young and slim, with masses of dark hair. It was possible she was the dark-haired woman Katie's husband had seen Paul with. She led me straight to her boss's office, a spacious room with large windows overlooking the busy main road. Far below us, traffic drove by with a barely audible hum.

'Mrs. Barrett,' a small man seated behind a very large desk greeted me. He stood up and extended his hand to shake mine. 'Our condolences once again. It was a terrible shock. We're all still trying to come to terms with what happened. Have you come to tell us about the funeral arrangements? There are definitely a number of my colleagues who would like to attend- with your approval, of course,' he added, seeing my expression.

It was an understandable enquiry, since more than a month had passed since Paul's death.

'I'm afraid the police haven't finished looking into things yet,' I replied.

I wasn't sure which of us was more embarrassed. He gave a delicate cough to cover the silence.

'Of course,' he said, as though it was normal for the police to be conducting such a lengthy investigation into the circumstances of a death. 'I understand. There are sometimes certain things that need checking.'

'My husband was murdered.'

'So, please, how can I help you?' he asked, sitting down and speaking slightly more briskly.

I dismissed a temptation to ask him for money, but his next question indicated that the thought had crossed his mind as well.

'Paul's death in service pension has gone through? There shouldn't be any problem with that.'

I nodded. No doubt the money was being paid into my account where it would accrue nicely until such time as I could touch it. Mr Edwards had no idea that I was under suspicion, with all my accounts frozen. Without thinking, I tucked my tagged ankle behind my other one, to reassure myself that the grey bracelet was concealed under my trousers. Mr Edwards cleared his throat and offered me a cup of tea. Tapping a phone, he summoned another young woman.

Stammering that it was later than I thought, I jumped up saying I had to leave. Promising that I would let Mr Edwards know the details of the funeral, I left, having learned only that Paul had worked surrounded by attractive young women. He had scarcely needed to go out clubbing to meet more. But of course, his liaisons had been furtive which only made his conduct seem even more shameful. I wondered if he had been hiding his affairs from his work colleagues, or from me, or perhaps both. He might have been conducting an affair with one of his work colleagues as well as with Bella, and Amelie, and possibly Nina, and goodness knows who else.

The next afternoon Ackerman and I went to see Nina. Her car wasn't in the drive and there was no answer when we rang the bell. We waited. Several hours passed while we sat in the car without speaking. By five o'clock I was growing anxious. I didn't have much time. At last Nina's car drew up outside her house. She didn't notice us climbing out of Ackerman's car and follow her up her front path to her door. I felt like a criminal stalking my victim, but it seemed I had no other choice. As she reached her front door, she spun round and glared at me.

'What the hell are you doing here?' she demanded. 'I thought I made my feelings clear. And who the hell's this?' She turned to Ackerman. 'You can bugger off as well. Get away from me!'

Ignoring her outburst, I introduced Ackerman as my friend. He immediately stepped forward and began smooth talking my irate friend.

'If you would be kind enough to give us one moment of your time,' he said, 'we won't keep you long. You must understand that we are trying to avoid a miscarriage of justice. I believe your friend here is innocent-'

'So am I!'

'I've no doubt you are, and no one is suggesting otherwise. But surely you appreciate that Julie is under suspicion-'

'Suspicion? She downright accused me of sleeping with her husband behind her back! How's that for suspicion?'

As before, Nina's outrage seemed genuine.

'The police are accusing her of murder,' Ackerman reminded her quietly. 'It's not quite the same.'

Nina's black eyes gleamed angrily. 'Someone must have done it, and it certainly wasn't me. No one has even suggested I was involved. Listen, Ackman, or whatever your name is, this whole thing has got nothing to do with me. I was a friend of Julie's, that's all. We're no longer friends. Now please leave.'

Ackerman nodded. 'Hopefully you'll be friends again, once this has all blown over.'

'Listen, I was a good friend to her, until she spread lies about me.'

'I didn't spread any lies about you,' I burst out. 'I asked you to your face whether what I'd heard was true. I never mentioned it to another living soul.'

'What about your friend here?'

Ackerman shook his head. 'I know nothing about your conduct, and I'm not interested in your private life, nor have I levelled any accusation against you. Now, may we please come in for a moment and talk about this?'

Nina hesitated, then glared at me. 'You can say whatever it is you have to say right here. You're not coming into my house.'

Ackerman sighed. 'Very well. I would like to ask you one question, if I may.'

'Go on then, ask. But I might not answer.'

He inclined his head. 'That's your prerogative.'

'Thank you very much,' she snapped.

I was growing edgy. It was past five and I had to be home in less than an hour.

'Were you with Julie at any time on the night of her husband's murder?'

'She knows perfectly well I was. We went out, all three of us, Julie, me, and Katie, and we had dinner together. She could have told you that.'

'And Julie had a few drinks? From what I've heard, that wouldn't be unusual,' he added, with a smile of complicity at Nina. 'Our witness says she was staggering about in the street, obviously drunk.'

'Hang on a minute-' I began, but he silenced me with a warning frown.

Meanwhile, Nina's demeanor towards him had changed. She smiled, staring at him as though I wasn't there. Seeing what he was doing, I kept quiet.

'It's not unusual for people to become violent when they're drunk,' he added then muttered something else that I couldn't hear, and she laughed. 'So, then you took a taxi home?'

'That's right.'

'And you took your friend Katie home first?'

'No,' Nina said. 'They dropped me off first.'

Ackerman leaned forward slightly. 'They dropped you off first? You're quite sure about that?'

'Yes, that's what I said. We'd gone to a Chinese restaurant in Eastcote not far from here, and I live the closest. You can check with the taxi driver if you don't believe me. I've got a record of the cab booking on my phone, with the time of the pickup, the registration number of the vehicle, and I can even send you the name of the driver and his photograph, because the cab firm always send that information and I haven't deleted the text. At least, I don't think I have. And even if I can't find it, the taxi firm will have a record of the booking and the time of the pickup. Why are you so interested in the taxi journey anyway?'

'A woman was seen entering Julie's house with her on the night her husband was killed.'

She snorted. 'And I suppose Katie invented that little detail, did she?'

'No,' Ackerman said quietly. 'This has nothing to do with your friend Katie.'

'She's not my friend,' Nina muttered, with a dark look at me.

'A witness saw two women going into Julie's house that night, a witness who thought the second woman might have had dark hair.'

'Oh, and so I'm the only dark-haired woman in London, am I?'

'The point is, whoever got out of the taxi to help me home went inside my house.'

Nina glared at me. 'I don't care who went into your house. It wasn't me. And I thought I made it clear that I don't want anything to do with you again. Ever. Now get off my property before I call the police.'

She went inside and slammed the door. I was dismayed by her continuing hostility, but Ackerman was smiling.

'Come on, then,' he said.

'Where to?'

'We're going to pay your friend Katie a visit.'

'I have to get home by six. If I break the conditions of my bail they'll lock me up again.'

He grinned. 'By the time we finish with your friend, you won't have to worry about your curfew anymore.'

'I can't risk it.'

He scowled in disbelief. 'You're saying you want to leave this until tomorrow? Really?'

'Listen, Katie works in a primary school and she finishes work at about three fifteen. She could be home by three thirty. Let's go and see her then, when we've got a bit more time.'

He nodded. 'Very well. Come on then, let's get you home.'

Chapter 42

The following day seemed to pass really slowly, even though I didn't get out of bed until eleven. Too wound up to eat, I sat around for three hours drinking tea and fretting.

At last, Ackerman came around at half past two and by three o'clock we were sitting in his car once more, waiting. This time we were parked a few doors away from Katie's house, watching out for her.

'Is that her?' Ackerman enquired a couple of times as cars drove past.

At twenty to four, I spotted her getting out of a car and scurrying up the road towards us. I jogged my companion's arm.

'That's her.'

He grunted, and we got out of the car and met her on the pavement. Although she looked taken aback, she seemed glad to see me.

'Julie! This is a pleasant surprise.'

She certainly didn't look like a woman who had murdered my husband, but there was a chance she might be able to throw some light on what had happened that night when we entered my house.

'And who's your friend?' she asked.

'This is Ackerman.'

'Ackerman?'

'Yes.'

It hadn't occurred to me until that moment to wonder about his first name. I had accepted his alias as just that.

'His name's Ackerman,' I repeated.

'Okay. Ackerman it is. I'm pleased to meet you.'

She held out her hand and he shook it. He appeared to be at ease, but I had the impression he was watching her closely.

'Are you coming in?'

She turned and led us inside.

'I'll put the kettle on.'

We all went into the kitchen and Ackerman stood while I perched on a stool.

'So, it's nice of you to pop in like this,' Katie said as we waited for the kettle to boil. She gave me a sly look. 'This is all rather sudden, isn't it? Where did you two meet?'

Realising that she was under the impression that Ackerman was a new boyfriend, I hurried to explain that he was just a friend.

'He's helping- ' I said, but he silenced me with a shake of his head.

'You know the police have accused Julie of murdering her husband?'

'Yes, I heard. It's ridiculous, isn't it? I mean, I know Julie and I'm sure she would never do anything like that. Still,' she lowered her voice, addressing Ackerman, 'I suppose they must have some reason for suspecting her? They did find him dead in bed, didn't they? It's going to be hard for Julie to prove she had nothing to do with it.' She sighed. 'It's a mess.'

'You were in a taxi with Julie on the night her husband was murdered,' Ackerman said quietly.

She didn't answer and I had the impression that she was now watching him. They were playing a game I didn't fully understand.

'I gather Julie was drunk that night? She was seen leaving the restaurant in quite a state.'

Katie laughed. I wasn't sure, but I thought she sounded nervous.

'Quite a few witnesses saw her,' he went on. 'But you were with her. So, how drunk would you say she was?'

'She was very drunk,' Katie conceded, with an apologetic glance at me.

'Your other friend, Nina, told us she left the taxi first, so it must have been you who was responsible for helping Julie to get home safely that night?'

He paused. Like me, he must have been expecting her to protest that she had done no such thing, but she hesitated.

'A witness saw you entering Julie's house with her on the night in question, anyway,' he added, as though it wasn't important. 'It was kind of you.'

'Yes, I saw her home safely. Someone had to. She could barely put one foot in front of the other,' she replied. 'I wouldn't trust anything Nina says. I could tell you any number of occasions when she's lied, but you can't blame her. She can't help it. She's a complete fantasist, but she can seem very plausible, so you do have to be careful around her. In fact, she told Julie a dreadful lie only a few days ago, didn't she, Julie?' Registering my silence, her expression altered. 'Didn't she, Julie? You know what a liar Nina is.'

'One of you is lying,' I agreed, 'but is it Nina, or you?'

She gave another nervous laugh. 'You know it's not me.'

'The thing is, a witness saw me entering the house with you just before Paul was murdered.'

'You see,' Ackerman added, 'the problem is that Julie was barely capable of standing when she arrived home that night.'

'What are you saying?'

'Our witness states she watched you help Julie into the house because she couldn't walk unaided and couldn't even stand without support. So that raises the question, how did Julie manage to overpower and kill her husband, given that she could barely stand up without help. And if it wasn't Julie who killed him, who else was there with her? Whoever it was must be the killer the police are looking for, don't you agree?'

Katie shook her head. 'I don't really understand who you are, or what you're doing here. I'd like you to leave.' She turned to me, her eyes burning with a curious intensity. 'Not you, Julie. Of course, you're welcome to stay. We're still friends, aren't we?'

She stood up as though preparing to escort Ackerman out of the house. But instead of moving towards the door, she twisted round and seized a knife that was hanging on a rack on the wall. Ackerman raised his arm to block her blow. I watched in horror as he staggered backwards, blood streaming from a wound on his forearm. With an inhuman screech, Katie leapt at him and slashed at the side of his head. His legs buckled under him and he fell to his knees. He knelt for a second before he pitched forward, and his forehead struck the floor with a loud thud. After that he lay still, while a pool of blood appeared on the floor beside him.

'Ackerman!' I called out. 'Ackerman!'

I wished I had found out his first name.

'It's a shame you killed your friend,' Katie said in a curious flat voice. 'He was only trying to defend me against your vicious attack.'

With a loud grunt, she slashed at her own forearm with the knife.

'What have you done?' I shouted, beside myself with terror.

She laughed. 'He could see you meant to kill me, so he tried to stop you, and now I have to kill you before you finish what you came here to do.'

'That doesn't even make sense. No one will believe I killed him. We were working together. He came here with me- '

'Did he? Or did he follow you here because he realised what you were planning to do and wanted to prevent you from killing anyone else? Or perhaps you both planned all this together for the money, and Bella found out. Only he thought better of it. He tried to argue you out of getting rid of me, because what did I have to do with all of your sordid mess? You didn't know about my affair with Paul.'

'What?'

If I hadn't been so terrified, I would have been tempted to laugh at the thought of Paul and Katie together.

'Paul would never have been interested in you. He went for young blondes.'

'Of course, you never suspected your good-looking husband might be having an affair with a frumpy overweight woman like me, did you? But he was screwing me for months. He even told me he loved me. I believed it too, until you told us he was having an affair with Bella. How could he do that to me? As soon as I heard that, I knew.'

'Knew what?'

'That he had to die, of course. Him and that young cow Bella.'

'So it was you that killed them both?'

'Of course it was me.'

She glared wildly around, as though looking for Paul, so she could vent her anger on him again. Her eyes came to rest on me and I shuddered at her maniacal glare.

'You thought your new friend, Ackerman, was turning against you, and you saw that as another betrayal. That's why you killed him, before you attacked me.'

She brandished her knife at me, grinning as she waved it in front of my face. I stared at her bloody hand, calculating how to grab the blade without seriously injuring myself.

'That's a lie!' I cried out. 'It's all lies! Everything you've said is a lie! It doesn't even make sense. No one's going to believe you, and you'll be locked up for the rest of your miserable life!'

I didn't know what I was saying, I was so shocked.

Katie smiled. 'Only the survivor will be able to tell the truth about what happened here today. That person's version of the truth will be *the* truth, and no one will be able to contest it, because there will be no other witness. Only one person is going to survive this.'

Grasping the truth in her words, I pounced. Avoiding the knife, I seized her arm and twisted it until she dropped her weapon. We both lunged, but I reached it first. Plunging the blade into her chest, I sank to the floor and crouched beside her, mesmerised by the quantity of blood spurting from her wound. There was so much blood.

My surge of elation gave way to horror. I don't know how long I stayed there, staring at her white face and struggling to comprehend what had happened. Losing Paul had been painful, but our relationship had come to an end before his death. In some ways this loss was starker. Katie and I had been close since we were five. I couldn't remember life without her. It causes unspeakable sorrow, of course, but no one's surprised when a marriage breaks up. We expect our friendships to last.

By the time the emergency services arrived, Katie had bled to death.

It was a policeman who discovered Ackerman was still breathing. Feeling helpless, I watched them carry him into the ambulance.

Chapter 43

It was always difficult to work out what Inspector Morgan might be thinking.

'Let me get this straight,' he said, his expression inscrutable as ever. 'You broke the terms of your bail by staying out after six, and your excuse for that infringement is that you couldn't go home because you were killing your friend? Have I got that right? Is that what you're telling us?'

'My client has already answered that question in her statement,' Andrew's voice cut in before I could respond. 'This was a clear case of self defence. You've seen the medical report. The man who was there looking after my client's interests sustained severe lacerations to his limbs and head. These injuries were caused by Katie Collins who violently assaulted him before turning on my client. Unfortunately, he's unable to give a coherent account of what happened that day, but my client's statement is quite clear, and all the evidence bears out what she said. The woman who killed her husband and his mistress is herself dead. My client killed her in self defence. I would have thought you'd be delighted to close your case.'

I nodded. 'That's right. She went crazy. First off, she attacked Ackerman. I mean, she just went for him. He didn't stand a chance. By the time I realised what was happening, he was lying on the floor, bleeding. I thought he was dead. I didn't have time to call for help because she turned on me next, screaming and slashing at me as I tried to defend myself. I managed to wrestle the knife from her, but it was pure luck that I stabbed her in the chest or she would almost certainly have killed me.'

'That was certainly a lucky blow for you,' Morgan said. He looked thoughtful. 'And you were lucky to escape injury yourself when the other two people who were present when this incident took place were subject to such violent attacks. After all, here you are chatting to us while the others, well, one is in hospital, and the other is in the mortuary.'

I nodded again and muttered about having seen the attack coming and being nimble enough to dodge away, while Ackerman had been caught off guard. Although Andrew assured me they couldn't hold me for long, the police kept me locked in a cell for another day. I grew frantic with worry, but they took no notice of my loud insistence that they release me immediately.

It wasn't clear to me how long I might have remained in custody, but the following day Ackerman recovered sufficiently to make a statement after which Andrew had no difficulty in getting all charges against me dropped. Even though he had been unconscious when I grabbed the knife from Katie, Ackerman confirmed that she had tried to kill him, after she confessed to murdering my husband and his mistress.

Exonerated, I went home dazed by my release. I had grown so accustomed to the tag on my ankle that my leg felt strangely naked without it. The solicitors who had been working on Paul's probate while I was in prison advised me that I was finally able to get hold of at least some of Paul's estate. They assured me the rest would follow soon. I was at liberty, I was a wealthy woman- and I was all alone. It was now no longer in question that Katie had killed both Paul and Bella.

Imagining what might have happened if she had succeeded in killing Ackerman as well, I shuddered. There was a good chance I would have been convicted of murdering all three of them. I couldn't imagine the impact such a sentence would have had on Dan. Our relationship would almost certainly have been over. He would have continued living with his grandparents and I might never have seen him again. Just the idea of it made me feel like crying. Whatever else happened, I had to get him back home with me as soon as possible.

Reckless of the expense, I went straight to King's Cross and booked a ticket on the next train to Edinburgh. The journey seemed interminable but at last I reached my destination, the house where my son was living. It felt as though many years had passed since I was last there. Trembling with almost unbearable excitement, I rang the bell. When Stella answered the door, she started back, clearly surprised to see me. With a cold glare, she asked me what I wanted. From the way she addressed me, we could have been strangers.

'What are you doing here? Aren't you supposed to be at home at this time? You shouldn't be here at all.'

'What do you mean, what do I want?' I replied, seizing on her words. 'I've come to take Dan home.'

'I don't think that's going to be possible.'

For a moment I thought my heart had stopped.

'Why... not?' I stammered.

I couldn't say any more. If anything had happened to my son, my life would lose its meaning. I felt my eyes water, but she assured me that Dan was fine. Having escaped a threatened prison sentence, it seemed that I now faced a different kind of challenge.

'Dan wants to stay here with us,' my mother-in-law announced with an air of finality. 'We've applied for custody- '

'What?'

'We've started the process to legally adopt him.'

'Adopt him?'

'Yes. Mark and I are adopting Dan.'

'You can't do that. He's my son.'

'I think you waived any parental rights when you were arrested for killing *my* son.'

'I didn't kill Paul, and you're lying if you suggest for one moment that I did.'

'The police think you killed him.'

'No, they don't. That's why they've released me. My innocence is no longer in question. It never really was. The police now know Paul was killed by a woman called Katie Collins, and they're satisfied I had nothing to do with it. There's no substance to that accusation against me at all, and there never was. Now, I'd like to see my son, please.'

She shook her head. 'It's too late. We've already sent off all the paperwork, and put the wheels in motion- '

'To hell with your paperwork,' I retorted, losing my temper with her. 'I want to see my son.'

'Dan doesn't want to go anywhere. He's happy here with us.'

I noticed she lowered her voice and it occurred to me that he might be in the house.

'Where is he? Is he there?' I demanded, deliberately raising my voice. 'I want to see Dan. Where is he? Dan?'

Stella shifted her weight, in an attempt to block me from entering, as though she was afraid I might try to barge past her. Her movement infuriated me.

'Where is he? Is he here?' I shouted as loudly as I could, hoping Dan would hear me. 'I want to see Dan right now!'

'He's not here-' Stella said, unaware that Dan had just appeared in the hall behind her.

'Mum?' He stepped forward. 'What are you doing here?'

His expression was difficult to interpret but I thought he looked pleased to see me, so I called out to him.

'Dan! It's all right. The police have found out who did it. They've let me go. They know it wasn't me. I'm innocent. It's all over. We can go home now.'

To my huge relief, his face broke into a broad grin.

Stella shook her head. 'No, he's not going anywhere.'

'Dan's coming home with me,' I told her.

'No.' She turned to Dan. 'We've started the adoption process. You can stay here with us.'

He threw me a helpless glance.

'That's up to Dan,' I said, trying to sound confident. 'He's free to choose whether to stay here for the rest of his life or come back home with me.'

I could see my own panic reflected in Stella's face. Feeling as though I couldn't breathe, I waited to hear Dan's reply. He stood in front of us looking pale and tense, like a lost child.

'I want to go home,' he bleated at last.

'Home?' Stella sounded almost angry. Or perhaps she was afraid. 'You have a home here with us, Dan.'

'I want to go back to London with Mum. That's what I want.'

There was an edge of determination in his voice that I had never heard before. In the time he had spent in Edinburgh, my boy seemed to have outgrown his naiveté. It was inevitable that he would have changed, after a separation of a few weeks.

Taking me to one side while Dan was upstairs packing his few belongings, Stella told me that she and Mark were going to take legal advice, but we both knew there was nothing they could do to persuade Dan to stay with them in Edinburgh once he had decided to come back home with me. All I could do was assure her that she and Mark could come and visit us whenever they wanted.

'Just give us a few days' notice,' I added, 'so we can make sure we'll be around. And we'd love to come and see you at Christmas, if we can. Dan feels really close to you and Mark, and we can't thank you enough for what you've done for him while all this has been going on.'

She must have heard the hostility in my voice, and seen the distance in my eyes. I wouldn't forget her efforts to take my son from me.

'We're convinced he should remain here with us,' she insisted. 'We can give him the stability and security he needs, and he has a place lined up at the college here.'

For all her fighting talk, she was forced to bow her head in defeat when Dan repeated that he wanted to return to London with me. That was just as it should be. With his father gone, his place was at home with his mother. The nightmare was finally over.

Mark dropped Dan and me at the station. Stella didn't come with us. She said she had to clear up at home, but I suspected she couldn't hold back her tears any longer. I would have been heartless not to feel sorry for her. Having lost Paul, she had almost held onto Dan but now he had vanished from her life as well. For nearly fifty years, she had been a mother and a grandmother.

Now that had been snatched away from her, leaving her bereft. There would be no more chances for her. She knew we were unlikely to visit her again.

In joyous contrast, my own sorrow lifted now that my son had been miraculously restored to me. I said nothing about the funeral arrangements on the train home, instead talking to Dan about his hopes and plans for college. We needed to move on from our grief and start thinking about the future. He knew what subjects he wanted to study, and thanks to Stella and Mark's efforts he had a place at college lined up in Edinburgh. As soon as we were home, I was going to contact all the London sixth form colleges offering those subjects and find him a suitable place. If necessary, I would enlist the help of the student disability service, but one way or another, in September, Dan was going to start college. I had spent too many years battling on his behalf to allow his steps to falter now.

Once we were home, Dan and I agreed that we wanted a quiet funeral, so I chose not to contact his former workplace. His colleagues were strangers to us and, as far as I was concerned, the fewer people who attended my husband's funeral, the better. Any of the women he had met might have had sexual relations with him.

So on a bright morning in September we buried Paul quietly. The flesh I had loved for so many years didn't deserve the quick passage of a cremation. I wanted him to think of him rotting slowly, as a penance for having destroyed my happiness.

Early autumn leaves had begun to fall; a few fluttered around us in a skittish breeze as we stood at the graveside. Apart from Dan and I, only Stella and Mark were there to watch the coffin slowly lowered into the earth. Dirt to dirt.

Chapter 44

Even though Paul's friend, Miles, was very helpful, it still took months for the probate to be completed, but at last I was done with lawyers and paperwork and waiting, and free to do whatever I wanted with the estate I had inherited from my husband.

As it transpired, Paul had been more prudent with his investments than I had suspected. There was a lot more money in the estate than I had anticipated mainly because, unknown to me, he had bought a flat in central London which had gone up in value by a substantial amount over the ten years he had owned it. The equity on that was nearly enough to buy another flat outright, in a different area. When he heard about it, Dan was keen to take over the flat in Camden himself, but I wouldn't hear of it. He was too young to live by himself.

'But Dad must have wanted me to have it,' he insisted. 'Why else would he have bought it?'

'I'm sorry, Dan, but it's just not going to happen. It might have seemed like a good idea when your father originally bought it, but the property market has moved on since then and it's become a bad investment,' I lied.

The truth was that the flat in central London was going up in value faster than our house in the suburbs.

'You'll have your own place one day with the money we get for it, I promise. But it won't be this flat, because we're going to sell it and invest the money in something more in line with today's market. Trust me, I've taken financial advice on this and I'm doing what's best for you, to safeguard the money that's going to come to you eventually.'

It would have made sound financial sense to let it, at least in the short term, while I decided what to do, but I lost no time in getting rid of Paul's flat. I could guess what he had used it for and wanted nothing to do with it. With the proceeds from the flat, which was snapped up at the modest asking price, I put my own house on the market and had no problem finding what I wanted. I justified the move to Dan by telling him I couldn't bear to stay in the home we had shared with Paul. That, at least, was true, although not for the reason Dan supposed. So, within a year of the probate coming through, Dan and I were settled at a new address.

We decided not to move away from the area as he wanted to stay in familiar surroundings, but having discussed our feelings with a bereavement counsellor, we both agreed we wanted to live in a place where we wouldn't be reminded of Paul in every corner of every room. We had no photos of him on display in our new home. Protected by his grandparents in Edinburgh, Dan knew nothing about Bella, or Amelie, or his father's relationship with Katie whose motive for killing Paul had been glossed over. Sticking as closely to the truth as possible, I told him that Katie had killed his father in a jealous rage because he had rejected her advances.

'But why?' he asked. 'What did she have to do with him? I thought she was your friend.'

'That's what I thought, and I've been asking myself the same question, over and over again,' I replied. 'I think Dad was kind to her, and she mistook his good manners for personal interest in her, so she fell in love with him and wanted him to leave us for her. Of course he refused, and she was so angry with him, she lost her temper and killed him.'

'So, are you saying it all started because he was nice to her?'

'No, that's not what I meant at all. We should always try to be nice to other people. But she fell in love with your father, and tragically she was insane. Thankfully there aren't many people like her around, so you don't need to worry. You can carry on being nice to people.'

I wasn't sure what else to say to him. Meanwhile, he joined a sixth form college, and his life moved on. It was very difficult, but slowly the trauma of losing his father in such terrible circumstances faded to a horrific memory and preoccupation with his studies, and his social life, took over and he looked more cheerful. Having lost my job, I made no attempt to regain it, or to find a replacement. Paul's death had left me relatively well off, so I didn't have to work and could devote myself to taking care of my son.

It was about eighteen months after Paul's death that I came face to face with Nina in the supermarket one afternoon.

'How are you?' I gave her what I hoped was an enthusiastic smile.

She returned my gaze coolly for a moment, without answering.

'It's been a while,' I went on awkwardly. 'We must meet and catch up.'

'Yes. Why not?'

'How about this afternoon?'

'I'm busy.'

'What about tomorrow?'

'Busy tomorrow.'

'Well, when are you free? I can make just about any time that suits you.'

'I'm busy all the time,' she said flatly and turned away.

'Nina, listen, I'm sorry for what I said to you.'

She turned back to glare at me and spoke very softly. 'Why don't you jump off the roof of the nearest high building? Is that clear enough for you?'

I shrugged. 'Please yourself,' I muttered, and hurried away before she could see how much she had upset me. The police hadn't released me from the jurisdiction of a court so that Nina could to sit in judgement on me. We never saw one another again after that chance encounter.

A few weeks later, I spotted Tracey on the street. We both looked away in tacit agreement not to acknowledge one another. Neither of us had any wish to renew our acquaintance now we were out of prison. The memory of my cell felt like a vaguely recollected bad dream. I didn't want to think about it anymore than was really necessary, and clearly she felt the same.

My former friends were dead or had drifted away. Even the memory of Paul was fading. My life would have moved on with a neat finality, had Ackerman not returned. I was hardly pleased to open the door and see him standing there. He looked even more disreputable than I remembered him, like a tramp in his oilskin and scuffed shoes. While I hesitated over what to say to him, he invited himself inside.

'So, you've moved,' he commented unnecessarily, looking around the neat hall which I had just had decorated. 'Very nice. I was going to call on you before now, but I saw that you were moving and thought I'd give you time to sort yourself out. Visitors are a nuisance when you're in the throes of moving to a new house, aren't they?' His hoarse voice grated unpleasantly. 'There's always so much to do.'

'I don't know why you're here,' I replied, terse in my dismay. 'The case on my husband is closed. I have no further need of your services. I'd like you to leave.'

'Oh, this isn't a social call,' he assured me. 'But in consideration of my services, there is still the question of the outstanding money.'

'Don't tell me you're expecting the balance of your fee? You didn't exactly do anything to deserve it.'

He raised his eyebrows. 'You can't have forgotten I was nearly killed while I was working on your case. We'll have to adjust my fee to take that into account. Danger money.'

'That was hardly my fault. You're supposed to be the professional. You should have known she was violent. And don't forget I was attacked too, while you were being paid to protect me.'

We glared at one another for a moment, but Dan was due home soon and I wanted Ackerman out of the house. With no time to bargain, I made a snap decision and offered to pay him half of the balance of his outstanding fee.

'I'm sure you'll agree that's a very generous offer,' I added in as firm a tone as I could muster.

Ackerman laughed at me. 'You're hardly in a position to haggle.'

Kicking the front door closed behind him, he took a step towards me, his mud-coloured eyes glittering.

'It's going to cost you a lot more than that to silence me.'

Chapter 45

Staring at Ackerman's unshaven face, I was momentarily speechless with fear for my own safety. While he had been working on my behalf, his rough exterior had inspired me with confidence. Now he had become a formidable opponent.

Hiding my apprehension, I tried to sound bold. 'What do you mean?'

He gave a little grunt, as though satisfied by my response. 'That's more like it,' he said. 'Shall we go and sit comfortably and talk about this? There's no call for any antagonism, not after all we've been through.'

I wanted to throw him out of the house, but wasn't sure how to persuade him to go, and in any case, I was bothered by his suggestion that I would want to silence him. Before anything else, I needed to find out exactly what he meant by that.

'This is all very nice,' he repeated, looking around as he followed me into the living room. 'I see you've done very well for yourself. Your husband's money came through, I take it?'

'You seem to be congratulating me on becoming a widow,' I replied.

Ensconcing himself in one of my new leather armchairs, he grinned up at me. 'Come on, Julie, he wasn't exactly a model husband, was he? There's no need to play the grieving widow. Now, shall we get down to business?'

Astonished, I listened as he demanded an outrageous sum of money. For a moment I couldn't speak, watching him lean back in his chair, a complacent smile on his lips.

'You're... crazy,' I stammered at last. 'I wouldn't dream of giving you so much. You're trying it on, but this is my money we're talking about, mine and my son's. You don't have a claim on any of it, not a single penny. I only offered to pay you at all because you're in such a sorry state. Now, either you accept my offer, or you leave with nothing.'

I stood up.

Staying put, Ackerman leaned forward and spoke very slowly, enunciating each word distinctly in his gravelly voice. 'Unless you give me exactly what I want, I'll tell the police you killed Katie, after you tried to kill me.'

'What?'

In my surprise, I could think of nothing else to say.

'I'll go to the police,' he repeated, still speaking very slowly as though he was explaining something to a child. 'I'll say I've recovered and remember exactly what happened. After you killed your husband and his mistress, you confessed to Katie. But she broke your confidence and told me your secret. Feeling betrayed, you killed us both. Only unfortunately for you, I survived to tell the truth.'

'That's nonsense, and you know it.'

'Your word against mine.'

'Why would I have wanted to kill you?'

'Because Katie and I knew what you had had done and you needed to silence us. I tried to restrain you, so you attacked me first, and left me for dead, and then you killed Katie. She was screaming hysterically while you were attacking me, and incapable of doing anything to stop you, and I was too badly injured to prevent you from killing her. But my injuries hadn't blinded me. I'll tell the police I saw what you did.'

'Do you really think anyone's going to believe I overpowered you?' My attempt at laughter sounded pathetic.

'I don't think you're going to risk another murder charge.'

Understanding what was at stake, I panicked. Whatever happened, I had to stop Ackerman going to the police. Dan would never cope if I were arrested again.

'That's why you didn't make any attempt to stop me bleeding before the police arrived, and didn't call an ambulance straight away, because it wouldn't have suited you to have me resuscitated.' His smile spread slowly across his face, starting with his eyes. 'You wanted me dead. In fact, you were relying on my being dead because I was the only witness to your stabbing Katie to death. You never expected me to survive.'

'No one's going to believe a word of that,' I told him, but he must have heard the uncertainty in my voice and seen it in my face.

'If you don't do exactly what I want,' he went on, 'you'll be locked up for all three murders. You smothered Paul after drugging his wine, so that was clearly premeditated. You strangled Bella, and stabbed Katie. Quite a collection, and all because your husband was unfaithful. And of course, there's the attempted murder.' He spread his hands out in an expansive gesture, as if to say, 'Here I am.'

'This is... blackmail,' I stammered. 'You'll never get away with it.'

He didn't bother to answer.

'You're just making all this up to scare me into paying you more,' I said.

'You won't do it. Your story wouldn't convince anyone. And anyway, you'll be locked up as well. Don't forget, you made a statement after Katie died to say she had confessed to killing Paul and Bella. Are you really going to say you lied to the police?'

'I'll say I was confused, thanks to the injuries I sustained when you attacked me.' He heaved an exaggerated sigh. 'I was in hospital when I made that statement. It never should have been taken seriously. Thankfully I've made a full recovery. But you're right, it's taken a while for my memory to return. That's not unusual in such cases, you know. And now I'm ready to come forward and tell the truth.'

'No one's going to believe you,' I insisted. 'How could your testimony possibly be reliable? You're... you're brain damaged!'

'Do you really want to put it to the test?' he replied, still smiling.

I did my best to dissuade him, but he remained adamant that he wanted his money. If I persisted in arguing with him, I really believed he would go to the police. Having been reunited with Dan, I couldn't risk losing him again.Knowing Dan would be home from college in an hour, I agreed to pay Ackerman whatever he wanted if he would only go away and leave us alone.

'I don't have the money here,' I told him, 'you'll have to wait.'

'I've waited long enough.'

'There's nothing I can do right now. Come around tomorrow morning and I'll have the first instalment here for you.'

'Until tomorrow then,' he agreed. 'Now, how about a cup of tea before I go? It looks as though our association is going to be continuing for a while, so we might as well be on good terms, and I'm parched.'

He looked as though he hadn't eaten a decent meal for a while, and his request gave me an idea. If I could persuade him to see me as a friend, he might become reasonable, and reduce the amount he was demanding.

'Did we ever stop being friends?' I asked, returning his smile nervously. 'I know if it weren't for you, I'd be in prison right now. You were the only one who stood by me.'

'That's more like it. So, we just need to regularise my payments. Think of it as paying for my ongoing support. A retainer, if you like.'

I nodded. 'Wait here and I'll bring you some tea, and I've got some cake.'

He raised his eyebrows. 'Cake, eh? You never used to offer me cake.'

'I didn't used to be able to afford it.'

He grinned at me as I stood up. 'Cake is the icing on the cake.'

Hurriedly I went to the kitchen. I wanted Ackerman gone before Dan came home.

My visitor was sprawling in an armchair when I rejoined him and placed a tray on the low table. As Ackerman picked up the pot to pour himself a cup of tea, his hand slipped. The pot had been filled from the kettle only seconds earlier so the tea was still virtually boiling. Ackerman let out a high-pitched screech as the scalding liquid spilled in his lap. Still screaming, he leapt to his feet.

'Get in the kitchen and pour cold water on it!' I yelled at him.

His eyes blazing, he pushed past me and hobbled to the kitchen, bent double in agony. Consumed with pain, he didn't look where he was going and slipped on a patch of water on the floor. As he toppled backwards, his head hit the edge of the granite worktop with a loud crack. Following close behind him, I froze.

Ackerman lay on his back. Leaning over him, I saw a thin line of blood trickle across the floor and form a small pool beside his head. His eyelids fluttered involuntarily but I don't think he saw me there, watching him. His breath came in laboured gasps, and then he was silent.

Shaking, I called the police.

'There's been an accident,' I blurted out, almost incoherent with shock. 'My friend has fallen and hit his head. I think he's dead.'

Epilogue

There seemed no reason to mention Ackerman's threatened blackmail to the police.

'He was a good friend of mine,' I concluded my statement. 'I can't believe what happened. I'm devastated.'

Detective Inspector Morgan stared at me in silence for a long time when I finished speaking. 'That makes three unexpected deaths in your presence,' he remarked at last.

Despite his implied suspicion, the Detective Inspector was forced to accept that in all these tragic events I was a victim, not a culprit.

For all her craziness, Katie was right about one thing. The sole survivor's account was the true one.

Acknowledgements

I am very grateful to Betsy Reavley for the inspiration and warmth of her support, to Fred Freeman for his invaluable advice, my eagle-eyed editor Morgen Bailey and my proofreader for their guidance, Sumaira Wilson for her untiring enthusiasm and practical help, and to the wonderful Sarah Hardy and her team of bloggers for their generosity with their time: Kate Eveleigh, Jo Turner, Melisa Broadbent, Sharon Bairden, Shell Baker, Gemma Myers, Liz Mistry, Kate Noble, Dash Fan Book Reviews, Sally Boland, Diane Hogg, Linda Green, Susan Hampson, Karen Cocking, Joanne Robertson, Vicki Dickinson, Katie Jones, Philomena Callan, Michelle Ryles, Susan Corcoran, and Joni Gheen.

My thanks also to Dr Leonard Russell for his medical advice, and last, but by no means least, to Michael who is always with me.

Lightning Source UK Ltd.
Milton Keynes UK
UKHW04f1849191018
330854UK00001B/153/P